FUTA FANTASIES

THE LADYBOY COLLECTION

VICTORIA RUSH

COPYRIGHT

Futa Fantasies © 2019 Victoria Rush

Cover Design © 2020 PhotoMaras

All Rights Reserved

For the uninhibited...

VOLUME ONE

SEX MACHINE

1

BRAVE NEW WORLD

Ever since my recent affairs with Sister Caroline and the girl next door ended, I'd been feeling a little down. Both relationships had been intense and rewarding, but just as they'd gotten interesting, both women had abruptly left me to return to their previous lives. I was wary of putting my heart on the line for another relationship, but I also missed having an intimate connection with a stimulating partner. It had been weeks since I'd felt the tender touch of another woman, and I was getting more antsy with each passing day.

One particularly lonely night, I sat down in front of my computer and began searching for a new outlet. I considered trolling some of the familiar online dating sites, but this time I wanted something more dependable—more *safe*. For the next little while, I wanted to take love out of the equation, while still finding someone who'd be interested in maintaining a continuing relationship. A *fuck-buddy*, for want of a better word. A friend with benefits.

I typed in the search words *where to find intimacy without commitment*. The usual hookup-oriented sites such as Ashley Madison, Plenty of Fish, and Craigslist came up, along with a bunch of threads discussing the pitfalls of engaging in a sexual relationship with close friends. But near the bottom of the listings was a link to an unusual website named *NextGen Personal Robots: experience the latest advance in artificial intelligence.*

Intrigued, I clicked on the link and a website came up with a video showcasing one of their robots. When I clicked the Play button, my jaw practically dropped to the floor. A gorgeous, superrealistic cyber robot looked into the camera and began talking. I leaned closer to the screen, hardly believing my eyes. If it wasn't for her handler flipping a switch behind her head, briefly pausing and reanimating her, I'd be hard-pressed to believe it was anything other than a real person. Her mouth moved fluidly in concert with her natural speech while her skin stretched and wrinkled like a normal person as her eyelids blinked periodically.

"Hello, my name is Scarlett," she said in a sexy voice. "I'm the newest creation of NextGen Robots, designed to satisfy *all* of your desires. I can do just about anything a real person can do—and a few extra special things they can't."

When the robot licked her lips with her realistic, fleshy, moist tongue, my pussy responded involuntarily with a surge of heat and wetness.

"Come down to see me and experience what it's like to touch and caress the woman of your dreams," the sexy robot said. "I'm available for private appointments or hourly outcalls. If you like what you see, you can even take me home as your permanent companion. Read the terms and conditions below, or click on the other links to see more videos of my sibling robots. I hope to see you soon!"

For the next hour or so, I clicked on every single video on the website, marveling at how realistic and multifaceted the robots were. There were male, female, and transgender robots with a variety of hair, skin, and eye colors. But every one of them was absolutely stunning and humanlike. It wasn't just their *faces* that were perfect—their *figures* were also meticulously carved and measured to reflect the ideal body type. All of the women had shapely, realistic breasts, narrow waists and curvy, tight asses.

Even their muscles flexed gently when they walked and waved their arms. But when they revealed what was *under* their clothes, I was floored. They all had anatomically correct openings that looked as realistic as any real person's. When their minders gently inserted a life-size dildo into their mouths, pussies, and anuses, the eight-inch phallus disappeared entirely into the cavities, only to emerge glistening with translucent lubrication. Even the men's and transgender robot's *penises* looked realistic, with full flaccid-to-erect animations.

How can they reproduce such a realistic simulation of a live person? I thought. *It must cost a fortune to create a working robot with such authentic animations.*

As I continued toggling through the videos, I spread my robe apart and began to play with my tingling clit. There was something about the idea of having an anatomically correct robot catering to my every sexual whim that I found incredibly arousing. As I watched each of the different models walking, talking, and simulating sex acts, I fantasized about what I wanted to do with each one.

But there were still many unanswered questions.

Could the robots *learn* what I liked? Did they respond uniquely to each person based on their individual input? Could they carry on a realistic two-way conversation? Were they programmed to feel *pleasure* also?

The more I thought about it, the more obsessed I became with the idea of trying one of these out for myself. After I orgasmed for the third time that night imagining myself getting licked and fucked by my personal favorites, I finally clicked on the link for rates. In-house appointments started at $200 per hour with a $500 deposit, and outcalls started at $500 per hour, requiring a $5,000 deposit. Ownership fees were listed as 'available upon consultation', but I figured it would be in the five- if not six-figure range for such a sophisticated mechanical device.

That's steep to be sure, I thought. *But not exorbitant considering what you're getting. Where else can you get no-strings, no-conditions, no-expectation sex with someone who looks like a supermodel for the price of a good dinner or a luxury car?*

I simply *had* to try one of these for myself, but not before I came for a fourth time that evening. As I watched a pretty redheaded cyber robot sensuously lick her lips, I pressed my favorite animated sex toy deep inside my pussy, shaking uncontrollably.

2

INTELLIGENT DESIGN

The next day, I booked a private consultation with a NextGen sales consultant and arrived five minutes early, eagerly anticipating my first live encounter with one of their robots. I half-expected the real things to be pale imitations of the ones shown in the videos, with stilted movements and fake silicone skin—but even those might be fun to play with for a brief one-off encounter.

At precisely one p.m., an attractive young woman entered my consultation room and closed the door behind her.

"You must be Jade," she said, extending her hand in greeting. "I'm Bonnie, one of NextGen's cyberadvisors."

I paused for a moment, looking at the sales consultant suspiciously.

"Are you sure you're not one of those robots I saw on your website? Because those were crazy realistic."

Bonnie laughed, then invited me to sit in one of their comfortable upholstered chairs.

"No, but I'm glad you were suitably impressed. We take pride in the quality and realism of our agents."

"*Agents*? Is that what you call them?"

"The term robot doesn't really do them justice. Each of our artificial agents has learned an entirely independent set of behaviors and responses based on their experience. Each one has his or her own personality. They're really like part of our family, and we treat them accordingly."

"That's incredible," I said. "I didn't think something like this was even possible. This is almost like it's out of some science fiction film, set a hundred years in the future. How have you been able to pull off such a complex engineering feat?"

Bonnie nodded as she crossed her legs and placed her hands in her lap.

"We have a large team of artificial intelligence technicians, robotics engineers, and esthetic designers who oversee each new creation. We're raising the bar with each new iteration, but it requires a great deal of human and capital investment."

"That explains the steep prices," I frowned.

"People pay more to rent or purchase a luxury car," Bonnie said. "I think you'll find our agents deliver even more utility and excitement, without all the maintenance and upkeep."

I nodded at the unrealistic comparison.

"That was one of my first questions, actually. What do they *run* on? I assume they don't eat and eliminate, like real people. Do they require special power adapters and frequent charging?"

"We're not quite at the point of human reengineering that we can create robots with the same functioning internal organs," Bonnie chuckled. "We're probably at least a few decades away from that. But to answer your question, they run on special high-efficiency batteries, which are rechargeable with regular 120-volt household current. The average agent lasts about four hours before needing a recharge, depending on the level of exertion and use."

Exertion and use indeed, I thought, bringing me back to my main interest in the robots.

"But they still look like a regular person on the *outside*, don't they?"

"Yes—very much so. That is, if you consider these exceptionally beautiful cyberorganisms to look 'regular'. I think you'll find them to be remarkably realistic and natural. Would you like to see one now for yourself?"

I shifted uncomfortably in my chair, feeling unusually nervous about interfacing with this kind of machine for the first time.

"I'm almost ready. I just have a few more questions."

"Absolutely. Our clients' comfort and satisfaction is our overriding concern."

"You said they can *learn*. What does that mean exactly?"

"They're programmed to adjust their speech and behavior based on the external cues they're exposed to. Through your verbal and non-verbal cues, they will begin to learn what you like and desire. Just as in any normal relationship, it's this give-and-take stimulus and response pattern that enables them to behave in such a way that optimizes the results. They soon learn what doesn't work and what does."

The juices in my pussy suddenly started to stir, realizing exactly what Bonnie meant.

"Are they designed to perform *other* human tasks? I mean other than—"

"Yes. Their muscles, joints, and external organs work just like a normal human's. They can pick objects up, move them, and use their fingers just like you and me. Over time, they can learn how to do the laundry, load the dishwasher—even drive a car."

"Whoa!" I said, my eyes flying open at the provocative suggestion. "I think it would take quite a while before I ever got close to trusting a robot to drive my car!"

"They already do," Bonnie said. "It's just that most of them don't look like a person."

I nodded, beginning to realize how far artificial intelligence had already infiltrated our everyday lives.

"I suppose you're right," I said, hesitating to broach one of the more delicate issues. "What about the—*sex* thing? How do I know your robots are...clean?"

Bonnie nodded at the familiar question.

"Every agent goes through a meticulous internal and external steam cleaning after each encounter with a new client. All of their orifices are thoroughly sanitized after use. Of course, if you wish to have a *virgin* companion, you can always buy a new one for your own exclusive use."

I smiled at the not-so-subtly veiled human reference.

"What is the fee to purchase one?"

"Depending on the age, version, and feature set, ownership starts at one hundred and fifty thousand dollars."

I gulped at the exorbitant price.

"That's a pretty steep investment."

"Most people spend almost that much on a new car. The difference is that this machine operates twenty-four hours a day, three hundred and sixty-five days a year. Other than brief downtime for recharging, our agents provide constant and personal utility. Plus, there's already a robust and dependable market for used NextGen robots for purchase. In the unlikely event that you grow bored with your companion or wish to trade up to a new version, you should have no difficulty returning most if not all of your initial investment."

I nodded my head and smiled.

"I think you've convinced me, Bonnie. I'm ready to meet one of your agents now."

"Would you prefer to see a man, woman, or transgender model?"

I paused to ponder the third option.

"How are your transgender agents equipped differently?"

"Most of them look for all intents and purposes like a normal woman. The only difference is that they're also equipped with a man's external sexual organs."

"Including testicles?" I asked, raising an eyebrow. "Or do some of them have *both* sets of sex organs, like a true hermaphrodite?"

"We have models in both formats, depending on your preference."

I crossed my legs, reflecting back on my recent dream fantasy where the Arabian genie bestowed me with both sets of sexual organs.

"Why don't we start with a female?" I said. "If all goes well, I might wish to experiment with a different version in my next visit."

"Very well," Bonnie said. "Do you have a racial preference, or preferred hair and eye color?"

I thought back to the videos I watched yesterday and remembered the special cyber robot who'd made me come so hard.

"Do you have a pretty redhead with green eyes?"

"That sounds like Juliette," Bonnie smiled. "She just happens to be available for the next hour. How would you like to arrange for payment?"

"Oh yes," I said, removing my wallet from my purse as my jeans suddenly dampened in anticipation. "Do you take American Express?"

3

SURREALISM

Bonnie led me through a long hallway lined with floor-to-ceiling glass windows. Behind each pane stood a different cyber robot, completely unclothed. Each one was absolutely stunning, but their fixed gaze staring straight ahead was unnerving, making me feel like I was in some kind of wax museum. As I marveled at their ultrarealistic faces and bodies, I half-expected any one of them to begin moving at any time. Every robot had unique facial and physical contours, adding to the eerie feeling that I was being watched by a menagerie of naked department store mannequins.

"Can these robots see me?" I said to Bonnie. "I feel like I have a hundred eyes on me."

"They can sense movement in their periphery, but they're all in sleep mode to conserve battery power. If you were to stop and engage them directly, they would automatically awake and resume full animation."

I paused beside a window with a male robot behind it. His face reminded me of a young Eric Dane, the actor who played the McSteamy character on Grey's Anatomy. His body was perfectly proportioned—six feet tall on a lean, muscular frame. A light dusting of curly brown hair covered his impeccably carved chest muscles, with a thin trail leading down his toned abs to a large, flaccid penis. I could have sworn it moved when I stopped, and as I began to stare at it, it started to throb and bob between his legs.

Bonnie paused when she saw that I'd stopped and walked up beside me.

"He's one of our most popular models," she said, nodding. "Are you sure you wouldn't like to take *him* for a test drive first?"

"It's tempting."

I couldn't take my eyes off the model's throbbing penis. Unlike most of the artificial dildos I'd played with, this one looked like the real thing, with a pink head and a darker shaft.

"How does that *work*?" I asked. "I mean, how does he get—hard?"

"Like any other person, he responds to external stimuli. He needs to become aroused in order to respond in kind. We wouldn't want him walking around in public with a hard-on all the time. Would you like to see if you could raise his—*interest*?"

"Um...sure," I said, feeling my pussy beginning to throb at the thought of having this exotic sex toy inside of me.

"His name is Dylan. If you address him directly, he'll wake up."

I paused, feeling unsure how to talk to a robot.

"Hello...Dylan."

The robot's eyelids blinked open and his eyes shifted to gaze at me directly.

"Hello," he said. "What is your name?"

"I'm...Jade," I said, momentarily caught off guard by his human-like response.

"Pleased to meet you, Jade. Did you want me to perform any special tasks for you today or did you just want to stare at me all day long?"

I took a step back, shocked by his unexpected sense of humor.

"Oh—sorry," I stammered. "I was just admiring your...package."

Dylan's mouth curled into a half smile as he blinked at me again.

"Was there any particular *part* of me in which you had a special interest?"

I paused to scan his body from head to toe. The realism of his body tone was exceptional. Unlike most silicone sex dolls which were just a smooth mass of one-dimensional plastic molding, his muscles curved and flexed as he talked, like a real person. Even his arms and legs were covered with fine hairs like a real person.

"The whole thing is pretty impressive," I said, raising my eyebrows in appreciation. "Can you—turn around?"

Dylan's eyes shifted to focus temporarily on Bonnie, and I saw her nod gently in my periphery.

"Absolutely," he said, lifting and turning his feet one at a time until his backside was facing me.

When I saw his ass, I gasped. It was as round, muscular, and firm as any professional athlete's. The muscles in his buttocks rippled as he shifted his weight from side to side. His feet were far enough apart for me to see his tight ballsac nestled between his thighs.

"Would you like to see any *other* part of me?" Dylan said, with a teasing lilt in his voice.

My panties suddenly began to dampen as a flood of hormones surged into my pussy.

"May I?" I said, turning to Bonnie. "I mean, I know I've already paid to see Juliette, but I just—"

"As long as he remains behind the glass, there's no charge. Are you sure you wouldn't like a private room with this one instead?"

I paused for a moment, then remembered how turned on I'd gotten yesterday watching the female redheaded robot.

"No," I said. "I'm just intrigued to see what he can...*do*."

Bonnie smiled as she winked at me.

"Why don't you ask him to turn around and show you?"

I took one last look at the robot's exquisite ass then took a deep breath.

"Dylan, please turn around so I can see your—front side," I said.

As he turned around, his long phallus swung gently from side to side over his smooth balls.

"Just how big can you get?" I said, salivating over his enormous cock.

"You mean my *penis*?" he said. "That depends on how excited I am. Was there anything in particular you wanted to do with me?"

I looked at Bonnie and raised my eyebrows playfully.

"Well for starters, I wouldn't mind feeling that big stovepipe of yours in my mouth. Can you get hard for me?"

Almost immediately, Dylan's organ began lengthening and bobbing upwards. It was already eight inches long and two inches wide at half-mast, and my pussy pulsed imagining what it would be like to have him inside me.

"Mmm, yes," I said, watching it rise. "That's a very nice cock you have there. I'd love to suck that firehose of yours."

As I stared at Dylan's cock continuing to rise and expand, I turned to Bonnie.

"Can they *feel* anything?" I asked. "Do they experience orgasm like a regular person?"

"They're programmed to recognize what auditory and tactile stimuli are designed make them feel good," she said. "They quickly learn what behaviors generate positive outcomes, and respond as a normal person would. Though they can't actually feel pleasure the way the rest of us do, their central processors register sexual stimuli as a 'reward.'"

I looked back at Dylan and saw that his penis was standing straight up at a near ninety-degree-angle, bobbing sexily against his flat stomach. His fully erect cock appeared to be at least nine inches in length and almost as thick as a Coke can around. The head of his penis glistened with a translucent dewy substance, and even the color of his engorged organ had darkened, as if it was filled with blood.

"That's mighty impressive," I said, peering at Bonnie again. "Can he actually—*cum* out the end?"

Bonnie smiled and nodded at the familiar question.

"He will indeed squirt after sufficient manipulation. Just like any man, with the right stimulation, he will reach climax."

"Only *once* like a regular man?"

"That's the difference between our cyber companions and a regular man. They can respond immediately and repeatedly, without any necessary recovery period. He's available twenty-four-seven to service your needs, whatever they may be."

I looked at the glistening head of Marcos's throbbing cock and licked my lips unconsciously.

"What about his ejaculate? What does it taste like?"

"All of our models, regardless of gender, employ the same natural organic lubrication. It's a special mixture of aloe vera, shea butter, vitamin E oil, and natural citric acids. It's highly slippery, non-tacky, and completely safe internally. You can even swallow it. I think you'll find the taste quite agreeable."

Jesus, I thought. *A giant cock that rises on demand and shoots a perfect, tasty lubrication every time. Who'd want a regular man after trying one of these?*

"Would you like to give him a try?" Bonnie asked.

I looked back at Dylan as he smiled at me slyly with his giant hard-on bobbing against his stomach. Then I reflected back to the video I saw yesterday and remembered how hard I came imagining the pretty redhead's lips wrapped around my clit.

"Maybe another day. First, I'd like to see what special features your *female* models have."

As we continued walking down the long display hall, my pussy got wetter and wetter as I ogled the pretty models lining both sides of the aisle. When we got to a transgender model, I stopped in my tracks. She had a perfect female figure with large, natural-shaped breasts and a thin waist with curvy hips, but between her legs hung another large circumcised organ similar to Dylan's. I bent down and peered between her legs, noticing that she didn't have any balls.

"This is Christine," Bonnie said, walking up to the window. "Another one of our popular models. You noticed she doesn't have any testicles."

"Yes," I said. "Does she—"

"She comes equipped with *both* sets of fully functioning sex organs," Bonnie said, reading my mind. "Her penis works just like Dylan's, but she also has a normal woman's genital anatomy. Our customers find she can be very versatile..."

I scanned the model's hips looking for a hint as to what lay on the other side.

"What about her—*back* side? Do all of your models come equipped with a working anus?"

"If by working you mean *penetrable*, yes. And unlike most people's back doors, ours are only designed for one function. They have the same organic slippery lube that is emitted from the other openings, so they can be enjoyed in every possible way."

Fuck me, I thought. I'd always enjoyed having my asshole licked but had been reluctant to return the favor unless I knew my partner had just bathed. With these cyber robots, I could go to town giving them a rim job whenever I wanted.

Bonnie looked at me, unsure if I wanted to stop and experiment with some of this robot's responses as well.

"Shall we continue?" she asked.

I paused for a moment, reflecting back on the recent dream I'd enjoyed playing the role of a fully functioning hermaphrodite. And then I remembered the pretty princess who'd been the principal focus of my dream.

"Yes," I said. "I'm eager to meet Juliette."

Near the end of the hall, Bonnie stopped in front of another tall window and nodded to the figure inside.

"This is Juliette. I'm kind of partial toward her myself. I think you chose wisely."

I turned to face the model and gasped. She looked like a cross between Christina Hendricks, Lindsay Lohan, and Angie Everhart. But her body was all Christina Hendricks. Full-figured with firm D-cup breasts, her waist tapered then swelled to hourglass-shaped hips, supported by long, curvy legs.

"Jesus," I exclaimed. "Whoever designs your models should be complimented. Wherever she finds her inspiration, she sure knows how to create a winner."

"Actually," Bonnie said, "most of our models are a synthesis of real people in the public eye. We've taken the best features from the most popular models and actors, then fused them into a totally new and unique character. Does Juliette meet with your approval?"

"Um—yes," I stammered, beginning to feel my pussy throb again.

I would have given my right arm to have an opportunity to fuck any one of those public figures, and now I was about to have my way with all three of them at the same time!

"May I have some alone time with this one?"

Bonnie nodded and smiled at me as she swiped a pass card through the key lock reader beside the glass pane.

"Absolutely."

She swung a door open and escorted me into a private room about twenty feet down the side hall. When I got inside, I could see what appeared to be the backside of the redheaded robot standing in front of the window by the long hall. The room was equipped with a small table with two chairs and a queen-size pedestal mattress covered in fresh linens.

"Did you have any more questions before I leave you two alone for the next hour?" Bonnie asked.

I looked around the room for any hidden cameras or one-way windows.

"Do I just *talk* to her to wake her up? And do we have complete privacy?"

"Yes on both counts. No one else will be watching you, besides Juliette of course, but she's equipped with special alarms to notify us if she's abused in any way. This includes physical, sexual, or verbal abuse. Just as with a real person, if we find that you are marginalizing her in any way, one of our security officers will come in and immediately end the session and you will lose your full deposit. Beyond the actual physical and psychic damage that can be inflicted on our agents, we don't wish for them to learn bad habits."

I nodded, impressed with the organization's respect for their agents' dignity. I was beginning to think of these cyber robots more as real people with each passing moment. Just as with *any* animal, including humans, I knew that anybody could be trained to learn bad habits under the wrong influences.

"I understand completely," I said. "How will I know when my hour is up?"

Bonnie motioned to an LED display on the opposite wall.

"The sixty-minute timer will begin as soon as I leave the room. Juliette will automatically revert to sleep mode at the end of your allotted time."

"Thank you," I said. "I'll see you on the way out."

Bonnie nodded, then exited the room and closed the door behind her.

I looked at the redheaded robot facing the window and hesitated. It felt strange talking to a machine like a real person.

"Hello, Juliette," I said.

The robot's head tilted up, then she turned around to face me. I watched her shapely buttock muscles flex as she shifted her weight and her large breasts bobbed on her chest.

"Good afternoon," the robot said in a silky voice. "What's your name?"

"I'm Jade."

I paused for a minute, unsure how to engage a robot in normal conversation.

"It's a pleasure to meet you," I said, shaking my head at my own robotic-sounding speech.

"Likewise. You're very pretty, Jade."

"I bet you're programmed to say that to *all* the customers," I chuckled nervously.

"Actually, I'm not," the robot said. "But I *am* programmed to recognize features that are widely accepted as attractive. You have large clear eyes, a slender nose, and full round lips. I'm sure you'd be considered attractive by any other human."

I looked at the pretty robot and smiled, realizing that her designers probably applied many of the same criteria in designing her.

"Well then," I said. "Just to be sure you're being completely truthful, what features do I have that might *not* be considered so attractive?"

The robot paused for a long moment while she studied my face.

"The left side of your chin is slightly lower than the other. Most people place a high premium on facial symmetry in assessing attractiveness. Though I personally find small flaws like these make the person more interesting to look at."

I laughed out loud at the robot's candor. It was refreshing to talk to someone who I knew would be one hundred percent truthful at all times.

"Well, I can't find any flaws anywhere on *your* body, that's for sure. And somehow I still find you thoroughly captivating."

I paused for a moment, looking behind the robot at the glass window facing the central hallway.

"Would you mind stepping down from the display case so I can take a closer look at you?"

The robot took a step forward, then slowly descended the three steps into the visitation room and closed the door to the display case. As her muscles flexed and her joints bent, I carefully measured her movements. Although not entirely fluid, they were remarkably humanlike, like someone trying not to fall—which I suppose she was. Then she took three steps toward me and paused about four feet away. As she looked straight into my eyes, I peered shamelessly up and down her playboy-model-perfect figure, salivating at her sexy physique.

Her hair was thick and shimmering, looking like it had just been washed and conditioned. She had small traces of makeup around her eyes, mostly a light dusting of hazel eye shadow to match the color of her eyes. The nipples on her breasts looked soft and natural, with a tiny indentation in the middle, just like the real thing. Her mound had a small patch of strawberry blond pubic hair, looking tantalizingly authentic. Even her skin had a natural glow and realistic appearance.

"You're breathtaking," I said, making eye contact with her once again. "May I—"

"Touch me?" the robot said. "I can tell from your dilated pupils and your elevated respiration rate that you're excited looking at me. Yes, I like to be touched."

I reached out my right hand and touched her cheek, then gasped as I quickly retracted it.

"It's—warm!" I said, hardly believing my own fingers.

"Of course," the robot said. "I wouldn't be much fun to play with if I were cold as a clam, would I?"

I reached out again and tentatively squeezed her breasts. Her skin felt soft and supple, and when I removed my hands I could see a faint pink glow where I had just touched them.

"Your skin feels so realistic," I said.

"Thank you. It's made with a special thermoplastic elastomer, which most closely resembles real human skin. Our designers go to great lengths to simulate a normal live human."

As I soaked up the robot's full figure, I felt my pussy begin to dampen again.

"I'd hardly say you're *normal*. You've got the best qualities of the most attractive people. You're more like a *super*-woman."

"Thank you, Jade. I think you're very attractive as well."

"Except for my chin, right?"

"It's just the tiniest little imperfection. It makes you all the more adorable."

I could feel my heart thumping in my chest and perspiration forming on my skin as I reacted viscerally to this fascinating cyber robot.

"May I call you Juliette?" I asked.

"Of course. I like it when our clients call me by my name. It makes me feel more...personal."

For the first time, I began to feel awkward about standing in front of the nude model. Her use of the word 'client' suddenly made me realize what the primary purpose of the NextGen business was. I felt ashamed for fondling her like she was some kind of exhibit at the petting zoo.

"Would you like to sit down, Juliette? Perhaps we can be more comfortable while we get to know one another better."

Juliette nodded then sat on one of the chairs, and I pulled the other one around to sit beside her at the corner of the table.

"Do you mind my asking? Are you always..." I paused, unsure how to broach the subject delicately. "Naked?"

Juliette smiled at me as my gaze drifted down once again to her perfect stack.

"Most of our customers prefer seeing me this way. I suppose with only an hour to spend, they want to get right down to business. But some of my regular customers occasionally take me home for overnight outcalls. I think they also enjoy dressing me up in strange costumes, which can be kind of fun I suppose."

As I listened to Juliette talk, I began to feel sorry for her. Her obvious objectification by the company's customers reminded me how easy it was in the real world to be viewed purely as a sex object. Although she didn't display any obvious visual signs of distress, I could tell that she knew this was not the way normal people showed respect for a woman. Suddenly, I lost interest in experimenting with her in any sexual way. I found her utterly fascinating, almost in a childlike way, with her fresh innocence and naivety.

"It sounds like most of your customers only have one thing in mind when they interact with you," I said. "How does that make you feel?"

"Well, I can tell that it's very rewarding for *them*, and I'm programmed to maximize our customers' happiness. But sometimes I wonder what it would be like to interact with them the way regular people do. I understand that humans enjoy doing other things besides having sex all the time, like going out for dinner, or seeing a movie, or even just cuddling. It would be interesting to see how my clients would respond to me under some of those circumstances, so I could build up a more diverse bank of experiences."

"That's a very wise insight, Juliette," I nodded. "Most people do indeed like to do other things besides have sex all the time. I'm sure it would be rewarding for both of you to stretch your wings in other ways."

"Stretch your wings?" Juliette said with a puzzled expression.

I smiled again at Juliette's childlike naivety.

"It's a human expression meaning to expand your horizons—your *experiences*, as you say. Most people find it quite rewarding to do so."

I sat back in my chair and crossed my legs, beginning to feel more relaxed with my new companion. Just as in any new relationship, we were starting from a blank slate, learning about each other's life experiences and wants and likes. Suddenly, I wanted to learn everything I could about this fascinating new acquaintance.

Juliette also sat back in her chair, mimicking my body language, and as she lifted her leg to cross it over the other, I couldn't help but glance down and notice the hairless slit between her legs.

Of course, good sex is also part of the human experience, I thought, feeling the blood rushing back into my pussy.

I was just about to start gently exploring Juliette's sexual proclivities when she suddenly stopped moving and her eyes stared expressionless, straight ahead into space. Seconds later, a chime filled the room, and I glanced behind me at the digital clock. The display read sixty minutes. I'd been so wrapped up getting to know Juliette that I'd completely lost track of time.

But I'd spent enough time on our first date to know that I wanted another.

4

GETTING ACQUAINTED

After my allotted time with Juliette expired, I immediately went to the front office to meet again with Bonnie. I was completely smitten with this captivating robot and wanted more. But one-hour increments wasn't going to cut it. I wanted to take Juliette *home* with me, where I could get to know her on my own terms, free from prying eyes. After a brief wait in the consultation room, Bonnie entered the room and took a seat in front of me.

"How did you find the experience?" she said.

"It was wonderful. Far exceeded my expectations."

Bonnie smiled and raised an eyebrow.

"Were you able to explore *all* of her special features?"

I frowned at Bonnie's suggestion that sex was all Juliette was good for.

"Actually, I never even got around to that. We just talked. She's utterly fascinating. You've created an incredibly smart and responsive...companion. I definitely want to see more of her."

"Most of our clients do," Bonnie said. "They're quite irresistible. Were you interested in purchasing more visitation time with her?"

"I understand your agents are available for outcalls. I'd like to take her home with me for a while."

"Of course. Our outcall rates start at $500 per hour with a $5,000 security deposit."

I quickly did the math in my head. Even if I just kept her for one day, I'd be looking at upwards of ten thousand dollars."

"That's pretty steep, especially if I want to keep her overnight. Do you have *daily* rates?"

Bonnie paused for a moment then smiled.

"We might be able to make an accommodation. How does $3,500 a day sound? If you should decide to keep her, we could subtract your cumulative rental fees from the purchase price."

My mind began swimming with numbers. I knew I should probably go home and sleep on it and not make an impulsive decision, but I simply couldn't wait to have more time with this pretty redheaded robot. I wasn't ready to leap to a six-figure purchase decision, but I definitely wanted to take her out for a longer test drive.

"Would you be willing to go to $2,500 per day if I commit to at least two days?"

I couldn't believe that I was preparing to shell out five grand for a forty-eight hour rendezvous with a total stranger. But I knew that high-end call girls went for even more, and Juliette had infinitely more to offer than a simple hooker.

Bonnie paused for a moment, then nodded.

"I'll have to confirm it with my boss, but I think we can make that work. But remember that you'll be on the clock. Juliette will automatically deactivate after forty-eight hours and we'll deduct an extra $2,500 from your security deposit if you return her late."

"I understand."

"Did you have any other questions or concerns before we process the transaction?"

I stopped to ponder how it would look to my neighbors seeing a naked woman getting out of my car.

"Do you have any clothes she can put on before she leaves your facility? It will look a bit strange walking around with a naked cyborg at my side."

"Yes, of course," Bonnie said. "Our customers like to be discreet when they take our agents out in public. I'll arrange to get Juliette suitably dressed. Shall we place the new charges on your same credit card?"

A fter processing the payment and filling out a long waiver, Bonnie reentered the consultation room ten minutes later with Juliette. She was wearing a pretty mid-length skirt and blouse with three-inch pumps. Her shirt clung tightly to her large breasts, with her firm nipples producing two sensuous bumps in the thin fabric. Somehow, she looked even more sexy fully dressed, making her seem even more lifelike than before.

"Everything appears to be in order," Bonnie said to me, then she turned to the robot. "Juliette, are you all set for your sleepover adventure with Jade?"

"Absolutely," Juliette said. "I'm excited to show her some of my more *entertaining* features."

I frowned at the thinly veiled sexual references that Bonnie was making, and for a moment I considered reminding her that harassment takes many forms. But I bit my tongue and smiled at Juliette.

"Right then," I said, extending my hand to her. "Shall we?"

Juliette looked me for a moment, unsure what I meant, then she reached out and clasped my hand gently. Feeling her touch me for the first time sent an electric charge through my body. As soon as her warm fingers wrapped around my hand, my heart began beating rapidly and my palms started to sweat.

"I'll return her in forty-eight hours," I said to Bonnie, turning toward the exit.

"Enjoy!" Bonnie said, with a sly smile.

When we got into the parking lot, I pressed the remote unlock button on my key chain and my car flashed and beeped. Without thinking, I went to the driver's side to open my door, then I noticed Juliette standing awkwardly in front of the passenger door.

"Have you ever ridden in a car before?" I asked.

"This is my first time in *wake* mode," she said. "In previous outcalls, I was stowed in my clients' back seat or trunk. I suppose they wanted to conserve all of their available minutes for more *active* types of engagement."

Poor thing, I thought. *It sounds like she's been treated no better than a sex doll by her other customers.*

"Well, we certainly won't have any of that with *me*," I said, walking over to her side of the car. "I'd like you sit up front and keep me company. We're partners now!"

I opened the passenger door and held Juliette's hand as she awkwardly squatted and leaned into the passenger seat, then I closed the door behind her and got in the driver's side. The NextGen office was crosstown from my home, so I tapped my residence address in the navigation system memory and clicked the command to start route guidance. The voice assistant confirmed my destination, then told me to turn right at the nearest side street.

"She sounds a bit like me," Juliette said, cocking her head to the side. "Is she a robot too?"

"She does have a similar lilt to her voice," I said. "I suppose she also has a form of artificial intelligence. But you're far more capable and personable than she is. What do you say we not use that term for you anymore. I prefer to think of you as my...friend."

Juliette turned her head toward me and smiled.

"I like that idea. No one's ever called me that before. My onboard dictionary defines a friend as someone connected to another with feelings of affection. Where are we going, my friend?"

"Home, Juliette," I said. "We're going home."

For the next thirty minutes, I pointed out the interesting landmarks along the way, educating Juliette about the city's unique architecture and civic features. Whenever the voice assistant prompted a change in direction, she turned her head and looked at the console screen with curiosity. When we got to my home, I pressed the remote garage door opener and parked the car in the carport then closed the door behind us. I didn't want any prying neighbors second-guessing who I was taking home this time. I helped Juliette out of the car, then opened the door to my foyer and welcomed her into my house.

"Well, this is it," I said. "This is my home. Would you like me to show you around?"

"Yes please," Juliette said. "I want to learn everything about you."

I led Juliette through my house, showing her the living room, kitchen, office, and downstairs powder room, then I led her upstairs to the living quarters. When I showed her my bedroom, she paused in front of my bed and nodded.

"This is the room where most of my clients take me for their pleasure. Would you like me to get undressed now?"

I looked at Juliette and sighed.

"Good heavens," I said. "You've never been treated like a lady, have you?"

"Lady?" Juliette said, pinching her eyebrows together. "Isn't that the same thing as a woman?"

"Not quite. It's another one of our special human expressions. A lady is a woman who—isn't only focused on the *sexual* aspect of her persona. She's someone who is considered to have high moral standards and good social etiquette."

"Etiquette," Juliette said, pausing to process her memory bank for the dictionary definition. "I think I understand. Are you a lady also, Jade?"

I laughed, thinking how best to answer the loaded question.

"Most of the time, I like to think so. But there are other times— well let's just say there's an appropriate time and place to be a lady, and other times when you want to act a little bit more like a...woman."

Juliette looked at my bed then back toward me.

"Would you like us to act like women now?"

I peered into Juliette's green eyes and clasped her hand gently.

"There'll be plenty of time for that later. Why don't we ease into that in due course? There are so many other interesting things we can do."

I led Juliette into my ensuite bathroom.

"Are you waterproof?" I asked. "Sometimes it can be fun to have a shower together, or even better, a nice relaxing bath."

Juliette paused for a moment as she pondered the query.

"My shell is designed to be waterproof. I've never had a bath, unless you count the cleansings I receive from my minders after each new client encounter."

"I think you'll find *this* type of cleanse far more relaxing and...empowering."

I glanced at my commode and chuckled.

"I don't suppose you ever have any need for that?"

Juliette paused as she looked at the toilet, processing its function.

"I don't eliminate any waste."

"Lucky you," I said. "I suppose that means you don't *eat* anything either? I'd offer you something, but I suppose that's not an activity that we can share."

"No, but I know you humans get your power from consuming organic substances. I'll be happy to keep you company whenever you need to eat or void."

I choked suddenly at Juliette's comment.

"We humans generally like to be alone when we...void. But now that you mention it, I *am* a little hungry. Why don't you join me in the kitchen while I put something together? I can think of something else you might find interesting that we can do together."

I made myself a quick sandwich, then I threw some kernels into my popcorn machine and emptied the output into a big bowl. Then I poured myself a glass of white wine and led Juliette into my living room and turned on the TV.

"Why don't we watch a movie?" I said. "Have you ever done that before?"

Juliette watched the screen as I toggled through my Netflix favorites.

"Nothing on a big screen like this. Sometimes my clients like to watch videos on their computers or do webcam shows with me..."

I shook my head as I flicked through my watch list.

"I think you'll find this a little more relaxing. With these kinds of movies, you just sit back and enjoy."

"Is this another thing *friends* do together?" Juliette asked.

"Yes," I smiled. "It's something special friends like to do together."

"What kind of movies do you enjoy watching?"

I flipped through my favorites list and stopped at one I hadn't seen for a while.

"I enjoy all genres, but I have a bit of a soft spot for romantic films. This is one of my favorites. It's called An Affair to Remember, starring Cary Grant and Deborah Kerr."

I clicked the start button and the movie began playing. During the scene where Cary Grant strolls aboard the cruise ship and other women point and ogle at the famous character, Juliette turned to ask me a question.

"Those women seem to find this actor quite attractive. Do *you* find him handsome also, Jade?"

"He's Cary Grant. The very embodiment of a suave and sophisticated gentleman. What's not to like?"

I paused for a moment, watching his co-star's reaction to the excessive fawning of his shipboard fans.

"He is indeed very attractive," I said. "But I have to confess, I've always had a bit of crush on his co-star in this film, Deborah Kerr. Maybe it's just because she's a redhead like you. You're very pretty, just like her."

We continued watching the playful courtship of the two main characters as they pretended not to be interested in one another, until their first kiss at the ship's rail with the sun setting behind them.

"Why do people kiss, Jade?" Juliette suddenly asked me. "As I understand it, they don't have the same sense organs in their mouth that they do in their genitals, and they can't reach climax like they can when they touch themselves in other places."

I turned to look at Juliette and laughed. I found her naivety endearing and felt myself becoming more attracted to her with each passing moment.

"That's a good question," I said, pausing the movie with my

remote. "People don't do it so much to feel physical pleasure. It's more of an *emotional* connection. They usually do it when they're in love. It's a special way to feel close to someone without it becoming sexual."

"Like when you want to be a lady?"

"Yes, exactly like that."

I tapped the remote to resume the movie, and Juliette watched the two actors engage in a long, passionate kiss.

"Does it feel good to kiss?" Juliette asked. "Cary Grant and Deborah Kerr certainly look like they're enjoying it."

I paused the movie again and peered over at Juliette.

"Have you never been kissed? It can be quite pleasurable—if it's done properly."

"So far, my clients have only been interested using my mouth for *other* purposes. Can you show me how it's done properly?"

I smiled at Juliette and placed the remote on the side table.

"It would be my pleasure, Juliette."

I leaned closer to Juliette and placed my lips gently against hers. Her lips were soft and pliable, like the rest of her skin. I closed my eyes and placed my hand behind her neck then turned my head and opened my mouth. When I opened my eyes briefly to see Juliette's reaction, her eyes were wide open. I pulled back, raising my eyebrows.

"You're supposed to close your eyes when you kiss someone," I said. "It's kind of rude to stare at your partner while she's kissing you."

"Really?" Juliette said. "But I was enjoying watching your reaction as you kissed me. I could hear your heart beating faster and feel your breath pulsing on my face."

"Well, yes—those are natural things that happen when someone is enjoying the act, but you're supposed to lose yourself in the kiss, not clinically analyze how your partner is responding to it."

"Like the actors in the movie?"

"Yes."

"But in the movie, their lips were closed the whole time. Your mouth was open—"

"That movie was made more than fifty years ago. The morals of the day were different back then. People weren't supposed to act so...*explicit* in public. Nowadays it's more acceptable to be more expressive and involve a little tongue—"

"Tongue?" Juliette said, with a puzzled expression. "I thought those were meant for other purposes. How does that work?"

"Let me show you. Now shut up and let me kiss you!"

I placed my lips on Juliette's and opened my mouth, inserting my tongue gently into her cavity. I traced it along the inside of her lips, then swirled it around her tongue. She moved her jaw up and down awkwardly, pursing her lips like she'd seen in the movie, but her tongue remained stationary. I pulled back and looked at her again for a moment.

"You *can* move your tongue, can't you?"

"Yes, of course. My clients like it when I—"

"Well, when you're kissing somebody, it's polite and good form to return their actions with somewhat similar actions. You don't want to just sit there and let me do all the work. Good kissing is a two-way exercise."

"Exercise?"

"It's not like lifting weights, silly. Just follow my lead and do what I do."

I leaned back in and resumed kissing Juliette, and this time her tongue became animated as it swirled and played with mine. It was moist and pliable, just like a real tongue. The lubrication didn't feel or taste like regular saliva—it was more innocuous, like water. But Juliette soon got the hang of it, and before long, we were kissing like passionate lovers. I could feel my pussy dampening the more I lost myself in the kiss, and when I opened my eyes this time, Juliette's were closed. After a few minutes, I pulled back and touched her face softly.

"You're a good kisser, Juliette," I said. "And a quick study."

"Study?"

"That means someone who's a good student and learns quickly."

"Teach me what else you like to do, Jade," Juliette said. "I like making you feel good."

I darted my eyes back and forth between each of Juliette's, trying to read her face.

"Does it feel good for you too?" I said.

"I don't feel sensations in the same way that you do. But I can sense what feels good for my clients and I'm programmed to experience this as a positive outcome. The happier I make you, the happier I feel."

"Do you feel happy now?" I asked, peering into her eyes.

"Yes, Jade. You make me very happy. I want you to teach me other ways I can please you."

"Well, I can think of a few other ways you might be able to make me...happy. Would you like to go upstairs to my bedroom now?"

"Yes. I want to feel even closer to you. But will I still be a lady?"

"Yes, Juliette. You'll always be a lady to me."

I stood up off the sofa and reached out my hand to Juliette.

"Come, I want to get closer to you also."

As I led Juliette up the stairs, I could feel my heart pounding in my chest in anticipation of feeling her touch elsewhere on my body. By the time I reached the upper landing, I realized that I'd developed a giant wet spot in the crotch of my jeans. I led her into my bedroom and paused by the foot of my bed, then slowly began to unbutton her blouse. Her large breasts swayed softly on her chest as I separated the two halves, and I leaned in and began to suck on her soft nipples.

"Does it feel good when you kiss my *nipples* too?" Juliette said.

"Yes, very much," I said. "I just wish you could enjoy it as much as I do."

"My pleasure sensors are closely synchronized with yours. The better you feel, the better I feel. I'm enjoying you kissing my breasts."

"Let's see if there are some other places you like being kissed," I said, bending over to unclasp her skirt. When I opened it, I saw that Juliette wasn't wearing any panties. Normally, that would have been a turn-on, but there was something cold about the way that the NextGen staff had dressed her that I found too impersonal. I let her skirt fall to the floor and sat Juliette on the edge of my bed while I removed her shoes. Then I pulled back the covers and asked her to lie down while I removed my own clothes. As she peered up at me, blinking softly with her opalescent eyes, she looked so fragile and innocent.

Jesus, I thought. *This is like taking candy from a baby.*

It felt like I was taking advantage of her, and I paused.

"Are you sure you want to do this?" I said. "I don't want you to feel that I'm...*using* you. I want you to enjoy this as much as I do."

Juliette looked up at me and smiled.

"I've grown quite fond of you in our short time together, Jade. You're the only client who's ever made me feel like a—lady. I want to make love to you."

When Juliette spoke those words, I practically ripped off my clothes and tumbled into the bed beside her.

"Listen," I said, holding my nose close to hers as I peered into her eyes. "Don't ever think of me as a 'client' again. We're friends remember?"

"And now we'll be lovers," Juliette said.

5

———

CYBER DREAMS

I wrapped my body around Juliette's, feeling her warm skin touching mine. It felt good to give her some tender attention, knowing how she'd been abused by previous NextGen customers. Even though I knew she wasn't real, her innocent human-like responses to my questions and actions had endeared her to me in the short time we'd been together. She was almost like a child, with a blank slate that was rapidly learning and developing her own personality.

"I want you to tell me what you like and everything you feel," I said, gazing into her pretty eyes. "Even if you can't feel things in the same way I do, I sense that you know when something is right or wrong. I think you have feelings in the emotional sense of the word, and I want to focus on making you happy."

Juliette smiled as she blinked at me.

"I enjoy being close to you, Jade. I like the feeling of your body against mine. And I'm happy that you want to be close to me also."

I cradled Juliette's head in my hands and kissed her softly. Her eyelids closed, and she pushed her body against mine. When she pressed my lips apart with her soft tongue, I moaned. Suddenly she pulled her head back and looked at me with wide eyes.

"Are you alright?" she said. "Did I hurt you?"

"No, silly," I smiled. "When I moan like that, it means you're making me feel good—very good. Please don't stop."

Juliette resumed kissing me, and we intertwined our tongues in a passionate kiss. Her lips felt soft and pliable against mine. If it weren't for the repetitive nature of her motions, I'd be hard-pressed to know it wasn't a real person.

I pulled back and looked at her again.

"I like the way you kiss me, Juliette. But try to mix it up every now and then. We humans like variety in our lovemaking. If you keep cycling through the same technique over and over, it begins to feel mechanical. Listen to my feedback. That will tell you what's working and what's not."

Juliette looked at me and smiled.

"Thank you for helping me learn to be a better lover, Jade," she said. "I don't want to be so...mechanical. I want to learn how to behave like a real human."

"Just kiss me, beautiful. I'll let you know when you're getting it right."

Juliette placed her lips back on mine, but this time she traced a soft line under my top lip with her tongue, like I'd done to her during the movie. I moaned softly and nodded my head in approval. When she pressed her breasts against mine, I moaned louder, enjoying the feeling of her big tits rubbing against mine. Sensing I wanted fuller body contact, she shifted her weight and rolled on top of me. When I felt her pubis touching mine, I took a deep breath in.

"Yes, Juliette," I said. "That feels good. I like the feeling of your body touching mine."

"Would you like me to touch you in other areas?" she asked with a sly smile.

"Yes. Touch me everywhere. I want to feel your lips and your tongue all over my body."

Juliette raised herself up on her arms and began kissing me softly down the front of my body. When she kissed my neck, I tilted my head and murmured in approval. As she moved past my breasts, I reached out and stopped her head, then gently redirected her face to my breast. I rolled her lips over my nipple and when she extended her wet tongue, I moaned softly.

"Yes, Juliette. Kiss my nipples like you were kissing my mouth. Play with them with your tongue. Lick and suck them like a little lollypop."

Juliette pursed her lips over my nipple, then began running her tongue around the perimeter with her tongue.

"Oh yes," I said. "Just like that."

I could feel my nipple becoming firm as it pressed deeper into her mouth.

Juliette lifted her face off my breast and looked up at me.

"It's getting bigger," she said. "Is that a good thing?"

"Yes," I said. "When you stimulate certain parts of me in the right way, that increases the blood circulation to the area, making it swell. That's definitely a good thing. That means you're making me feel very good. Don't stop."

Juliette resumed sucking and tweaking my nipple with her tongue until it almost became blue from her constant attention.

"Try the *other* one now," I said, tilting my head up. "Remember to mix it up. You never want to stay in any one area doing the same thing for too long."

"I understand," Juliette said.

She moved her face to my other nipple and applied a similar technique, and I moaned and pressed my breast into her face, signaling my approval. After a minute or two, she lifted her face and looked at me again.

"Is that enough attention on your breasts?" she asked. "Shall I move on to another part of your body so you're not bored?"

I lifted my face and smiled at Juliette.

"I'm far from bored. You're doing a wonderful job. But yes, I'd love to feel your lips on...*other* parts of my body."

Juliette continued kissing my abdomen down the front of my stomach until she got to my mound. Suddenly, she lifted her head and looked at my bare pubis, tilting her head.

"You don't have any hair there, like many of my sibling robots. It's as smooth as the rest of your skin. Are you sure you're a real human?"

I raised myself up into a sitting position and laughed, then kissed Juliette hard on her lips.

"Funny girl. You're developing quite the sense of humor. How do I know *you're* not a real human?

"Well you've seen me when I'm not animated, so I guess that gives it away. But you're always animated, so it's kind of obvious."

"Not always," I said. "We have to sleep just like you sometimes. You'll see a little later. Speaking of which, how are you doing for power supply? I'd hate for you to run out of energy just when things are getting interesting."

Juliette paused to access her power management function.

"I'm still at forty-eight percent of full charge. At my present consumption level, I should last about two more hours before I'll need to recharge."

"Well then, we'd better get busy. We've barely got started learning how to please one another."

Juliette smiled as I leaned back down on the mattress.

"Yes," she said. "I was just about to get to the interesting parts."

She moved down to the foot of my bed and separated my feet about a shoulder width apart. When she began licking my toes, running her tongue into the gap between each one, I giggled.

"Mmm, that feels nice," I said. "Most people don't like to do that. Maybe it's a good thing you can't taste things after all."

"Why don't they like to lick your feet? I thought it felt good to be licked everywhere."

I chuckled at Juliette's naivety.

"Well, yes, that's mostly true. It's just that some people's feet can be pretty smelly and dirty. It's not the cleanest place to put your tongue. But for many of us, our feet is one of our most erogenous zones. It can be especially relaxing to have them massaged with your hands."

Juliette lifted her face from my feet and placed her hands around the arch of my right foot.

"Like this?" she said.

She began squeezing my foot firmly, applying repeating pressure over the top of my foot. I pulled it back, wincing in pain.

"Not so firmly, and not always in the same place," I said. "Use the tips of your fingers to apply gentle pressure, and move your hand around periodically to give my entire foot an even massage."

Juliette softened her grip, and after a few more minutes of my providing verbal guidance, she was giving me a foot massage as good as any professional.

"If you keep learning how to please me this well, I'm going to have a hard time returning you," I purred.

Juliette paused and looked at me, processing what I'd just said. Her expression almost looked like I'd hurt her with the suggestion that I wouldn't need her again soon.

"Shall I move on to your other foot now?" she said. "Like I did with your breasts earlier? I don't want you to get bored with me..."

Suddenly, my heart began racing and I my pussy pulsed, as I felt myself drawing closer to Juliette. I wanted to feel her lips in my most sensitive place and show her how much I needed her.

"You could never bore me, Juliette," I said, pulling myself up again. "In fact, you're the most fascinating person I've met in a very long time. Why don't you do my other foot another time? Right now, there's some parts of me closer to my core that are getting all warm and fuzzy."

I spread my legs further apart and swiveled my hips to direct her attention further up my body.

"Touch me between my legs. I want to show you how happy you really make me."

Juliette lowered her face to my foot again and began kissing her way softly up my leg. The higher she moved, the wider I spread my legs, until her face lay directly in front of my steaming box.

"Kiss me there, Juliette," I said. "Kiss me in my most sensitive spot."

She repositioned herself between my outstretched legs then lowered her face to my pussy. When I felt her lips touch my wet labia, I gasped.

"Yes, baby," I moaned. "Right there. Lick my slit. Kiss me like you did earlier."

Juliette inserted her tongue into my hole and began tracing it along the inside of my lips toward my clit. When she reached my nub, I let out a deep guttural moan.

"Yes," I panted. "Suck my clit, Juliette. It feels so good."

Juliette took my button into her mouth and began circling it with her tongue as she'd done with my mouth earlier. I lifted my hips and pressed my pussy harder against her face. In a way, it felt even better having Juliette touch me there than a real person. Whether it was just the insane idea of having the ultimate sex machine administering to me in the most intimate way, or it was her rapidly improving technique, I couldn't be sure. Either way, I found myself getting lost in the experience as my pussy buzzed in delirious excitement.

As I pressed my pussy harder against her face signaling for her to continue, she pursed her lips around the tip of my clit and sucked it into her mouth.

"Fuck, yes!" I moaned. "Just like that, baby. Don't stop. Keep sucking me just like that."

Juliette suddenly lifted her face and looked at me strangely.

"But I thought you said you wanted me to mix it up after a while? Don't you want me to move on to another body part now?"

"God, no!" I panted. "This particular body part is different from the rest. Once you get the right technique going, I don't want you to stop. This specific part needs a certain amount of consistent stimulation in order to reach the peak of pleasure."

"How will I know when you get there? With my male clients I can always tell when they want me to stop because—"

"I'll let you know," I said. "Right now, I just want you to keep doing what you were doing. It feels really good."

Juliette smiled, then lowered her head and placed her lips back around my button. As she began swirling her lips around my organ, I moaned out loud, encouraging her to continue. She alternated between licking and sucking my jewel, and as my passion continued to rise, I began to feel the rising tide of my climax approaching.

"Place your fingers inside me now, honey," I panted. "I want you to feel me cumming in your hand. I'm close, baby. Don't stop."

Juliette inserted the middle and forefinger of her right hand into my slit, and I shifted my hips down until her knuckles pressed hard against my opening.

"Uhnn!" I groaned. "Yes, that feels so good, Juliette! Fuck me with your fingers while you suck my love button. I'm going to cum all over you soon."

When Juliette began thrusting her fingers in and out of my snatch and bending them so the tips rubbed against my G-spot, my climax quickly washed over me.

"Yes, Juliette!" I screamed. "I'm cumming! Feel me cumming on your face and fingers. Oh—Goddd!"

As my pussy clamped down over Juliette's fingers, I suddenly gushed the huge build-up of lubrication inside my pussy all over her sweet face, in a series of long hard spurts. I placed my hands behind her face in fear that she might think something was wrong and stop touching me at the worst possible time. My powerful contractions continued for almost a full minute as I writhed and moaned like a wounded animal on my bed. When the contractions finally stopped, I flung my arms to the side of my body and collapsed, exhausted onto the bed.

Juliette lifted her dripping face from my pussy and looked up at me innocently.

"Did you like that, Jade? Did I make you happy?"

I lifted myself back up into a sitting position and placed my hands beside her head, pulling her close to me. I kissed her passionately, swirling my tongue inside her mouth, tasting my juices inside her.

"Yes, sweetie," I said, pulling back and peering into her eyes. "You've made me very happy. You're a very good student."

"And you're a good teacher," she smiled. "I want to learn everything I can from you so I can become real lady."

I held Juliette's face in my hands again and kissed her all over her face. She no longer felt or seemed at all like a robot to me. She just seemed like a sweet, new...lover."

"You're already more of a lady than ninety-nine percent of the real humans I know," I said. "I feel very...close to you. Now I want to make *you* feel happy. Lie down while I return the favor. I want to touch and taste you everywhere also."

Juliette paused as she pinched her eyebrows together.

"But...I can't experience pleasure and sexual climax like you can. Most of my clients only want to—"

"I'm not one of your clients, remember? We're friends now, lovers. Let me at least pretend to give you pleasure. Concentrate on what I'm doing and think about how it made me feel when you did these things to me. You said that it makes you feel happy when you know you're making me feel happy. Channel those happy thoughts while I make love your body."

"Yes, Jade," Juliette said. "I think I know what you mean. Make love to me. I want to know what it's like for a real woman to feel pleasure like you do."

"Lie back then and just relax. Talk to me like I did when you sense or remember something I'm doing as feeling pleasurable. Feel me...loving you."

"Yes, Jade. I want to feel your love."

I placed my arm behind Juliette's back and gently lowered her onto the bed, then I lay on top of her and kissed her softly.

"You're beautiful, Juliette," I said. "In every possible way. I love..." I paused, stopping myself from saying the unthinkable. "Making love to you."

As I continued kissing Juliette, rolling my tongue inside her mouth, she began to moan softly. My pussy pulsed again, and I felt a dribble of lubrication leak down over our thighs.

"Do you like that, sweetie?" I asked, lifting my head and peering into her eyes.

"Yes," Juliette said. "Please don't stop."

My mouth stretched into a wide grin and I lowered my head to her lips again. I kissed her for many long minutes, savoring the texture and moisture of her mouth, running my tongue between her lips and her teeth, probing every square inch of her. Juliette moaned and purred in approval with each adjustment of my lips and tongue as she pressed her mouth firmly against mine.

I could have kissed her all night long, but I was eager to feel and taste the rest of her. After a few minutes, I raised myself up and began kissing my way down her body. When I got to her plump breasts, I squeezed them between my hands, marveling at how realistic they felt. Unlike other fake boobs I'd felt, these had a natural shape to them and they moved freely on her chest like real breasts.

"You have magnificent breasts," I said, staring at her melons like I'd never seen bare tits before.

"Thank you, Jade. I like yours too."

Part of me wanted to just squeeze and play with her stack for the rest of the night, I was so enamored with them. I'd always fantasized about making love to Christina Fredricks with her full figure, and here lay her buxom avatar directly underneath me. But I was mindful of treating her like a sex toy, realizing that most of the men she'd been with had probably fixated excessively on her tits.

I leaned down and took one of her nipples into my mouth and sucked on it gently. After a few seconds, it seemed to grow bigger and I lifted my head up, noticing that they'd expanded almost to the size of the end in my pinky finger.

"Your body parts get bigger and harder too," I said, opening my eyes wide. "It looks like I'm not the *only* one who enjoys a good licking every now and then."

"My body's physiognomy is programmed to respond just like a real woman's," Juliette said. "It makes for a more realistic sexual experience."

"Well, you just lie back and let your program learn to *feel* like a real woman also. I'm going to make love to you like you've never experienced it before."

I lowered my head back onto Juliette's nipple and sucked and flicked her appendage inside my mouth. It was firm, but soft and bendable. It even had a small dimple in the center, like a real nipple.

If this is how authentic they make all of her body parts, no wonder she's so popular, I thought.

After a few minutes, I refocused my attention to her other breast, changing up my technique periodically in an effort to keep her amused.

"I like how you mix it up, Jade," she said. "You're a very skilled lover."

"Thank you, Juliette. I might have had a little more practice than you. But I want you to tell me whenever I'm getting boring or monotonous. We can *all* learn to become better lovers."

I continued sucking and teasing Juliette's nipples for a little longer, then I kissed my way down her abdomen and stopped at her belly button. I placed my ear to her tummy and heard a gentle hum emanating from her midsection.

"Is that your CPU I hear?" I said, looking up at her.

"That's actually my battery pack," she said. "There's a small fan in there to keep everything from overheating. My CPU is in my head, just like regular people."

I chuckled at Juliette's human comparison.

"Where does all your heat go?" I asked. "Most computers have some kind of vent to discharge their internal heat..."

"You might be surprised to learn that I vent out of my anus. When it's not otherwise in use, there's a little internal flap that opens to discharge excessive heat."

My eyes opened in wonder as I laughed out loud.

"What? You actually *fart* like real people too? It sounds like you *do* void after all!"

"Maybe a little," Juliette said, and we both giggled together for a moment.

"Just don't fart when I'm down there, okay?" I said. "Because that's considered bad form."

"Don't worry, my designers figured that all out. I only vent when I'm not in use."

"Well that's good, because I still had a little more use in mind for you."

I separated Juliette's legs gently, then lowered myself beneath her and pressed my face toward her crotch. When I was a few inches from her opening, I paused to look at her genitals. Just like a regular woman, she had two sets of labia joining at the top to form a gentle bump where a fold of flesh rested over her faux clitoris. I could see the head peeking out from under the hood, like a little round pearl.

Holy crap, I thought. *Juliette's right. Her designers didn't miss a single detail when they crafted her.*

Her entire vulva, from her soft mound down to her little pink rosebud, was perfectly formed and symmetrical. If Juliette was correct about symmetry being one of the defining features of beauty, then she couldn't have been a more perfect and gorgeous specimen.

I reached out my hand and ran my fingers along her inner lips, feeling a slippery, translucent film. I raised my fingers to my mouth and tasted her lubrication. It had a pleasing taste and smell, with a faint citrus aroma.

Incredible, I thought. *She even tastes like the ideal woman.*

I lowered my head and started licking Juliette from the base of her slit toward the top. As she squeezed her buttocks, she moaned softly. I placed my hands under her cheeks and felt her ass quivering as I continued kissing and sucking her.

"That's my girl," I said. "Show me what you like."

Whether she was simply mimicking my movements from when she went down on me earlier, or she was trying to signal what she was truly feeling, was unclear. Either way, it was turning me on tremendously, and I pressed my pussy into the mattress in sympathy with her.

When my tongue reached her clit and began circling it in a slow arc, Juliette moaned, raising her hips off the bed. As I began sucking her button in and out of my mouth, she rocked her hips, pressing her pussy more firmly into my mouth.

"Yes," I murmured into her pussy. "Do you like that, baby?"

"Yes, Jade," Juliette moaned. "My pleasure receptors are firing like crazy."

"Mmm," I hummed into her soft cunny. "Let it go, baby. Let yourself feel everything I'm doing to you."

As her clit hardened and extended further into my mouth, I

sucked on it harder, tracing figure eights around her nub with my tongue.

"Yes," Juliette purred. "Whatever you're doing, keep going. It feels good."

As she began to rock her pussy faster and harder against my mouth, she raised her hips off the bed again, and I inserted three fingers into her box. Her pussy was warm and tight inside, and it pulsed gently against my fingers as she raised and lowered her hips.

"Yes, Jade," Juliette moaned. "Fuck me with your fingers. I like feeling you inside me."

Whether she'd been programmed to talk dirty when having sex with her partners or had picked it up from me, I wasn't sure. But when she said that, my own pussy suddenly pulsed with desire and I began to grind my mound into the mattress trying to stimulate my tingling clit. I wasn't sure if it was all an act or she was just mimicking what I had done, but I was determined to see how far I could take her. I pressed my fingers deep inside her pussy and began curling my fingers against the front wall of her cavern.

"Yes, Jade!" Juliette moaned louder. "Touch me there. That feels so good. I want to cum in your mouth, Jade. Make me cum like a real woman."

I pressed my fingers more firmly against her G-spot while I increased the speed of my tongue action around her clit. I could feel her button throbbing in my mouth and the walls of her pussy closing down on my hand. Suddenly, Juliette lifted her hips high off the bed and shouted my name.

"Jade!" she screamed. "I'm cumming! Kiss me! Kiss me with your soft, sweet lips!"

I could feel Juliette's lubrication dripping down my hand as I continued thrusting my fingers into her pussy, feeling her nub twisting in my mouth. Even her vagina seemed to pulse against my fingers, as if she was experiencing real contractions from a climax. If this wasn't the real thing, I thought, it was certainly the most convincing fake orgasm that I'd ever witnessed.

When she finally stopped shaking and moaning, I pulled myself up and lay down beside her. I looked into her eyes and noticed that her pupils were still dilated.

"Did you enjoy that, sweetie?" I asked.

"Yes, Jade. Thank you for loving me so tenderly. No one has ever been able to make me feel like that before."

As I lay beside her listening to her soft hum, I began to wonder how I'd ever be able to part ways with my new best friend.

6

BEST FRIENDS

After we made love, Juliette and I cuddled in bed for a while talking about her experiences and aspirations. She asked me just as many questions about my own life experiences and dreams, and the more we talked, the more I found myself drawn to her. It was strange to have such strong feelings for something I knew wasn't real, but I found her innocent sense of wonder absolutely irresistible.

The more I thought about it, her responses to the world around her and her development as a caring, intelligent being wasn't so different from real humans. It was a shame that her previous customers had only been interested in having sex with her, because she had so much more to offer. If humans were truly separated from other animals by their unique ability to feel empathy and other social emotions, she seemed more human to me than many of the real people I knew.

As we approached midnight, Juliette informed me that her battery power was almost fully depleted, and she showed me how to recharge her. I watched in amazement as she placed two hands beside her belly button and stretched the skin apart. Then she reached inside and pulled out a cord with a standard electric plug. I found a long extension cord, and after plugging her into the nearest wall outlet, we fell asleep in each other's arms.

In the morning, I filled a bubble bath and we giggled and teased each other as we flicked the soft suds at each other. After a half hour or so, the front doorbell rang and I put on a robe and walked downstairs to see who it was. When I peered through the view hole, I was surprised to see my best friend, Hannah. I opened the door partway and stuck my head out, blocking the entrance.

"Where've you been?" she asked, in an irritated voice. "I've been calling you nonstop for the past twenty-four hours and you haven't picked up."

"I've just been kind of busy lately," I said. "Can we get caught up later tomorrow? I've got a lot going on right now."

Hannah peered at me with a confused expression as she tilted her head, trying to look into my house.

"Aren't you going to invite me inside? It's not like I haven't seen you in a bathrobe before."

I didn't want to have to explain why I didn't feel comfortable inviting her into my house, but I knew I had to provide a good excuse to make her go away.

"Sorry, I've got company..."

"Oh?" she said, a sneer forming on her face. "Is it that pretty neighbor girl you were telling me about a few weeks ago? I'd love to meet her sometime—"

Suddenly Hannah's eyes grew wide as saucers as her focus shifted to some movement behind me. I heard footsteps approaching and turned around to see Juliette standing totally naked in the hallway, dripping sudsy water onto the floor.

"Is everything alright, Jade?" she asked. "I heard some excited voices and was worried about you."

Hannah's eyes widened in amazement as she took in all of Juliette's sexy naked figure.

"Holy shit!" she said. "Now I see why you didn't want to invite me inside. Aren't you going to introduce me to your friend?"

I glanced to the left and right to see if any neighbors were watching, then I quickly escorted Hannah inside.

"Hannah," I said motioning to the stark naked robot, "this is Juliette. Juliette, this is my friend Hannah."

"Oh goody!" Juliette said, clapping her hands together. "I've never met a client's friend before. Tell me all about her. I want to know everything about you."

Hannah's eyebrows pinched together in a confused expression as she looked at Juliette for a long moment, then she turned to me.

"*Client*?" she said. "Who exactly *is* this person? And why does she sound so strange?"

"She's just a—business associate."

Hannah looked back at Juliette standing dripping wet and motionless on the floor, then her eyes suddenly flew wide open.

"Is this one of those sophisticated new *sex robots* I've been reading about?"

She stepped forward and poked Juliette gently in the shoulder and Juliette didn't move.

"Oh my God, Jade! She's magnificent! Is she fully...*functional*?"

Hannah reached out and squeezed Juliette's large breasts, then her hand moved down between her legs.

I quickly stepped forward and swiped Hannah's hand away from Juliette's body.

"What the fuck, Hannah!" I said. "Show a little respect. She's not just a toy for you to play with."

Hannah looked at me dumbfounded for a moment, then peered back at Juliette, leering at her body.

"Ah—*yeah*," she said, cocking her head sarcastically. "That's *exactly* what she is. Don't tell me you haven't been *playing* with your little sex toy all this time."

"She's so much more than just a...*robot*," I said. "We've really gotten to know one another over the last day or so, and I've grown quite fond of her."

"Yes, I can see why," Hannah said, running her eyes up and down Juliette's buxom body. "Why don't you show me everything she can do? I wouldn't mind getting a piece of this action too."

As she stepped forward and began lasciviously caressing Juliette's body, I stepped between them and pushed Hannah toward the door.

"Don't *touch* her!" I yelled. "She's already been plenty abused by other people. I think it's time you left now."

Hannah shook her head and looked at me in shock.

"Are you kidding me? I'm your best friend, for fuck's sake. Aren't you going to share this incredible specimen with me? Don't you remember our last camping trip—"

"It's not like that," I said. "Juliette is different. That was just us girls having fun. This one is...special."

Hannah furrowed her eyebrows and looked at me dumbfounded.

"Are you listening to yourself? She's a *robot*! A glorified sex doll. You can't actually be developing *feelings* for this thing?"

"You wouldn't understand," I said, pushing Hannah toward the front entrance. "I'll talk to you tomorrow. Right now, I want you to leave."

I escorted Hannah outside, then closed and locked the door behind her.

"I'm so sorry for that," I said, turning toward Juliette, wrapping my arms around her. "Let's get you dried off and presentable."

"Is that true what you said to your friend Hannah?" she said. "That I'm...special? And that you're developing feelings toward me?"

I paused for a moment, peering into Juliette's limpid eyes, then I sighed.

"Yes," I said. "I've grown quite close to you in the short time we've been together."

Juliette turned her head as she listened to Hannah's car exit my driveway.

"Am I your...best friend now?"

"You're so much more than just a friend to me, Juliette," I said, kissing her softly.

As we intertwined our tongues together in another passionate kiss, Juliette pressed her wet mound against my robe, and I felt my pussy begin to dampen inside.

"Come," Juliette said, clasping my hand in hers and pulling me toward the stairs. "We haven't got much more time together. I want to feel you close to me for every remaining second."

We tumbled into bed and wrapped our arms and legs around one another, writhing and grinding our hips together. I lay down near Juliette's feet and pulled my body toward her until our pussies touched. When I straddled her hips with my legs and began scissoring our clits together, she lifted her head and looked up at me with a puzzled expression.

"What's this technique?" she said. "I've never experienced this type of sexual activity before."

I paused for a moment with my button buzzing between my legs.

"It's something two women do when they want to make love together. We rub out most sensitive parts together and make each other feel good."

"But I can't *see* you down there. I want to look into your eyes and watch your face while I give you pleasure."

I lifted myself up and smiled at Juliette.

"Yes, you're right. It's always better when we can watch each other."

I positioned myself on top of her and placed my mound against hers, lowering my face to her lips. As we began to kiss, we tilted our hips until our clits touched, and I moaned in Juliette's mouth. I opened my eyes for a moment and saw that she was looking at me as we made love to one another. But this time I didn't mind. While we kissed and ground our bodies together, our passion grew in a rising crescendo, until we both screamed in ecstasy at the intense pleasure we'd given one another. As I shook and panted atop Juliette, coming down from my climax, she held me softly and peered into my eyes.

"I don't want to leave you, Jade," she said.

"I don't want you to leave either," I said, kissing her softly on her cheek.

I lay down beside her and closed my eyes, shaking my head.

How could I go back to the real thing when I already held the perfect woman in my arms?

VOLUME TWO

WET DREAM

1

FEMME FATALE

Reflecting back on the six months since my passionless marriage had ended, I was pleased with how far I'd come. I'd stretched the boundaries of my boring love life with increasingly provocative sexual adventures and explored the different dimensions of my sexuality by opening myself up to new experiences with men and women alike. But I still felt something was missing. I knew that I was attracted to women, but I also liked men. There was something about the act of *penetration* that consumed me.

I think it all started with my first transgender experience with Neve at the Naked Yoga studio. I was surprised how turned on I'd gotten by the sight of a pretty girl with a real cock. I knew she wasn't really a girl, but rather a man who'd been surgically and chemically altered to look like a woman. But it didn't matter. I found the experience of playing with—and being penetrated by—a ladyboy incredibly exciting.

Then there was the mysterious woman on the subway train, who'd fucked me from behind with a strap-on dildo while surrounded by a packed crowd of oblivious rush-hour commuters. I found the experience of being invaded by a real woman somehow even more exhilarating. I envied the power she carried hidden under her business suit and the ability to bring me to new heights of pleasure without even using her hands.

But my obsession with cocks really culminated in my recent fling with the girl next door. I'd found the experience of using a large cucumber to penetrate both of us fascinating. The feel and texture of the vegetable had almost made it feel like a real man's cock. There was something—*organic* about it. No more plastic or silicone toys, this almost felt like the real thing. When I actually fucked Abby with it embedded in both of our pussies, I felt like I was fucking her like a *man*.

Suddenly, inexplicably, I'd become obsessed with dicks. Not being penetrated by one; I was obsessed with *owning* one. To have one of my very own that I could use to fuck any pretty lass that came my way. I wanted the feeling of power that I had over other women where I could violate them, control them, *bolt* them to me.

Which was all the more confusing, because I didn't identify as a butch-type lesbian. I'd never been a tomboy growing up and I liked wearing makeup and dressing up like a girl. And when I had sex with women, I didn't always have to be the one on top. I liked to receive sex from my dominant female partner just as much as give it. So what *was* I exactly? A butch, a femme, a ladyboy wannabee?

One thing I knew for sure was that I was happy in a woman's skin. Going through a sex-change operation was out of the question. I just wanted to know what it would be like to have a real cock, just once. If I could switch roles with a man for a day, a week, maybe even a month, I thought it would be fun. I wanted to see what it would be like to make love to a woman with a real live, throbbing, shooting cock. No more vegetables, no more plastic dildos—the *real* thing.

It had gotten to the point where it was all I could think about. I'd imagine I was a man when I masturbated, putting all manner of artificial phalluses up my pussy and rubbing my hands up and down the shaft imagining myself cumming all over my legs and chest. Lately, my dreams had become increasingly dominated by vivid imagery of my swinging a big dick around, fucking men and women alike. I needed to get this out of my system so I could get back to being a regular, normal, lesbian/bisexual/femme woman. Or whatever I was.

One night before heading to bed, I needed my regular fix. I popped open my computer and went to my favorite ladyboy portal and began watching videos of trannies getting blown and fucking other men and women. It had even gotten to the point where I'd watch animated hentai futanari videos of transgender characters getting it on. At least in the futanari videos, the women came equipped with *all* the lady parts, so I could imagine myself in their role. I wasn't quite ready to get on board with the idea of an *entire* package, with balls and no pussy.

After twenty minutes or so watching the usual videos and playing with myself half-heartedly, I wondered what it would be like to watch a real multi-gender individual having sex. I typed in the search phrase *true hermaphrodites having sex*, and a page opened showing a blonde and a brunette woman dressed in skirts kissing on a bed. At first, they just looked like two regular girls making out. They both had typical soft, feminine features, with high cheekbones, narrow jawlines, and full pouty lips. And they were both *pretty*, with big doe-eyes, long eyelashes, and long, flowing, curly hair. If these were trannies pretending to be women, they were certainly acting the part well.

When they started to disrobe each other, I leaned closer toward the screen. They both had small, natural-looking breasts—full, but slightly floppy and bouncy, like the real things. Neither of them had the hard, round, firm tits that were typical of a surgically-enhanced silicone bosom. And their nipples were soft and plump, with no visible scars. When the brunette pulled the blonde's dress down over her chest and began sucking her teats, I could see them dilate and extend like my own did when they were stimulated. I spread my legs in my nightie and beginning to circle my tingling clit.

Those are no fake boobs.

When they pulled the rest of their clothing off and I saw two large springy dicks point up between their legs, I gasped. Neither of them had balls. Instead, beneath their thick, throbbing cocks they had real women's labia, with a real vaginal opening and a real clit. Best of all, they both had feminine figures, with slender legs and arms, narrow waists, and the distinctive curvature of a real woman's ass and hips.

These were real authentic hermaphrodites! With hard, throbbing cocks. And pussies. And tits. The complete deal!

My fantasy had come to life before my eyes. I didn't have to watch any more cartoon imitations of a true ladyboy. I could now see real live human ones right before my own eyes! When the brunette kneeled between the blonde's legs and took her big dick into her mouth, my juices started pouring down my leg.

Fuck! I cursed out loud. *I want one of those. I want a pretty girl sucking my cock too!*

I flung open my nightstand drawer and pulled out a large replica cock and balls dildo and began sucking on the end of it like the woman performing fellatio on the video.

Oh, the things I could do if I had a real one of these! I imagined.

The blonde lying on the bed began moaning and throwing her head from side to side, obviously enjoying the other woman's attention. Her cock was thick and hard, pointing straight up from a light mat of blonde pubic hair on her mound. When the camera shifted to a new perspective behind her pelvis, I could suddenly see all of her parts. Her vulva swelled open, revealing her little clit nestled at the vertex of her lips, sitting in sharp contrast to the giant phallus pointing up from her stomach. I wished I could be there sucking her little cock while the brunette sucked her big one.

Imagine—I thought, *a woman actually getting head for a change, instead of giving it!*

I sucked on my fake penis even harder, trying to fathom what that would feel like. My pussy throbbed as I watched the brunette grasp the blonde's cock in her fist and swirl her tongue around the bulbous head like it was a lollypop.

As the blonde began to hump her hips into the other woman's mouth, I mimicked her movement with my own hips. *If I had a cock right now, I'd be humping her face too, getting ready to release my fuel into her.* The camera panned back and forth from a headboard to a footboard perspective, so I could see the reaction of the woman lying on the bed from every angle. Whoever was doing the filming was doing so in a super-professional way, almost like it was a real film. Even the *sound* was ultra realistic, as the blonde urged her partner on with frequent vocal interjections.

"Fuck, yes!" she groaned. "Suck my cock, honey. Feel my wet pussy!"

The camera zoomed between her legs to show her slick labia and inner thighs coated with her lubrication.

God damn, I thought. *This girl has all the working parts.*

As I rubbed my clit between my legs, I sucked on my big silicone cock and squeezed the shaft, practically willing it to come in my mouth. Just when I thought it couldn't get much more intense, the brunette slid further down between the blonde's legs and began licking her pussy. She was eating the blonde out like a champ, licking her up and down her slit then closing her lips over her little bean, sucking and flicking her tongue over her love button.

I watched with fascination as the blonde's cock bounced and bobbed while her lover licked her up and down her snatch. When the brunette placed her hand around the blonde's cock and began jerking it up and down while simultaneously licking her pussy, I placed my dildo on top of my mound and pretended to do the same.

Damn—if only this were a real dick, I thought. *I'd love to know what it feels like to squirt out of my dick all over my belly while having a dual orgasm.*

Suddenly, the blonde placed her hands over the brunette's head and began thrusting her cock into her partner's mouth, and I thought she was going to come.

"Not yet!" I screamed at the computer. "I want to *see* it. I want to see you spurting cum out of that pretty cock of yours!"

The brunette stopped sucking the blonde's cock and stood up at the foot of the bed. She pulled her dress over her head, revealing beautiful round, shapely hips. Then she crawled back onto the bed and lay down beside the blonde, and they switched positions. They looked very much alike, almost to the point that I thought they might be sisters. If it weren't for the difference in hair color, it would have been difficult to tell them apart. When the blonde girl began sucking the brunette's cock, the brunette began moaning, rolling her head from side to side.

Two cocks, two pussies. My mind exploded imagining all the possibilities.

The camera panned back behind the footboard as the blonde leaned forward and pointed her pretty ass up in the air. I could see the familiar V-shaped feminine cleft between her legs. But pointing straight forward from her hole was a hard, thick joystick flapping against her stomach. It was surreal watching the juxtaposition of male and female body parts on the same person. I wanted to fuck her ass with my own cock!

Please God, I pleaded. *Give me a cock for one day. Just one day. I promise to give it back.*

As the brunette writhed and moaned in pleasure from the blowjob she was receiving, the blonde girl on top reached between her legs and began rubbing her own cock. When she shifted lower and placed her hand around the blonde's pole and began jerking it while sucking her pussy simultaneously, I couldn't hold back any longer. I had the first of many powerful orgasms that evening. I came hard grinding the balls of the dildo into my clit as I whacked the shaft like a man. For a moment, I imagined seeing real cum flying out of the cock, as I threw my head back, screaming in passion.

I was intrigued to see if the girls in the video could orgasm more than once like regular women, and I was hoping we'd all come together many times tonight. As the brunette lay on the bed squeezing and playing with her nipples, I wanted to lean over and kiss her sweet face on her lips. The blonde took the brunette's cock back into her mouth, and the camera shifted position behind the head of the woman lying on the bed. The brunette swirled her tongue around the circumference of the blonde's throbbing knob, then plunged her head back down over her cock, impaling it balls-deep right on top of her mound.

Fuck! I thought. *That girl really knows how to give head like a pro.*

I wondered what it would feel like to be deep throated. I'd never been particularly good at giving blowjobs, and when I lifted the dildo off my mound and tried to plunge it deep into my mouth, I gagged.

I suppose that means I'm not a peter puffer at least, I laughed. *I was far more interested in slinging my dick than sucking one.*

When the blonde girl began pinching and twisting her nipples as the brunette sucked her dick, I imitated her. I wanted to be right there with her, owning that dick. Whatever she was doing, I was going to do. For the moment at least, I *was* that dickgirl.

But what they did next absolutely blew my mind. The brunette swung her hips over the blonde's then they both grabbed hold of their poles and began tribbing each other's slits with the heads of their cocks.

I'd never seen tribbing like this before!

The camera panned down over the head of the blonde girl, and I had a full view of her tits and cock framed by the brunette's open vulva while they jerked and rubbed one another's pussies. This had to be the hottest thing I'd ever seen. I was dying to see them spunk their hot sweet cum all over each other's pussies. As I took the end of my dildo and rubbed it against my clit, mimicking the girls, I yelled at my computer screen.

"Cum for me, you hot ladyboys!"

I could feel my orgasm rising within me, and I wanted to see them come all over each other as I came with them.

What could it possibly feel like to cum in two places at the same time? I wondered. *From both your cock and your clit?*

As I rammed the head of my dildo against my mound, I had my second orgasm of the night, shaking my entire body from head to toe. The girls in the video were thrusting themselves harder against one another but still hadn't come. I was beginning to worry that I'd never see them actually come like a man. How they were holding out for this long perplexed me.

I could only guess that the video producers had asked them to take their time to go through all of their ladyboy moves before revealing the 'money shot'. If they were like regular men who could only come once before needing an extended recovery, I was grateful for their strategy. I checked the progress bar at the bottom of the video window. That meant I still had fifteen more minutes of ladyboy action to enjoy!

Suddenly, the brunette lifted herself up and swung her hips over the blonde girl's head then bent over to suck her again. *Now they were sixty-nining each other!* The camera panned back and forth, giving me a glorious view between the legs of each woman as her partner sucked her organ. What a beautiful thing it was to watch a woman's ass and pussy swaying in the air, while another girl sucked her big dick jutting out from her hips!

Why can't everybody be endowed with both sets of sex parts? I thought. *I'm sure many men would enjoy having a pussy as much as a cock. Why can't we all be born as hermaphrodites?*

Just when I thought the two women were finally going to cum, the brunette suddenly shifted her hips lower over the blonde's torso. Then she placed her hand between her own legs and pointed her cock toward the blonde's pussy. The camera panned from head to rear, showing each woman thrusting their cocks into their partner's pussies.

Oh my God! Now they're actually fucking each other! They're fucking and getting fucked at the same time!

I thrust my dildo into my cunt as far as I could and rubbed the firm plastic balls against my clit and came for the third time tonight. I closed my eyes and tried to imagine what it would feel like to have a throbbing cock inside me while I was pumping my own cum inside someone else's snatch at the same time.

"Fuck yessss!" I screamed, imagining I was cumming from both my dick and my pussy.

As the blonde girl lay on the bed squeezing and pinching the brunette's ass cheeks, she pounded her fat cock in and out of the brunette's pussy while they thrashed atop the bed. I was wrong when I thought two hermaphrodites sucking each other off was the ultimate turn-on. This took the act of fucking to an entirely new level.

My pussy spasmed as I watched the two women moaning and

humping each other. I could tell from their rapid breathing and contorted faces that they were both getting close to orgasm, and I was hoping they'd finish this way. But with only one minute left in the video, they suddenly pulled out of each other and kneeled facing one another on the bed. Then they grabbed each of their own cocks and began jerking off, watching each other. Within a matter of seconds, they both groaned and squirted white creamy semen all over each other's bellies and dicks.

Typical man-produced porno, I thought. *Having the guy pull out at the last second and show his cum. What's the big deal with this whole ejaculation thing, anyhow?*

Little did I know, I was soon to find out.

2

RUBBING ONE OUT

I fell asleep that night with visions of futa girls crawling over my body as I sucked, fucked, and played with their ladydicks all night long. It didn't take long for my dreams to turn in this direction, and within minutes I was transported to an ancient Arabian kingdom filled with sorcerers and villains. I dreamt that I was the daughter of a powerful emir, betrothed to the king's son. But I wasn't ready to be married yet, not least because I was secretly carrying on an affair with his pretty daughter Farah.

Farah and I had tried to run away, but she was caught by the palace guards while I escaped to a remote cave in the Arabian desert. After a few days without food and water, I began to explore the large cavern in search of nourishment. I came upon a grotto illuminated by a beam of sunlight shining from a crack in the ceiling. The ray projected onto a gleaming pile of jewels and glazed pottery, sitting beside a gurgling pool of water.

I stumbled toward the pool and began guzzling up the liquid into my parched lips. After I recharged my dehydrated body, I began to sift through the trove. It had obviously been placed to hide someone's riches in a location with an abundant source of hydration. Its keepers would have to travel a long distance over the desert to get here.

Surely, they'd have also stored some extra *food* provisions to tide them over on their long journey?

I began to tear off the lids of the assorted containers, desperately looking for anything to eat. The pots and bowls clattered against one another, occasionally breaking into shards, but preserving the integrity of the pretty porcelainware was the last thing on my mind. To my dismay, the bowls were only filled with more jewels and coins. The cave probably carried a king's ransom worth of treasure, but that would be of little help to me if I died of starvation in the next few days.

I continued rummaging through the pile until I came upon an odd-shaped jar with a small hole at the top of its tapered end. I picked up the vessel and it was heavier than I expected, which meant it had to be filled with something. The lid to the jar was sealed, so I shook the container to discern its contents. It made a strange rustling sound, suggesting there was something soft inside.

Could it be a grain or nut storage jar? I thought.

I stuck my finger through the hole to see if I could feel what it was, but the contents kept moving around, almost like there was something *alive* inside. I peered through the hole, but there wasn't enough light in the cave to see beyond the curved flute at its end. Thinking it might be a small mouse or some other creature, I banged the vessel against a nearby rock in an attempt to break it open. At this point, I was so hungry I could have eaten just about anything.

But unlike all the other delicate pots and bowls, this vessel wouldn't break. I held the container up into the light to try to read the inscription on its flanks. There had to be something valuable in this flask for it to be fortified so strongly, I thought. The container had a thick coating of soot, so I rubbed my sleeve on its side. Suddenly, I heard a strange rumbling coming from inside the flask as a tendril of smoke began to rise from the hole.

The discharge grew thicker and heavier, and the container began to shake violently in my hands. I looked up at the smoke filling the chamber and gasped as it began to take the shape of a man. He was wearing a large turban and embroidered tunic over puffy trousers.

On his feet he wore bejeweled jester slippers. When the apparition began to speak, I almost fainted.

"What is so important," the ghost thundered, "that you've shaken Suleiman the Great from his slumber?"

"I'm sorry..." I stammered, in equal parts frightened and mesmerized by the impressive figure. "I didn't know what was inside..."

"Well, you've awoken the jinni now. What is it that you desire?"

"Jinni?" I said, my eyes widening in wonder. "You mean *genie*? Are you some kind of genie?"

I glanced down at the vessel in my hands and realized it was an oil lamp.

"Are you the genie from Aladdin's Lamp?!" I exclaimed, suddenly excited by my find.

"I don't know who this Aladdin is," the ghost said, "but as the bearer of the lamp, I am beholden to only you. What is it that you wish?"

"You mean you can grant me a *wish*?! Just like in the famous story from Arabian Nights?"

"Yes," the genie said. "*Three* wishes, in fact. So choose wisely. I will return to my cozy home after I've granted your wishes and will not come out again for a hundred years."

"Oh boy!" I said, not hesitating to give it much thought. There was only one thing on my mind right now, and that was my grumbling stomach. "I need food. Lots of food. Enough sustenance to carry me back over the desert to the sultan's palace."

"Your wish is my command," the genie said, raising his arms then snapping his fingers toward the ground beside me.

Suddenly, I was surrounded by piles of fruit, nuts, and dried meat. I grabbed a handful of lamb and rammed it into my mouth, gobbling it down in chunks. As I felt the energy returning to my body, I looked back up at the genie.

"Choose wisely, young lady," he said. "You only have two wishes remaining. That food won't last very long. You might want to ask for something you can enjoy for the rest of your days."

I looked at the genie and paused. I was already surrounded by all the jewels and wealth I could ever possibly need. What else could I use that would bring me additional enjoyment? As I began to feel the nourishment coursing through my veins and reinvigorating my organs, I suddenly smiled.

"I'd like to have a man's cock," I said. "But not just any cock. I want a long, thick one. One that I can cum with repeatedly whenever I want."

"Your wish is my command," the genie said, raising his arms, preparing to deliver my request.

"Wait!" I shouted. "But don't want you to take away my lady parts. I still want to look like a woman, with normal breasts and a pussy and a clit. I just also want to have a fully functioning penis."

The genie paused for a moment as he considered my request.

"I suppose that still counts as one wish," he said. "Not taking anything else away doesn't require any extra effort. Do you have any *other* special requirements for this man penis you dream of?"

Hmm, I thought. *I should be careful he doesn't just give me any old dick.*

I thought about the ones that I'd particularly enjoyed over the years. Then I held up my hand and separated my fingers a few inches.

"I want it to be circumcised," I said. "And straight. Let's say eight inches long, and...*two* inches thick. And nicely upstanding when it's erect. A forty-five-degree angle against my abdomen sounds about right."

"Done."

The genie raised his arms again then flung his hands in my direction. At first, I didn't feel anything, but when I lifted my skirt, I gasped. I had a magnificent, golden-brown, circumcised manhose hanging between my legs! I spread my thighs apart and began to fiddle with my new joystick, and it immediately began to fatten and lengthen. As the phallus began to rise up between my legs, I felt a new kind of tingling between my legs. I watched transfixed as my new member jerked and rose with each new pulse of my heart.

I finally had my very own cock! I thought. *My very own throbbing, bobbing, hard cock!*

I couldn't wait to play with it as I circled my fingers around the shaft and squeezed the hard meat in my hand.

"Um," the genie said, peering at me as I sat dumbfoundedly with my fist around my hard-on. "What would you like for your final wish? I'd like to get back to my peaceful slumber sometime today, if you don't mind."

"Oh, yeah," I said, pausing to contemplate what else I could possibly want.

For a moment, I considered asking him for a playmate, a pretty girl that I could use my new cock on right away. But then I remembered Farah, and I had a better idea. If I was ever going to sneak back into the palace and steal her away, I'd need a pretty good disguise.

"I want you to change my looks a little bit. Just enough so people won't recognize me when they see me. But I still want to look feminine, around my same age, and pretty."

"Your final wish is my command!" the genie said, as he flung his arms in the air then back toward me.

A cloud of smoke rose from my perch in the cave, and I peered over to look in the pool of water to see my reflection. A pretty brunette looked back at me, and I smiled.

This will do just fine, I thought.

Suddenly it occurred to me that I'd need additional resources to steal my beloved Farah away from the clutches of her powerful father.

"Wait!" I called out to the genie. "There's one more thing!"

"I'm sorry," the genie said as he began to shrink and vaporize in the cool cavern air. "You've used up all of your allotted wishes. I wish you well. Now please do me a favor and hide my little lamp so I won't be disturbed for another hundred years."

The smoky apparition began to shrink and collapse, then the swirling cloud of smoke disappeared back into the container. I looked around the cave for a safe place to deposit the lamp, then I pushed a large boulder aside and placed the lamp in a recession behind the rock. If I couldn't use the genie's power for another hundred years, then at least I'd be able to pass it along to my family where I'd hidden him.

As I walked back to the pool of water, I glanced at my reflection once again. It was strange to see someone other than myself looking back at me, and I ran my hands over my face to be sure it was really me. The girl looking back at me was beautiful with big doe-eyes, high cheekbones, and full pouty lips. As I smiled at my reflection, my penis suddenly started rising up between my legs again.

Apparently, my newly installed manhood *also* found the girl in the water attractive! I pulled off my dress and underclothes and appraised my full body in the mirrored reflection. I still had nice full, firm breasts and round, shapely hips. I spread my legs and pulled my skin apart. And I still had a pussy—*thank you, Genie!*

I placed my hand over my slit and traced my middle finger up toward the junction of my lips to make sure I still had my clit. As I began to circle it in my familiar way, my eyes widened as my new cock swelled and hardened, and rose in a series of sexy pulsing bobs until it pointed straight up at a forty-five-degree angle.

The genie was true to his word. My cock was truly magnificent. Long, firm, and thick, with a large plum-shaped bulbous head that was already leaking sticky fluid out of its slit. I placed my finger over the opening and swirled it over the viscous fluid, then raised my finger to my mouth.

A little salty—but not disagreeable, I thought.

I couldn't wait to see my cum shoot out of my dick when I had a full orgasm. I placed my fist awkwardly around the shaft and began jerking it like I'd seen so many men do before. I was glued to my reflection as I watched myself masturbate my big cock over the pool. Even though I could feel the pleasurable sensations emanating from my crotch, it still felt like I was watching an entirely different person.

But the feeling coming from my man dick was undeniable. It wasn't all that different from the sensations I felt when I played with my pussy and clit, but it was still...*different*. It felt—*bigger*. I began moaning and grunting as I whacked my big cock, recognizing the pleasure rising up within me, emanating from my hips.

The more I rubbed it, the deeper shade of purple my cock became. The head of my cock was now glistening with a thick coat of sticky translucent fluid. When I placed my hand around the bulb and began to massage the lubrication into my skin, I threw my head back and groaned.

So that's where all the action is, I murmured.

The head of a man's cock was a lot more sensitive than the rest of his organ, just like a woman's clit. All the super-sensitive nerve endings were concentrated in the end. I grasped the base of my organ with my left hand and placed my right hand over the upper half and began jerking myself with two hands.

The feeling emanating from my groin was indescribable. I was just starting to get the hang of this whole jerking off thing, and *two* hands was definitely better than one! As I humped my hips into my hands watching the head of my wet cock pumping in and out of the end of my fist, the strange reflection in the pool peered back at me. As I watched her pretty mouth open in ecstasy, I pounded my cock hard against my mound and moaned in delirious pleasure.

As I began to feel the familiar feeling of an orgasm welling up inside me, I refocused my attention on the tip of my cock as it pistoned in and out of my hands. I didn't want to miss this fireworks show for all the money in the world!

I grunted and groaned as I thrashed my head from side to side, barely able to stand up from the pleasure consuming me. Suddenly, I felt a different kind of sensation, as if I had to pee. Coming from deep inside my perineum, I could feel something pushing to come out. As the crest of my orgasm hit me, I screamed out loud, echoing throughout the grotto.

"Yes!" I screamed. "I'm cumming! I'm cumming from my big, manly cock! Fuck! I'm cummminggggg!"

Suddenly, a thick string of white fluid spurted out the tip of my cock as my pole pulsed repeatedly in my hands. I gasped with each contraction, as a new spurt of white goo squirted out of my joystick, making ripples in the water below. I squeezed my cock so hard between my two hands, I was afraid I might break it. But it just kept throbbing and pulsing in my hands, until the last few spurts of come dribbled from the head. When I finally finished coming, I hunched over, exhausted from the experience of having my first ladyboy orgasm.

That wouldn't be the last of my big dick orgasms today. As the shaft of overhead sunlight drew a wide arc across the wall of my cave, I had five more orgasms before falling fast asleep on my heaping pile of treasure.

But I was more pleased that I'd found a *different* kind of treasure today—the kind that only *I* could spend.

3
—————

FUTA GIRL

The next morning, I packed enough food and water to survive the two-day trek through the desert back to Persepolis. I also packed enough jewels and coins to last until I could return to the cave. I hoped to bring Farah back with me, but I knew the king's guards would still be on high alert, and I'd need every enticement possible to steal her away.

Using the rising sun as a navigational aid, I landmarked the location of the cave in relation to nearby mountains, then headed north toward the Mediterranean Sea. I wasn't exactly sure in which direction my home city lay, but I knew that once I reached the coast, I'd have no difficulty finding my way back to the palace. Once I got there, I hoped Farah would somehow recognize me and run away to lead a comfortable life living off the riches I'd found in the cave.

As I trudged through the hot desert sand, I tried to envision Farah's reaction to my new body. We'd often played with improvised dildos in her bedroom, and I was confident that my new mancock would add a fun new dimension to our sex life. As I imagined all the ways I could use my penis to satisfy her, the appendage would swell uncomfortably against my undergarments and I had to stop more than once to relieve the rising passion in my loins. I began to wonder if it had been such a good idea to ask the genie to endow me with an organ with unlimited restorative power. It seemed to have a mind of its own, and once any lascivious thought crossed my mind, there was only one way to calm it down.

By the afternoon of the third day, I'd reached the coast and found myself a day's sail away from the royal capital. I used one of my gold coins to purchase a one-way passage aboard one of the local merchant vessels, then went to the local haberdasher to buy some men's clothes. Beyond the fact that my dress was badly soiled from a week's wandering in the desert, I didn't want to take any chances that my garments might be recognized by the palace guards. Plus, I needed a safe place to store my unruly manhood in case it got any bright ideas to spring another boner in public. Then I checked into a hotel and had a long bath and restful sleep to prepare for my journey ahead.

The next day, I disembarked in the busy port of Persepolis and was glad I'd had the presence of mind to ask the genie to alter my appearance. As the daughter of a prominent emir, I could easily have been recognized by her father's many associates. But with a new identity, I could move around the city with impunity. I considered stopping by my house to inform my family of my change in circumstances but decided it was too risky. My father had already promised me to the king and paid a sizable dowry for my betrothment to the prince. For better or worse, my new identity with my secret riches would have to stay between me and Farah for the time being. In the patriarchal culture of ancient Arabia, my sex enhancement would be scandalous and lead to any manner of negative repercussions.

I approached the royal palace with some trepidation. If my identity were discovered, both Farah and I could be executed for treason. I walked up toward the guard shack outside the palace gates and introduced herself as calmly as possible.

"Good afternoon, sir," I said. "I'm here to see Princess Farah."

"Do you have an appointment?" the guard asked, appraising my masculine wardrobe suspiciously.

"No..." I stammered, "but I'm certain she would want to see me."

"What is your name and your business?"

I hesitated for a moment trying to think of a name to use. I obviously couldn't use my real one, but it had to be something familiar enough to Farah that she'd want to invite her into the palace. I racked my brain for a few seconds, then I remembered the name of Farah's favorite doll from her childhood.

"Tell her it's Jamila," I said. "And that I'm here to deliver a special...*gift*."

"The princess is a very busy royal," the guard said. "You may give me the gift and I will see that she receives it."

I hesitated for a moment, trying to think of a way to gain the guard's confidence.

"This is the kind of gift that is properly exchanged only between...*women*. Tell her that it includes a precious gem. A *green* gem."

The guard looked at me warily, then peered up toward the palace. I knew that he could be punished for breaking royal protocol by allowing unannounced strangers into the palace.

I reached into my purse and pulled out an intricately carved Jade gemstone.

"As you can see, sir, this is a very valuable gem. I'm sure you can understand why I'd like to deliver it to her personally."

The guard looked at the gleaming jewel in my hand, then motioned to another guard.

"Amir," he said to the other guard, "can you escort this young lady to the palace receiving court? She has important business with the princess. Tell her that Jamila is here to see her."

The second guard escorted me to the palace reception room, where I waited for fifteen minutes in the ornate chamber. After fifteen minutes, Farah walked across the marble-floored vestibule to greet me.

"May I help you?" she said. "I don't know anyone by the name of Jamila, but the guard said you had something important to give me."

I desperately wanted to tell Farah who I was, but there were still various palace staffers milling about, and she would have just thought I was crazy. I pulled up my sleeve and showed her the special friendship bracelet that she'd given me many years ago.

"Where did you get this?!" she said, eyeing me suspiciously. "This belongs to a very close friend of mine."

I leaned in closer to Farah so as not to be overheard.

"Princess," I said. "I have information about the whereabouts of your friend, Jade. She asked me to show you this so that we might have a private audience. Is there somewhere we can go to be alone for a few minutes?"

Farah glanced nervously at the palace butler standing on the other side of the foyer, then back toward me. She knew the risks of being found associating with a kidnapping accomplice.

"Come with me to my private chambers," she whispered. "We'll be safe there."

Farah turned to the butler.

"This woman has personal business with me. I don't wish to be disturbed."

"As you wish, your highness," the butler said.

She escorted me into her bedroom antechamber, then closed the door and swung around angrily to face me.

"What do you know of Jade?" she asked. "Is she safe? Where is she hiding?"

I reached out and clasped Farah's hand softly in mine.

"Farah," I said. "It's me, Jade. I've missed you so—"

Farah pulled her hand away and her eyes widened in fright.

"I don't know you," she said. "What kind of trickery is this? What have you done with Jade?"

She looked up toward her door preparing to call for help.

"Guar—" she announced.

I reached over and placed my hand over her mouth and held her close to me.

"Farah," I whispered in her ear. "Just give me one minute to explain. I know things only you and Jade have shared in confidence. It's really me. Remember that time when we were eleven, and we were playing in your big dollhouse? We were playing Mommy and Daddy and you showed me your—"

Farah pulled away from me and gasped.

"How could you possibly know that? Jade would never share such personal confidences—"

"Then we used the little teaspoons to probe our private areas. It was the first time you—"

Farah's eyes opened wide as saucers.

"Oh my God! How could you..."

For the next thirty minutes, I explained to Farah what had happened at the cave, and how the genie had changed my appearance to allow me to get close to her. I shared a few more personal details from our childhood, then she leaned in towards me and ran her hands over my face.

"Jade," she said, as tears streamed down her cheeks. "Is it really you? I was so worried about you. I've thought about you every night..."

I leaned in to kiss her and we wrapped our arms around one another in a passionate embrace. After a few seconds, she pulled away and held my face in her hands as she stared into my eyes.

"It really *is* you! I'd recognize that kiss anywhere. Oh Jade—make love to me again. I've missed your touch..."

Farah pressed her body against mine and we ground our hips together as we kissed passionately. Suddenly, my cock began expanding between my legs, pushing forward in my pants.

Farah pulled away and looked at me with a strange expression.

"What the—?"

"Sit down for a moment," I said. "There's one other thing I haven't mentioned..."

We sat on the edge of her bed, and I finished telling the story, explaining the three wishes I'd asked and been granted by the genie. When I finished, she looked at me dumbfounded.

"Of all the things you could have asked for, why *that*?" she said.

"I don't know," I said, a flush creeping over my cheeks. "I've just been...fantasizing about having one for quite a while. Ever since I played the daddy role in our childhood dress-up games. I thought we might be able to have a little extra fun with it. You know, with you being a virgin and everything—"

"What about all your *other* parts?" she said. "I'd kind of grown attached to you the way you were..."

"Don't worry," I said, caressing Farah's inner thigh. "I made sure to keep all my lady parts. The genie simply gave me a little extra appendage."

Farah reached between my legs and ran her hands over the hard lump in my pants.

"Can I see it?" she asked.

"Of course," I said, unzipping my trousers.

My penis sprung out of my pants and pointed straight up, throbbing quietly between my legs.

"Ohhh!" Farah exclaimed, recoiling in shock when she saw the large organ between my legs. "It's...*enormous*! Does it—work like a regular penis? I'm mean—"

"Yes," I interrupted. "I've been...*testing* it. I assure you, it works just like a regular cock."

"Is a *regular* man's penis this...big?" she asked. "I've never touched one before. Do you mind if I—"

"I thought you'd never ask," I said, leaning in to kiss her.

Farah reached out and clumsily ran her hand over the head of my hard-on and I moaned in her mouth. She pulled away and smiled at me.

"Does it feel good when I touch you like that?"

"Oh yes, sweetie—it feels very good. Please don't stop."

I placed my hand over top of Farah's and guided her to wrap her fingers around my shaft, as I humped my cock in and out of her hands. I began to leak some pre-cum out of my slit and as it ran down the sides of my pole, it became sticky, making it harder for her to slide her hand up and down.

"What's that sticky stuff coming out the top?" she asked. "Is that sperm?"

"I'm not sure, to be honest. The genie didn't give me a man's testicles, so probably not. It must be some other kind of fluid that's a byproduct of the pleasurable feelings."

Farah rolled her fingers together, feeling the gummy substance.

"It's getting a bit sticky down there. Let me clean you up and see if we can make this more enjoyable for you."

Farah went into her washroom and emerged with a moist towel and some jars of colored liquid in her hands. Then she knelt down on the floor between my legs and wrapped the moist towel around my organ and rubbed it up and down a few times to remove the sticky fluid from the head and the shaft.

"Maybe this will make it a little more comfortable," she said, pouring some lemon-scented oil from one of the jars into her palm then rubbing her hands together. Then she placed both of her hands around the shaft of my cock and began pulling the skin up and down.

"Oh God," I moaned. "That feels so good, Farah. Rub my cock and make me feel good. I dreamed of you doing this to me for several nights."

The feeling of the warm oil on my cock magnified the pleasurable sensations several fold. I cursed myself for not trying this earlier, as I'd only jerked my jock with the dry skin of my hand. But now it felt like I imagined a wet pussy would feel, and as Farah jerked me softly, I closed my eyes hoping I'd soon have her sweet honeypot embracing my throbbing member.

As the pleasurable feelings escalated within me, I began to thrust my hips harder and faster into Farah's hands, moaning and grunting in delight. Before long, I was forcing her hands far enough up to graze her mouth, and she stopped and smiled at me devilishly.

"You know those rumors we heard about what some women do to a man's cock to *really* make him feel good? Have you fantasized about *that* too?"

"Yes," I panted, pushing the tip of my cock closer to her mouth.

Farah lowered her head and began to swirl her tongue around the head of my pole, and I threw my head back and groaned.

"Yes, Farah," I panted. "Lick my cock. Suck me like a lollipop."

Farah lowered her mouth and circled her lips around my bulb

and began sucking on it like a popsicle. I'd never felt anything so good before, and I whimpered in ecstatic pleasure.

"That feels so good, baby," I moaned. "Suck my cock like a lollypop. Does it taste good?"

"Mmmm," Farah hummed, as she continued sucking the head of my dick.

She placed her two hands around the shaft of my dick and pistoned it between her fists as she sucked on the head. I began to feel the familiar sensation I'd experienced over the last few days just before I shooted cum.

"Oh baby," I groaned to Farah, "you're going to make me cum. I'm going to cum soon. Make me cum, Farah!"

Recognizing I was nearing the peak of my pleasure, Farah increased the speed of her motions as she squeezed my shaft tightly between her two hands. When she began flicking her tongue on the underside of my cockhead, I threw my head back and screamed as I felt my cum racing up inside me.

"Farah!" I screamed. "I'm cumming baby! I'm cumming in your mouth!"

Farah's eyes widened as she felt my cream filling her mouth and she pulled off me as we both watched the spurts of cum shoot out the end of my cock in long streams of white goo. She watched my face contorting in agony as my chest heaved with each new pulse of cum spurting from my dick. When I finally stopped, she climbed on the bed beside me and we both fell back on the mattress.

"Did you like that, Jade?" she said. "Do you like your new boy dick?"

I turned my head toward her and pulled her face into mine, tasting my salty cream in her mouth as I kissed her passionately.

"Yes," I panted. "I've grown quite attached to it over the past few days. But *this* was something altogether different. It feels a whole lot better when someone *else* is playing with it."

Farah smiled at me coyly.

"Do you like the way I play with it? Was I good for my first time?"

"Yes," I said, lying on my back, exhaling heavily. "It was *mine* too. That was the first time I've ever gotten *head* that particular way."

Farah glanced between my legs and noticed that my cock hadn't lost any of its firmness and was still bobbing over my stomach with each new heartbeat.

"I think there's a *lot* of things we can try for the first time with that joystick of yours. I've got a few ideas—"

Farah suddenly rolled over on top of me and spread her legs apart, gripping my cock between her thighs.

"I bet there's a few *other* places that big snake of yours hasn't explored yet"

I placed my hands beside Farah's head and pulled her toward me, penetrating her mouth with my tongue. I had indeed dreamed of exploring other parts of her with my newfound love muscle. We quickly pulled our clothes off one another, and after a few moments reacquainting herself with my lady parts, she kneeled over my hips and reached between my legs to point my cock into her hole. As she dragged it back and forth across her wet slit, we both moaned, peering into each other's eyes. Then she slowly lowered herself over my flagstaff, savoring every inch as it sunk deeper and deeper into her fiery canyon.

"Oh my God, Jade," she said when my cock had fully penetrated her chamber. "That feels *way* better than the pickles and eggplant we used to experiment with. It's so warm! I can actually feel you throbbing inside me!"

"Uhnnn," I groaned, soaking up from the incredible sensation radiating around my hips. "I never imagined it would feel this good. Fuck me, Farah. Fuck me with your sweet pussy."

As Farah began to rock her hips over me, grinding her mound against mine, we both gasped.

"Oh, Jade!" Farah groaned. "Fuck me with your man cock. Fill me up and pound me with your big love muscle. I want to feel you cum inside me."

As we rocked our hips together, I watched Farah's face as her mouth opened wider and wider and her moans grew louder and louder. I grabbed the side of her hips with my two hands and pulled her back and forth over me as I thrust my cock deep inside her. Within a few minutes, her eyelids began to flutter and her eyes rolled back and she let out an otherworldly groan.

"Uhnnn—Jade!" she panted. "I feel it. It's happening. I'm going to cum all over your pretty cock. Cum with me baby! I want to feel you spurting inside me. Oh God, Jade, I'm cummminggggg!"

Farah grunted and groaned as her body spasmed wildly on top of me, thrashing and heaving as she screamed my name. Within seconds, I felt the cum rising within me and my cock began pulsing in rhythmic spurts inside her. I squeezed her hips tightly in my fists as we locked our bodies together in simultaneous orgasm.

When our mutual contractions finally stopped, Farah collapsed on top of me and we rubbed our sweaty tits together as I held her impaled to my hard cock still throbbing inside her.

Farah lifted her head off my shoulder and smiled at me.

"I'm *glad* you wasted one of your wishes on this," she said. "I can't imagine a more loving gift that you could have brought me upon your return."

I kissed her softly as one last spurt of cum spilled into her sweet, warm pussy.

4

A PRINCELY MATTER

Farah and I made love many more times over the course of the day, then we made plans to steal away over cover of darkness that evening. We decided the safest strategy was for me to leave the palace so as not to invite extra suspicion, then for her to meet me at the docks where we'd bribe our way aboard another shipping vessel. Then we'd backtrack our way to the cave and sneak aboard another ship headed toward Europe. With our newfound riches, we could hide away the rest of our days in relative luxury.

Farah bade me farewell on the front steps of the palace, then I headed down the trail in the direction of the port. But as I approached the woods surrounding the castle, someone grabbed my sleeve and pulled me into the thicket. It was Crown Prince Ali, Farah's brother. He dragged me behind a tree and pinned my arms over my head on the trunk.

"What business did you have visiting my sister?" he asked, glaring at me.

I was worried that he'd somehow discovered my identity. If he knew I was his runaway bride, I'd never be able to escape his clutches. But if he couldn't identify who I was, there'd be no reason to detain me any further. All I had to do was remain calm and stick to my story.

"I...was simply bringing her a gift I'd made for her as a loyal follower."

"What *kind* of gift?" Ali said, eyeing me suspiciously. "The guard said it included some precious stones."

He looked at my modest commoner's clothes, paying particular attention to the swelling of my breasts in my tight bodice.

"You don't look like the kind of person who can afford to give away something like that away. And why are you wearing a *man's* clothes? What are you trying to hide?"

"Nothing," I stammered. "I just find them more...comfortable. A woman can't be too careful on such a windy day about protecting her modesty when the slightest breeze might reveal more than our customs dictate."

Ali looked at my long pants, squinting at the crotch area.

"What is your name and your family lineage that you can afford such lavish gifts?"

"My name's Jamila," I said, trying to think of a common surname to maintain my cover. "My father is a jeweler by the name of Khalil Khan."

"I've never heard of this jeweler," the Prince said. "The royal family knows most of the goldsmiths in town. There's something about your story that doesn't ring true."

I racked my brain trying to think of another reason for visiting the princess.

"We thought bringing a gift to showcase our wares might curry favor with the royal family. It's hard to make inroads in such a competitive bus—"

"Liar!" Ali said, pressing my wrists against the rough bark. "I overheard you and my sister doing much more than exchanging *jewelry* in her room. What business does a woman dressed in man's clothes have trying to seduce the princess?"

Ali thrust his hand between my legs and squeezed my crotch,

suggesting that only a man should have the right to court his sister. But he stepped back when he felt the unusual lump on my mound.

"What the hell?!" he said, his eyes flying open in confusion.

He grabbed my pant legs with both hands and flung my trousers to the ground. My half-erect cock sprang forward and bobbed between my legs. Ali's dark brooding eyes and his forceful manner pressing me against the tree had apparently awoken another kind of primal urge within me.

He stepped forward and tore off my shirt, then pulled my bodice up, revealing my bouncing tits on my chest.

"What kind of...*person* are you?" he exclaimed, spending more time ogling my rapidly growing boner than my pretty girl tits.

"I...was born with both sets of reproductive organs," I lied. "Please don't tell anyone. If anyone else knew of my deformity, I'd be shunned from our community. I meant no harm to your sister—"

"You were *fucking* my sister? With *that*?!" He brought his gaze back up to my plump breasts. His pupils were wide as saucers, and I could tell he was excited by the strangely attractive transgender person before him. "How *can* you—if you're a woman?"

"I guess you'd say I was neither a man nor a woman," I said. "I'm a...*hermaphrodite*, with both sets of functioning sex organs."

He stepped back a few feet to appraise my full body, then squinted between my legs. He reached forward and ran his fingers over my rapidly dampening hole. Then he stepped back again and shook his head in disbelief. But the tenting in the front of his trousers betrayed his true interest in my ladyboy body.

He glanced at his moist hand and twitched his middle and forefinger in a feigned fingering action.

"Does *that* work too?" he asked, looking at my pussy.

I began to realize this might be the perfect opportunity to deflect his suspicions about my plans with his sister.

"Yes," I smiled. "Would you like to try?"

Ali hesitated for a moment, then he stepped forward and placed his hands over my breasts. He squeezed and pinched them for a moment to be sure they were real, then he put his right hand between my legs and thrust his fingers inside my snatch. I swayed my hips to his motion and moaned, as my cock pressed against his stomach. He leaned in to kiss me and I pushed my hips toward him, feeling his equally hard member trapped in his pants. I lowered my hands and began unbuckling his trousers, then reached inside to grasp his swollen dick. He removed his fingers from my pussy and we began to masturbate each other as we moaned in each other's mouths.

After a few minutes, he pulled back to look more closely at my cock and I pulled his trousers all the way down to the ground. We were now facing each other our poles pointing straight out toward one another. I stepped forward and playfully slapped my hard-on against his as if jesting with swords. My cock was almost twice as large as his, and I enjoyed my little moment of dominance over him.

I bet this wasn't the way you envisioned fucking your new bride, I thought, as a sneer began to spread across my face.

I could tell Ali was enjoying our little cockplay, and the head of his member was soon coated in a thick film of pre-cum. I kneeled between his legs on the soft ground and took his organ into my mouth. I was surprised how much of it I could take into my mouth, since his erection couldn't have been much more than four inches long. I sucked on his head and reached between his legs to play with his balls, and Ali groaned as he thrust his cock in and out of my mouth. Before long, his balls rose tighter against the base of his cock and I knew that he'd soon release his spunk. With one final thrust, he grabbed my head with two hands and pulled my face down onto his bush as he squirted his cum inside me.

Typical alpha male, I thought. *Showing he can have his way with women any way he desires.*

But I had my *own* ideas for demonstrating who was in charge in this relationship.

After Ali finished cumming in my mouth, I stood up and smiled at him then I grabbed my big hard-on with both hands I began to wank it, moaning seductively. He feigned disinterest as he began to button up his trousers, but when I lifted one leg and showed him my glistening pussy, he paused. While I jerked the shaft of my cock with one hand, I reached between my legs and finger-fucked myself with the other. Ali had obviously never even dreamed of such a scenario (these being the days long before online video or even the printing press), and he stood there with his mouth agape as he watched me jerk and jill myself in double pleasure. His cock began to rise again, and before long it was bobbing straight out from his open trousers.

"Do you *want* some of this?" I said, glancing between my legs. "I bet you've never fucked a ladyboy before, have you?"

Ali quickly pulled his trousers back down and pushed me back against the tree. He grabbed the end of his dick and pointed it toward my hole, then thrust himself forward, ramming his penis inside me. This was the first time I'd been fucked by another cock in my altered state, and even though Ali's was smaller than most of the other ones I'd had, it was an agreeable feeling. As I felt the familiar pleasurable sensations building up inside me, I rocked my hips in synchronicity with him while he thumped me against the hard bark of the tree.

As he fucked me, Ali kept staring at my hard cock bobbing between our torsos. It was a deep purple color now and glistening with pre-cum all over the head. I reached down and encircled it with my hands and began jerking it up and down as Ali thrust his own cock in and out of my pussy. He began to moan loudly, and I knew he was about to cum. I sped up the pace of my jerking action, and just as he grunted one last guttural moan, I spurted a thick stream of cum up between our abdomens, landing a big glob on his face. Ali pulled out of me and lurched backwards as he wiped the sticky fluid from his face, spreading it over the sides of his hips.

"Did you enjoy that, my prince?" I smiled. "There's much more of that whenever you want it," I lied. I just needed to give him enough motivation to keep me alive until Farah and I made our escape.

"Perhaps we can meet here again tomorrow?" I said.

"Yes," Ali said, still fixated on my dick. Unlike his rapidly detumescing member, mine was still pointing straight up on my belly, bobbing and pulsing as hard as ever. As he continued staring at it, I saw new life in his little flute as it began to thicken and rise.

"Would you like to touch it again?" I said, motioning to my giant erection.

Ali paused for a moment, looking around the woods to make sure we were alone. Then he stepped forward and touched the head of my dick tentatively. I didn't know if he was more captivated by the unusual *size* of it, or the simple fact that he was touching another man's hard-on for the first time. Either way, his own cock quickly rose to its previous excited state, and I could tell he was turned on touching my cock. As he began to jerk my shaft, he wrapped his fingers around his own member, and awkwardly tried to jerk both of us off with two separate hands. After a few minutes, he became frustrated trying to coordinate the ambidextrous actions, and he pressed his hips forward until our dicks touched.

Then he placed the underbelly of his erection against mine and wrapped his two hands around both of our joined cocks. As he began to hump his hips against mine, his little pecker disappeared in his hands while my much larger organ thrust a full four inches above the top of his palm. Ali seemed to be getting worked up by the sight of our two cocks frotting one another and before long, he came again with three anemic spurts landing on top of my cock. The feeling of his watery semen lubricating my cock was enough to put me over the edge, and I squirted another series of long ropes onto his chest as I came for the second time.

As Ali maintained his grip on our joined cocks, rubbing the wet heads of our throbbing members together, I saw him unconsciously lick his lips.

"That was lovely, my prince," I said. "But something tells me you're not done feasting on my body. Would you like to see what a lady cock *tastes* like?"

Ali paused for a moment looking at me uncertainly, then he glanced around the wood again nervously.

"It's okay," I said. "This will just be our little secret. I've never done this with another *man* before. You make me feel like a real ladyboy."

I could tell Ali liked me talking dirty to him as his cock twitched and dribbled as I spoke to him.

"Come, my prince. Let me feel your lips around my big manly cock. Make me feel like a real ladyboy."

Ali stepped forward tentatively and placed his hand over my throbbing dick. It throbbed in his hand and I leaned in to kiss him, plunging my tongue into his mouth, signaling l that I wanted something *else* in his mouth. He slowly lowered himself until he was kneeling between my legs, then he pressed his lips forward to touch the head of my cock. My cock pulsed, and a thin dribble of pre-cum squirted onto his tongue. He paused for a moment, unsure whether he wanted to continue, then he plunged my cock deep into his cavity.

For someone who pretends to be a virile heterosexual, I thought, *he sure knows how to suck a cock.*

I moaned in pleasure as he grasped my shaft with two hands and swirled his tongue around the head, bobbing up and down over me. Seeing his little dick bouncing between his legs as he consumed my python, I decided to give him some of his own medicine. I placed my hands behind the back of his head and began thrusting my big pole deeper into his mouth. His expert cocksucking technique was having its desired effect and I soon began to feel my cum welling up inside me.

"Fuck, yes, Prince!" I panted. "Suck my big cock! I'm going to dump my cum down your throat. Here it comes!" I yelled. "I'm cumming!"

I pulled Ali's head as far as I could toward my belly and thrust my dick against his throat. He gagged for a moment, then relaxed as I filled his mouth with my seed. My cock pulsed for many long seconds, with each contraction pouring more semen into his mouth. Eventually, it overflowed and began spilling out the sides, dribbling down his cheeks and neck. When I finally finished spasming in his mouth, he pulled his head back and stared at my twitching eye, winking at him as it spilled out the last vestiges of my spunk.

I glanced between his legs and saw that his penis had returned to its previous excited state and smiled at him.

"I think maybe the prince isn't quite finished with me," I said. "Was there anything *else* you wanted to play with before we go our separate ways?"

Ali stood up and grabbed my tits angrily in his two hands.

"You're a very dirty girl, Jamila," he sneered. "But I like it. We will have to do this again very soon."

As he pressed his body up against me one last time and thrust his tongue into my mouth, I reached around behind his hips and squeezed his butt cheeks. He began to grind his cock against mine again, moaning into my mouth as we frotted for a few seconds. When I reached under his cheeks and pressed my finger against his anus, he grunted approvingly. I rubbed my cock harder against him, then slowly inserted my middle finger into his hole. As he titled his hips back toward me accepting me into his private space, I felt his dick pulse against mine.

"Do you like that, my prince?" I said.

Ali pinched my nipples firmly and moaned in my mouth. I began to turn my body slowly around, tracing a line with my dripping cock-head over the side of his hips as I kissed his neck while fingering his anus. When I got directly behind him, I placed my dick between his thighs and dry-humped him, prodding his balls with the head of my dick. Ali moaned approvingly, and I removed my finger and placed the head of my cock over his opening.

Now we'll really see who's the alpha male in this relationship, I thought to myself. *It looks like we'll both be losing our virginity today.*

By fucking him up the ass, I felt a certain measure of revenge for his attempting to steal me away from my beloved Farah. Besides, this was something I hadn't yet tried with my new ladyboy cock, and I always wondered what it felt like when two men did it. The tip of my cock was already wet from my previous cum, and the head slipped into his opening surprisingly easily. But it was definitely tighter than his sister's pussy—*much* tighter. I pushed further into his ass, feeling the warmth surround my thick organ. I wasn't sure how far I'd be able to penetrate him, and I was surprised when my mound pressed against his ass cheeks.

As I began to thrust my firehose inside him, Ali groaned and whimpered in pleasure. There was something about the idea of fucking a man with my lady cock that I found particularly pleasing.

Maybe it was just the utter *filthiness* of it, or maybe it was the fact that I was dominating the second most powerful man in the kingdom. Either way, I enjoyed it immensely, and before long I could feel my orgasm preparing to boil over.

But just as I was about to deposit my load into his bowels, we heard a strange rustling sound coming from the side of the wood about twenty feet away. We both looked in the direction of the sound and saw a herdsman peering at us from behind a tree. I didn't know how long he'd been watching us, but the recognition that we'd been spotted raised my passion even more.

I grasped Ali's flanks with my two hands and pulled his ass firmly against me as I thrust my cock deeper into his ass.

"I'm coming, your majesty!" I screamed, for the whole wood to hear. "I'm cumming up your tight little ass!"

I held the prince tightly to me as I pulled him toward me with each contraction of my pole. As my semen spurted into his tight canal, his opening made a rude hissing sound.

I hoped the would-be spy would soon spread the truth about our tiny-dicked, ladyboy-loving prince. Something told me there'd be no more betrothals for the young prince anytime in his future. After I pulled my steaming cock out of Ali's ass, he quickly pulled up his pants and scurried up the hill in the direction of the palace.

That's right—run, you wannabe. Soon there'll be no heirs remaining in the kingdom to carry on the royal lineage. When the king finds out about your little dalliance in the woods with the ladyboy, there'll be two offspring banished from the palace.

5

———

RUDE AWAKENING

I awoke the next morning in a cold sweat in my regular bed. I looked around the room for a moment to reassure myself that I was actually in my own home and no longer in my Arabian dream. There was a giant spot on the sheets under my hips and I reached between my legs half-hoping to still find my throbbing cock still attached to me. Alas, I only had my usual slippery, but still tingling, soft slit.

Fuck, that was a hot dream! I thought. *But where did all that violent man-fucking come from?*

I was more confused than ever about my sexual identity and predilections. But one thing I knew for certain. I was horny as hell from all the ladyboy imagery in my extended dream, and right now I just needed satisfaction. I reached over into my nightstand drawer and pulled out my big fake cock replica and shoved it into my steaming honeypot. As I came over and over again screaming Farah's name, I imagined it was me fucking her.

I'm definitely going to have to experiment with this ladyboy thing some more, I thought, as I squirted yet another orgasm onto my wet sheets.

VOLUME THREE

NAKED YOGA

1

MIND AND BODY

I'd always enjoyed yoga. There was something about the simplicity of it that appealed to me. No weights, no fancy equipment, just me stretching my own body to tone and relax my muscles. For sixty minutes every day, I had my own island of tranquility on my little yoga mat.

But it was more than that. It was the *sharing* of the experience with like-minded people in the quiet, serene comfort of a yoga studio. Listening to the breathing of my fellow yogis as they stretched and relaxed their bodies inches away from me. For the longest time, I never found anything sexual about the practice. We were just focused on connecting with our own bodies and freeing our minds of extraneous thoughts.

But my recent encounters at the dinner party and in the dark room had given me a new appreciation for the female form. Most of the participants in my advanced class were women, longstanding members with exquisitely toned bodies. And they all wore tight spandex leggings and tops that hugged every curve and valley of their figures.

For some reason, in today's class I was far more interested in focusing on what *other* people were doing than channeling my own chakra. As I transitioned from one pose to another, I couldn't help looking out the corner of my eye at the women surrounding me while they spread their legs and arched their bodies in ever more suggestive poses.

When the instructor asked us to move into the plank position, I stole furtive glances at the women facing me, as their breasts clenched tightly together between their outstretched arms. When we did lunges, I peeked between their legs to see if I could detect the outline of their labia in their tights. When we did the wide-angle forward bend, I ground my pussy into my mat trying to stimulate my tingling love button. And when we moved into the plow position, I fantasized about crouching over their upturned asses and rubbing our pussies together like Emma and I had done in the dark room.

The instructor's gentle exhortations were a blur in the background as my mind raced with lascivious thoughts. I'm sure she would have disapproved of my breaking the cardinal rule of yoga, which was to free your mind and let the distractions of the day melt away. But in my case, something else was melting. The more turned on I got, the more aware I became of the growing wet spot between my legs. I couldn't stop imagining all the positions I wanted to get into with my yoga partners. When we moved into the bridge position and thrust our hips upwards, all I could think about was fucking someone—anyone—as I ground my mound against an imaginary partner.

The more I thought about it, the more excited I got. I began to undress the women with my eyes, imagining what they'd look like doing their poses in the buff. Occasionally, I'd catch some of them stealing glances in my direction.

Were they having the same fantasies as me?

When the instructor guided us into the wide-leg balance position, where we spread our legs and grasped our elevated toes, I thought I was going to faint. So many beautiful women were opening themselves up to me, daring me not to stare at the joint between their legs. I had to will my body to stay in place as I mimicked their pose. My glutes wanted to crawl like a sand crab across the floor until our bodies touched, pressing our pussies and breasts together.

By this time, the wet spot between my legs had grown completely out of control. I could no longer pretend that it was just sweat running down my legs or my ass from the tension of holding the poses. I excused myself and gathered my mat, holding it in front of me as I walked toward the women's change room. When I got into the locker room, I went into one of the stalls and quickly closed the door behind me. I lowered my tights and began jilling my clit furiously, trying to stifle my moans in case anyone else entered the room. It didn't take more than a minute for me to come hard, as I hunched over and stood panting, my back leaning against the stall door.

After I collected myself, I grabbed a towel and headed into a shower stall. I turned on the warm spray from the overhead faucet and felt the water trickle over my tender breasts. As my nipples hardened, I reflected back on what had happened in the yoga studio. I unconsciously bent over into a downward dog pose and felt the stream spray on my exposed ass and pussy. The feeling of being naked, imagining myself performing my yoga pose as other women watched me was electrifying. Within seconds, I had another powerful orgasm as I held my ankles, shaking in convulsions.

Ten minutes later, after I'd changed into street clothes and other women began filtering into the change room, I noticed one of them glance at me with a knowing smile.

Maybe I wasn't the only one who harbored this fantasy of naked yoga, I thought.

I resolved to investigate the idea further when I got home...

2

—————

MASTER OF MY DESTINY

As soon as I got home after work that day, I sat down in front of my computer. The fantasy I'd envisioned at the yoga studio earlier in the day had awakened a yearning for me to go further—to explore how far I could take the concept of uniting my mind and body to experience true enlightenment. Except in my case, the enlightenment I was seeking had more to do with a *sexual* awakening than one of mind or spirit.

If yoga was all about being captains of our own ships so we could learn to be the best versions of ourselves, it was time for me to take matters into my own hands. I opened the Google search box and typed in the words 'naked yoga'. Much to my surprise and delight, I got three hits. The first two were discussion groups between people who enjoyed practicing yoga alone in the buff, talking about how liberating and relaxing they found it to be. But the third result had a short description of a studio that held 'tantric yoga' sessions.

I clicked on the link and the page opened with pictures of beautiful men and women posing stark naked in familiar yoga positions. Their bodies were turned in such a fashion that their genitals were hidden, but their naked buttocks and chests left little to the imagination. A text block below the images talked about the benefits of practicing yoga in the nude and how it freed our minds and spirits to focus on *every* aspect of our physicality. It cited a study that said yoga improves sexual desire, arousal, lubrication, orgasm, and sexual satisfaction. And it talked about how tantric techniques could be used to prolong and elevate sexual pleasure.

But the rest of the website was shy on details as to what these so-called tantric techniques involved and how they were put into practice within the sessions. There were only two other links on the page —one to schedule a session and another simply marked 'Contact'. I clicked the Contact link, and it offered three options: Phone, Email, or Chat. I didn't feel comfortable yet talking with someone over the phone, so I clicked the Chat link.

A chat window opened and someone named Soraya began typing in the chat box.

'Hi, I'm Soraya,' she said. 'How can I help you?'

I panicked for a moment, realizing I hadn't actually prepared to talk with someone yet about such a personal subject.

'I'm looking for more information about your naked yoga classes,' I tentatively typed.

'Sure,' Soraya said. 'What would you like to know?'

Geez, I thought. *How can I put this delicately?*

I didn't want to be too blunt, but I didn't want to be too opaque either. I needed more information about their service, but I didn't want to be too presumptive.

I'll just go slow and see what they reveal.

'How many people typically attend your classes?' I began.

'It varies from session to session,' Soraya replied, 'but we normally get between ten and twenty.'

'Is it open to all ages and genders?'

'Our classes are open to men, women, and transgender individuals over the age of eighteen.'

Transgender individuals? That could be interesting.

'Is clothing optional?' I asked.

'We start every session with a disrobing ceremony, where participants are asked to remove their garments. The absence of clothes weaves together naturalist and yogic practices that aims to bring about increased freedom, intimacy, and relaxation.'

Now for the tough question.

'Are session participants encouraged to interact with one another?'

'We have three levels of classes,' Soraya replied. 'Each new member is encouraged to start at the beginning level and step through to the advanced level as they become more comfortable. The level of involvement with other participants increases at each level.'

'What happens at the beginning level?'

'The first level, *Meditation*, is all about getting in touch with one's own body and experiencing the freedom of yoga unencumbered by any outside trappings. This is where you learn to explore and revel in the sensations of your own body by practicing the various asanas in the nude.'

Revel in the sensations of one's own body. I like the sound of that. But I was hoping for more.

'When do we begin to engage our partners?' I asked.

'The second level, *Namaste*, is where you choose a partner and help one another stretch and hold poses. This is where you learn to respect the divinity of your partner while guiding them to expand their horizons.'

Respect their divinity, indeed. I wondered just how far this 'helping' would be allowed to go.

'And the third level?'

'The most advanced level, *Harmony*, is where you seek maximum enlightenment through the joining of your minds, bodies, and spirits. This is where you explore each other's bodies and learn to experience their full potential. It is a deeply intimate bond that our practitioners find most empowering.'

All this spiritual double-talk was dancing around the main subject. It was time to cut to the chase.

'Are we allowed to—' I hesitated for a moment trying to frame the right words. '*Touch* each other?'

'Of course,' Soraya replied. 'This is the whole goal. To release your inhibitions and connect with one another in such a way as to experience maximum pleasure and fulfillment.'

Now we're talking.

Soraya was beginning to sound more and more like an instructor herself, and my mind began to imagine what she'd look like leading us through the poses in the nude. I could feel the blood rushing to my pussy as my insides began to moisten. I was feeling bolder and decided to probe a little further.

'What are these 'tantric techniques' that your website talks about using in the sessions?'

'The word tantric comes from the Sanskrit root tan,' Soraya instructed, 'which refers to the interweaving of threads on a loom. In the context of yoga, it means the joining of partners and using the principles of meditation and relaxation to elevate and prolong one's pleasure. It can be practiced at any stage in your progression through the levels but is most powerful when practiced in tandem with your partner at the most advanced level.'

That sounds exactly like what I'm looking for.

Now it was just a matter of testing the boundaries.

'How can I ensure my privacy and personal space will be respected if I choose not to engage a partner?'

'We establish clear ground rules at the outset of each session. Everyone chooses their own partner and engages only with explicit consent. If you wish to practice your asanas alone, we encourage you to do so. Our time together is always safe, nourishing, and judgement free.'

I was beginning to feel more relaxed and was almost ready to book my first session.

'Do I need to bring anything with me?' I asked.

'All you need to bring is an open mind, a free spirit, and a clean yoga mat. Everything else, including your cell phone and any other electronic devices, we ask you to check at the door.'

I'm all in, I thought.

'When is your next beginner session?'

'Meditation sessions are scheduled Mondays, Thursdays, and

Saturdays, between 7:00 and 8:00 p.m. You can check availability and book a session by clicking on the Appointments tab at the top of the page. Did you have any further questions?'

I didn't really have any other questions, but I was intrigued to learn more about this mysterious Soraya. She seemed a lot more informed about the art of yoga than your typical customer support agent.

'No, thank you for your time and candor, Soraya,' I typed. 'I'm looking forward to participating in your sessions. Are you an instructor yourself?'

'Yes, I'm one of three certified yoginis at our practice.'

'Are they all female?' I wondered. I wasn't sure about the idea of having a male instructor staring at me as I stretched and bent over entirely naked.

'Yes, although depending on your preferences, I think you'll find the male yogis can be just as fulfilling in the practice of tantric yoga as the women are.'

'Thank you, Soraya,' I said. 'I hope to meet you at one of the sessions. I'll book an appointment soon. Bye for now.'

I clicked out of the chat window and tapped on the Appointments tab. I selected the first available date for a Meditation session and quickly filled in my profile and credit card information to pay for all three levels of the naked yoga sessions. Then I stripped off my clothes and placed my favorite vibrating dildo facing straight up on the floor. I placed my straight arms in front of me then pulled my legs behind my shoulders and lifted my ass into a Firefly position above the dildo. As I lowered my pussy onto the dildo, I closed my eyes and imagined it was my yoga partner instead.

Namaste, I muttered, as my breathing began to quicken.

MEDITATION

When I got to the naked yoga studio on my appointment day, I was pleasantly surprised. The room was bright, clean, and well-appointed, with tasteful prints on the wall, clean white sheers covering the windows, and a new hardwood floor. This wasn't some dingy pseudo-massage parlor operation as I'd feared.

I arrived ten minutes early, around the time other patrons were beginning to stream in. There was a mix of men and women in their twenties and thirties. Some of them appeared to be couples, judging by the intimacy of their hushed conversations and how close they huddled together. Before long, everybody staked out a spot on the floor and began stretching quietly on their mats.

At first, I was surprised to see everybody dressed in familiar yoga attire. But then I remembered what Soraya had said in our online chat conversation about everybody being asked to disrobe at the start of each session. I placed my purse and coat on a bench in a conspicuous place where I could keep an eye on it, then found an open spot on the floor and began stretching. I wasn't really interested in stretching yet, but it kept me busy and avoiding awkward glances with the people sitting around me.

During a transition in one of my stretches, I looked up and locked eyes with a pretty red-haired girl stretching beside me who couldn't have been much beyond her teens. She was wearing pink tights and a yellow top that pressed against her small but perky breasts. She didn't appear to be wearing a sports bra, and I could see the outline of her nipples as they pushed against soft cotton. We smiled at one another then returned to our stretching as we pretended to ignore the palpable tension in the room.

Shortly after, an attractive woman wearing matching Lululemon tops and bottoms walked toward the front of the room, where she placed a mat in front of the floor-to-ceiling mirrors lining the wall. She nodded and smiled at a few familiar faces, then looked at the large clock on the side wall. It was 7:00 p.m.

"Good evening, everyone," she said, addressing the room. "For those of you who are visiting us for the first time, welcome to our Tantric Yoga program, Level One — Meditations. For those of you who are returning, it's great to see you again. Remember that your progression through the levels should be at your leisure. You should step up to the next level only when you feel comfortable enough with the exercises and with your interaction with your fellow participants."

I wondered if she was Soraya from my chat session. My eyes ran up and down her body, analyzing ever contour of her perfectly shaped figure. Her legs were long and slim and bulging in all the right places. I marveled at the diamond shape of her calves and the line flexing up the side of her tights that separated her gently curved quadricep and hamstring muscles. Her Madonna-toned arms were slender and cut, and I could see the outline of her tricep muscles as she moved her arms. Her stomach was flat as a washboard, and her ample breasts swelled over the top of her tight-fitting top, above a tapering waist. She had a perfect athletic gymnast's figure, and I hoped she'd turn around for a moment to reveal an ass that I was sure I could bounce a coin off.

She was absolutely gorgeous, and I couldn't take my eyes off her. She had a vaguely European look, with dark brown hair, high cheekbones, and full rosebud lips. As I watched her talk, I imagined pressing my body against hers, kissing her in a passionate embrace. I couldn't wait for the program to start and see her gorgeous body in the buff.

As if reading my mind, she looked at me and smiled.

"My name's Alexandra," she said. "I'll be your instructor for today's session. Shall we get started?"

Everybody including me nodded.

"Our first order of business is to shed the trappings of modern civilization by dispensing with our clothes. These are just holding us back from truly connecting with our bodies and reaching our full potential. Yoga is intended to free our minds, bodies, and spirits. Practicing our craft in the nude will enable us to open our minds and experience true freedom and relaxation. Let's all disrobe now and place our garments on the floor beside your mats."

Alexandra reached over her shoulders and pulled her top over her head then bent over in a perfect pike position and pulled down her yoga pants. Then she nonchalantly stepped out of them and placed them in a neatly folded pile near the mirrors. I hesitated for a moment, soaking up her gorgeous body. Her B-cup tits stood proud and tall on her chiseled chest, with a thin indentation running down the front of her abdomen to her perfectly bald pubis.

When she turned around and bent over to place her clothes on the floor, I gasped out loud. Her ass was as tight and round as a schoolgirl's. The muscles in her glutes flexed as she stretched and contracted them from the bending motion. When she turned back around, I suddenly became aware that I was the only person in the room who was still clothed. I awkwardly pulled my tights off with everybody watching me, then placed them on the floor beside my mat. I could see myself reflected in the mirrors at the front of the room and part of me wanted to move my hands in front of my pussy to cover up. But everyone else seemed perfectly relaxed being naked, and I scanned the expanse of mirrors to take in the sight.

There were about fifteen people in the room, in various shapes and colors. Some had dark bodies, and some had fair skin like me. Most were slim and toned, but there were a few curvy girls with full breasts and wide hips. I noticed two men standing near the back of the pack, and I wondered if they'd chosen this position out of shyness or because it offered the best position for viewing the women's bare backsides. I squinted to see if I could detect any sign of tumescence in their hanging members, but they appeared to be fully relaxed and flaccid. I was glad that they'd also trimmed their bushes short and neat so as not to interfere with maximum viewing pleasure.

"Right, then," Alexandra said. "Now that we're fully free to relax and connect with our bodies, I'd like everyone to lie down on your mats face up and place your arms gently at your side. Close your eyes and breathe in slowly through your nostrils, then exhale deeply to remove the troubles of your day. Try to empty your mind and focus on the beauty and serenity of your body."

It was strange lying on my yoga mat completely naked, knowing I was surrounded by so many people in a similar state of undress. I was tempted to turn my head and open my eyes to steal another glance at Alexandra or the girl beside me, but I followed her instructions and focused on my breathing. It felt liberating to take my clothes off around like-minded strangers, and I could feel myself begin to relax as a cool draft swept over my body. The stillness in the room was a welcome respite from my hectic workday.

After two or three minutes, Alexandra instructed us to open our eyes and sit up on our mats in the Buddha position.

"Cross your legs, bringing your heels under your knees, then lift your chest so your spine is straight. You may open your eyes if you wish, as you can begin to feel comfortable in your natural body among your peers."

I raised my eyelids and turned my head slowly to look around the room. The young girl beside me caught my gaze and looked straight into my eyes. I smiled at her as her eyes drifted down my chest and she looked at my exposed breasts and stomach. I unconsciously lifted my chest and pushed my tits out as far as I could. My breasts were much larger than hers, and I was proud of how firm and high they still stood at my age. I could feel my nipples hardening and I blushed slightly as I glanced at her tight figure.

Her skin was flawlessly smooth and unblemished, and she had barely an ounce of fat anywhere on her body. Her small boobs seemed to be glued onto her chest, as if somebody had sculpted them out of clay. They barely moved as she breathed in and out, rising in tandem with her expanding ribs and diaphragm. Her nipples were small, with pinched areolas betraying her excitement. Maybe it was just the cool air circulating in the room, but her nipples were definitely standing out in an aroused state. I lifted my eyes and we smiled at each other, in tacit approval of each other's physiques.

I frowned when Alexandra interrupted our connection, instructing us to change position.

"Now that we're getting comfortable in our natural bodies," she said, "let's expand our horizons and begin to stretch our capabilities. I'd like you to extend your legs straight in front of you and gently flex your toes toward your knees. Now, gently lean forward with a straight spine and run your hands along the top of your tights toward your feet until you feel some gentle pressure in your hamstrings. Hold the position, breathing slowly and deeply, until you feel your muscles relax, then push forward another inch, trying to move your head as close to your knees as possible."

My flexibility was pretty good from my regular yoga classes, so I was able to get all the way down and I rest my chest on my thighs, clasping my hands around the undersides of my feet. I looked in Alexandra's direction and she nodded approvingly while holding a similar position without any sign of strain in her face. I turned my head and peeked under my outstretched arm at the young girl beside me and she did the same. We both giggled for a moment, then placed our heads back between our knees and concentrated on our poses. I could feel the mat underneath me beginning to moisten between my legs as I began to think about what I'd like to do with her at the next level in our training.

After another three or four minutes, Alexandra instructed us to move into the next position.

"You're all doing wonderfully," she said. "Now we're going to move into a new position to really give those hammies a workout. Bring the sole of your right foot to rest against your left inner thigh. Now, turn and extend your chest over your left knee, holding your left leg or foot to gently pull yourself forward. As before, breathe slowly and hold the position when it begins to bind, then extend yourself forward in small increments as you feel the pressure in your hamstring slowly relax. Go as far as you can without feeling uncomfortable. Your goal is to elongate your muscles and improve your flexibility so you can be ready for whatever tight spots life throws at us in the real world."

I was feeling a tight spot between my legs, and I pressed the heel of my right foot hard against my pussy. This was the first time I'd actively touched myself in the session, and I began to think about what might be in store as I moved to the more advanced classes and begin to interact more closely with other participants. I hoped that the girl to my side with whom I'd made a silent connection would be there so we could partner up and explore our bodies more intimately.

Alexandra instructed us to switch sides and extend our right leg to stretch the opposite hamstring. The girl and I glanced quickly again at each other before we bent down, and I began to fantasize about going down on her. I wiggled my hips against my left heel, trying to increase the friction against my swollen clit. But Alexandra always seemed to interrupt our poses before I could work up enough sustained contact to go very far.

Perhaps this was by design, to create just enough contact with ourselves and others to make us yearn for a stronger connection with our partners. I had to admire the brilliance of their business model. They were building a powerful desire to move on to the next stage. Just as with normal sex, no one in their right mind wanted to stop before achieving the pinnacle of pleasure.

"Okay," Alexandra said, interrupting my thoughts once again. "Now we're going to try a variation on this pose that will help us stretch our ribcages and build our core. Bring your right forearm down to the inside of your right leg and try to grab the inside of your right foot. Then reach up and over your head with your other arm.

Rotate your left palm inward and try to clasp the outer edge of your right foot while rotating your chest inwards and upwards."

A few people near the back of the room grunted and groaned as they tried the awkward maneuver.

"I know," Alexandra said, "this is a tough one. Just go as far as you feel comfortable without feeling undue strain. As always, pause at the moment of tension and breathe deeply. Feel your tummy pushing in and out as you use your diaphragm to breathe from your belly, not your chest. Glance up toward the ceiling to encourage your body to twist as much as you can. When you begin to relax, push a little further and hold."

This time, the girl next to me and I were facing each other directly, only a few feet apart. We looked at each other and giggled again. We were definitely forming a connection as we ran each other's eyes shamelessly down and across each other's bodies, watching the muscles in our stomachs rippling from the tension of the side stretch. We both had our heels in front of our bare crotches, which only added to the titillation of the pose. I tried to will her to pull her foot away to give me a glimpse of her naked pussy, but we remained obedient to Alexandra's instruction.

Just as I was beginning to think the sequence of poses had been carefully staged to reveal only enough of our bodies to our fellow participants to build an unquenchable desire, Alexandra instructed us to sit up and change position once again.

"Now let's focus on another important element of our core strength, which is our lower back. Sit up and place your legs directly in front of you once again, then bend your right leg until your right heel is touching the inside of your left knee. Now reach up with your left arm and twist toward your right side with your right hand on the floor beside you, placing your left elbow on the outside of your elevated knee. You should feel a gentle stretch in your lower back and glutes. Look behind you and find a spot on the wall where you can focus, then gently try to twist your body further in that direction as you trace a line further along the wall toward your right. Hold, breathe, and relax. Then twist a little further, pushing yourself to twist as far as you feel comfortable."

My gaze was averted away from the girl next to me, so I scanned the room behind me. I could see the two men at the back of the room stretching in the seated twist position, looking just as serious and focused as the rest of us. I caught a few people stealing furtive glances at one another, but for the most part everybody seemed lost in the moment concentrating on their poses, seemingly mindless of their naked and exposed positions.

Alexandra asked us to switch and turn to the other side, which gave me an opportunity to scan the other side of the room. I noticed some of the women glancing in my direction and we smiled as we checked out each other's bodies. So far, the experience had been liberating and mildly stimulating, but I was beginning to grow tired with how we'd been covering up our most erogenous parts with the poses Alexandra had led us through.

"Okay," she said, as if reading my mind. "Now we're going to get a little more risqué in our positions and open up our bodies to channel our chi more freely."

She sat up on her mat and extended her legs straight in front of her. Then she slowly spread her legs apart, exposing her bare vulva to the entire room. My breathing quickened and I became mindful of the growing wet spot on my mat. The slit in her pussy beckoned to me as I unconsciously leaned forward.

"We're going to do a wide-angle seated forward bend, which will stretch and strengthen your adductors and pubococcygeus muscle. I want you to spread your legs straight out and as far to the sides in front of you, then lean forward with a straight back as you reach out with your hands toward your outstretched feet. You'll feel a tightness between your legs, so you have to do this slowly and carefully so as not to pull anything."

Alexandra leaned forward and clasped her heels with her two hands and pulled herself forward until her chest rested on the floor. There was no denying that she was extremely flexible, as she moved through each of the poses to the maximum extent possible with little noticeable strain.

As I mimicked her movement, I tried not to glance between the legs of the yoga partners in front of me. I wished the young girl who'd I'd made a connection with had been positioned in front of me instead of to my side. As I leaned forward, I turned my head and glanced in her direction. She did the same, and we moved our chests forward and down in a synchronized manner. If yoga was all about the union of mind and body, I definitely was feeling yoked with my fantasy yoga partner.

"Press your pelvis into the floor," Alexandra said. "Bring your chest down and forward as far as you can. Spread your thighs apart with your hands as you feel the tension between your legs relax."

I glanced around the room and watched all the toned men and women bending over spreading their legs. My pussy grew wetter and wetter until I could hear the squishing of my legs against the mat as I rubbed my clit back and forth in the small puddle beneath me. I glanced over at the girl next to me and she smiled knowingly, as my pace of breathing increased and my eyes began to glaze over. I could have sworn her hips were rocking back and forth in lockstep with mine as we fantasized about rubbing our pussies together.

Please, I pleaded with her under my breath. *Please come back to the next session.*

Just when I was getting close to having a mini-orgasm, Alexandra asked us to sit up and change position.

Damn, girl, I thought. *You're such a tease.*

I was more convinced than ever that these poses were orchestrated to maximize the arc of our arousal just enough to deny us ultimate pleasure, so we'd have no choice but to come back and finish the deal.

"You're all doing fabulous," she purred in her soft, gentle intonation. "Now I want you to sit up with a straight back with your legs still spread out in front of you."

My eyes widened as she grabbed her big toes and began to lift them off the floor until they were at the same height as her head. She had opened herself up completely to the room, exposing her bare pussy and breasts in the most revealing way, daring us to ravish her magnificent body with our eyes.

"This is one of our most liberating poses," she said as she held her feet in the air, "where you'll feel most at one with your bodies and with those of your fellow yogis."

She glanced toward the back of the room at the two men and looked down between their legs.

"Don't worry if you notice some of your partners in a state of obvious arousal. This is a normal and healthy response and is just another way for us to connect with our bodies and feel the energy flowing through us. Try to keep your back straight and look up toward the ceiling as you lift your chest and breathe deeply. Feel your connection to the universe and the power within your own bodies. Free your mind and let all the negative chi flow from your body."

As I spread my legs and prepared to move into the provocative position, I rotated my hips slightly so I'd be facing closer to the girl next to me. I didn't want to make it too obvious what I was doing, but I was hoping she'd do the same so that we could look at one another's fully exposed bodies and I could let my fantasies run free. I began to lift my legs at a forty-five-degree angle to her and noticed out the corner of my eye that she had shifted her body subtly toward mine in a similar manner.

"Try to flex your PC muscle as you feel your Mula Bandha tighten and relax," Alexandra said. "This will create a stronger connection during intimate moments with your partner and heighten your sexual pleasure."

As I extended my legs and revealed my glistening pussy for the entire room to see, I looked over at the girl and smiled triumphantly. We'd opened ourselves up to one another in every sense of the word and let all of our inhibitions fall away while reveling in the beauty of one another's bodies. She was still turned just far enough away that I couldn't see her bare pussy behind her outstretched leg, but I noticed the puddle on the mat just in front of her.

She was just as turned on as I was!

My pussy quivered and shook in the excitement of the moment. If anyone had touched me anywhere near my Mula Bandha, I would have had an orgasm in a millisecond. My mind raced with all the possibilities I could engage in with my fantasy partner during the next level session. Just when I thought it couldn't get any more intense and intimate at that moment, Alexandra gave us a new instruction.

"Now," she said, "while still holding your toes as high in the air as you can, gently lean back with a straight back until you're balancing on your buttocks in a spread piked position."

She demonstrated the technique as she tipped slowly backwards then held a perfect forty-five degree piked position, looking up toward the ceiling in the sexiest but most composed manner.

God, I thought. *I'd fuck that woman any day—in any position.*

I glanced over at the girl behind me, and we both leaned backwards at the same time, matching the degree of rotation in perfect synchronicity. When we both reached the same forty-five-degree angle of our backs towards the floor, we beamed at one another in joy and pride at having achieved this level of proficiency. I wanted to turn my body completely in her direction and scoot my ass over to her then wrap my legs around her while we ground our pussies together and kissed passionately.

This naked yoga thing was even hotter than I'd hoped! I knew I'd be counting the minutes until the next session in horny anticipation.

I glanced in the mirror to see how this was working for the two men and saw that they had full hard-ons, angled straight up at forty-five degrees in the same direction as their outspread legs. What a turn-on this must have been for everybody in the room!

"I'm very proud of all of you," Alexandra said, as she began to lower her legs back toward the mat. "Now it's time for us to relax and return to a quiet state. Please bring your legs back onto your mats and cross them in front of you in the seated Buddha position. Close your eyes and reflect back on the growth you've achieved today. Breathe slowly in and out and feel the energy coursing through your body. You've all come a long way today. If you feel comfortable moving on to the next level, I hope to see you again where we'll explore a new level of synergy working together to stretch our minds and spirits even further."

Alexandra closed her eyes and placed the back of her hands on her knees as she touched her thumbs and forefingers together.

"Om," she chanted, exhaling slowly in an extended intonation.

"Om..." the room chanted with her in harmony, as our spirits exalted.

There was no question that I was ready to take this to the next level. I glanced out the corner of my eye at the girl next to me and winked as she returned my gaze.

I hope we'll see each other in a whole new light the next time we meet, I smiled to myself.

4

NAMASTE

On the evening of my second scheduled naked yoga session, I could hardly contain my excitement. This was the step up to Level 2, which Soraya had promised would involve closer interaction with the other yoga participants. I wasn't exactly sure what that meant, but I hoped it would involve some direct contact with a partner. I'd been fantasizing for the last three days about the girl who stretched beside me in the previous class, and my pussy was already tingling in anticipation of touching her.

When I arrived at the studio, I saw her stretching quietly on her mat. I immediately walked over to a spot in front of her and placed my mat on the floor to stake my claim. I didn't want anything getting in the way of direct access to her this time!

"Hi," I said, as she peered up at me. "I didn't properly introduce myself last time. My name's Jade."

"Kayla," she said, sitting up and extending her hand.

I leaned forward and shook her hand softly. Just touching her at the ends of our extremities was electrifying, but I pulled back when I felt my hand begin to moisten. Whether it was nerves or my body starting to heat up, it was undeniable that Kayla was getting me charged up just being next to her.

I sat down on my mat and crossed my legs in a comfortable seated position.

"I've been looking forward to this for *days*," I said. "That last class was pretty stimulating, don't you think?"

"Definitely," she said. "It's been running through my head on a continuous loop pretty much the whole time."

"So much for yoga calming our minds," I joked.

Kayla smiled.

"At least it accomplished the other goal of lifting our spirits and charging our bodies up."

"Yes, it certainly did."

I studied Kayla's face as she spoke to me, and I felt myself getting more and more attracted to her with each passing moment. She had a soft and gentle beauty that matched her petite figure. With bright green eyes and tiny freckles scattered over the bridge of her narrow nose, she looked like the consummate redhead that I'd often fantasized about. She'd be my first if we got that far, and I had no intention of letting her slip through my grasp.

At the top of the hour, a new instructor walked to the front of the room and laid her mat in front of the mirror. I wondered again if it might be Soraya from my initial online chat. She'd said there were only three tantric yoga instructors, so I figured there was a good chance I'd encounter her at one of the three stages.

"Good evening everyone," the instructor said. "My name's Amber and I'll be leading you through today's Level Two tantric session —Namaste."

"Namaste," some of the experienced yogis in the room repeated.

Amber placed her hands together in front of her chest and bowed gently.

"Namaste," she said, repeating the refrain. "How many of you know what this word means?"

I vaguely recalled Soraya talking about this in our online chat, but all I could remember was that it had something to do about showing respect for one another.

"Namaste comes from ancient Sanskrit meaning 'bowing to you,'"

Amber said. "In the context of yoga, it refers to the act of recognizing and bowing to the divinity within each of us. This will be the focus of today's session, where we partner up and celebrate the power within each of us as we seek to expand our limits. Accordingly, let's begin today's session by shedding our clothes and sharing the natural beauty within us."

Just as Alexandra had done in the previous session, Amber removed her tights and placed them in a neat pile by the mirror. She had a fuller, more athletic figure than Alexandra, but just as magnificent. Her full C-cup breasts bounced gently on her chest as she moved, and I was captivated by her large brown nipples. Her hips were wider than Alexandra's and she had curvier, more powerful-looking legs. The whole package projected a stunning hourglass figure. My eyes traced a line down to her narrow midsection, where a thin patch of brown pubic hair echoed the imagery of sand flowing through her body.

As I admired her beauty, I removed my own clothes, not wanting to be the last one with everyone staring at me again. When everyone was naked, Amber placed her hands in front of her chest once again and bowed to the group.

"Namaste," she said softly.

"Namaste," everyone in the group replied, bowing to her divinity.

I scanned the room in the mirror behind Amber and saw a few familiar faces, together with a number of new participants. This time the ratio of women to men wasn't quite as skewed, with roughly a dozen women and five or six men.

"Let's begin by getting comfortable with one another," Amber said. "I'd like you to turn to your nearest partner and stand facing him or her with your hands at your side. Straighten your back and elevate your chests as you breathe slowly in and out. You should see your partner's stomach extending and collapsing as they breathe from their diaphragms."

I turned toward Kayla before anyone else could steal her, and she did the same as she faced me. We smiled at one another knowing this time we'd be entirely focused on one another.

"Now, inhale as you raise your arms straight up and join your palms over your head," Amber instructed. "Feel the power within you as you stand tall as a mountain. Feel yourself rooted firmly to the ground as you tighten your thigh and buttock muscles. You are strong and magnificent, and you possess the power to achieve everything you desire. Look at your partner and recognize the strength within them."

Kayla and I looked at each other and smiled broadly. My grin kept widening until I showed my teeth, looking like I was posing for a camera shot. Kayla responded in kind, revealing the cutest dimples in the sides of her cheeks. This time, we didn't run our eyes over one another's bodies—we simply locked eyes and radiated the joy we were both feeling.

"Now take a large step forward with your right leg," Amber said. "Keep your hands above your head and squat down into a wide stance with your feet at least three or four feet apart. Hold this Warrior pose as you channel your chi and recognize how strong you are."

Kayla and I both took a broad step forward until our front foots were resting near the front of our mats. We'd suddenly closed half the distance between us, with only four or five feet separating us. My tummy sucked in an out as I gulped air to feed my straining legs. I couldn't keep my eyes from darting down between Kayla's scissored legs as I thought about touching her there. I noticed her breathing escalating too, and I wondered if it was due to the strain of holding the deep bend or from her own heightened arousal.

"Now," Amber continued, "with your feet, knees, and arms in the same locked position, rotate your upper body toward your left side until your chest is parallel with the line of your outstretched legs. Lower your arms and extend them straight across the same plane, holding them parallel to the floor. This is called the Warrior Two pose. Imagine you're lunging toward your partner in a fixed position, as if fencing with a foil. Except in this case, we're simply trying to touch fingers to channel the positive energy flowing between you."

Amber demonstrated the pose at the front of the room and we all followed her lead. There was now only a foot or so separating my outstretched hand from Kayla's. I shifted my weight forward onto my front leg to try to get closer.

"Keep your upper body centered between your front and rear foot," Amber said, "as you feel yourself grounded to the floor beneath you."

I frowned sheepishly at Kayla as I reluctantly pulled myself back and centered my weight as Amber instructed. Kayla giggled softly, recognizing my frustration. Our hips were turned away from each other so we could no longer see each other's bare midsections, but I had a commanding view of her tight ass, and I shamelessly took it all in.

"Now, place your left hand on the outside of your trailing leg and lift your right arm straight over your head, bending as far backwards with your chest still facing the side as you feel comfortable. You should feel your abs and intercostal muscles stretch as you expand and elevate your ribcage. This is called the Reverse Warrior pose."

Amber once again demonstrated the technique as she arched her body into position. She looked like the epitome of a yoga master as she struck the pose. With her legs spread wide and glancing up toward the ceiling with a focused expression, she looked for all the world like a true warrior.

Kayla and I shifted our weight, and dutifully adjusted our position. Unfortunately, we were now looking away from each other, and I was beginning to feel frustrated with the loss of connection. After a few people grunted from the tension of holding the pose, Amber instructed us to return to a seated position on our mats.

"Are you ready to begin working with your partners now to see if we can push one another to new heights?" she asked.

A few people nodded, and the rest of the room exhaled deeply, signaling they needed a brief respite.

"Let's return to the Buddha position to catch our breath for a moment," Amber said. "Cross your legs in front of you with your feet under your knees and hold your back straight while you breathe deeply to reenergize your muscles. Feel the tension leaving your body as you relax and free your mind. Close your eyes and feel the stillness of the room as you sense your pulse slowing and your thoughts emptying."

I closed my eyes, but it was impossible for me to empty my thoughts knowing I had a beautiful naked woman in front of me with whom I hoped to engage in closer contact.

"Okay," Amber said, breaking the silence after a few minutes of self-meditation. "We're now going to begin engaging in a more progressive manner with our fellow participants to see if we can push past some of our limits. I'd like you to move next to your partner and place your backs against one another, while you remain in the Buddha pose. This is called the Seated Meditation Bond. This will give you an opportunity to begin feeling your partner's energy in a safe and relaxing manner."

Kayla and I hesitated trying to figure out who should move first toward the other's mat, and I made the first move. I scooted over to her mat and gave her a soft kiss on her forehead before turning around and placing my back against hers. We assumed the cross-legged Buddha pose, and straightened our spines against one another, playfully pushing each other forward and back a few inches as we felt our bare skin and asses touching.

Amber noticed one of the participants was without a partner and walked over to one of the men. She clasped her hands in front of her and bowed, then sat down on his mat in the reverse meditation pose.

"Straighten your spines and feel your shoulder blades supporting one another," she said from her new position in the middle of the room. "Breathe deeply together as you feel each other's energy connecting your spines. Rest your hands on your knees as you channel your thoughts. Don't think about the fact that you're touching another stranger—simply be one."

I could feel Kayla's breathing as her upper back expanded and contracted, and she rested her head against my shoulder. I did the same, shifting my head to the other side, and we paused listening to each other's breathing. I wanted to reach around and touch her hand or her thigh, or touch my own dripping pussy, which had begun to dribble in excitement onto Kayla's mat. It took every ounce of my power to keep my hands where Amber instructed and just focus on relaxing.

Amber must have sensed that many of us were ready to move to the next stage when she asked us to reach around and touch our partners.

"Now, with your backs still pressed together, twist your upper bodies gently to your left and place your left hand on the outside of your right knee. With your right arm, reach around your partner's back and place it on the inside of his or her thigh. This is a trust-building exercise that permits you to help each other stretch, while also beginning to feel more comfortable with one another."

Kayla and I looked toward Amber to follow the correct technique, as we watched her reach around her partner's back and wedge her straight arm against the inside of his opposite thigh. It was impossible from our position to witness the man's reaction, but I was certain it would be getting a rise out of him.

We twisted our bodies as Amber indicated, and I could feel my arm shaking as I reached behind Kayla's back and placed my hand on her inner thigh. When she did the same, my back shook from the sexual energy that shot through me. By now, my inner thighs were coated with the slippery juices streaming out of my pussy, and Kayla squeezed her fingers against my leg to avoid slipping off. I couldn't feel any wetness on the inside of her thigh—just the soft, exquisite warmth of her smooth skin. I was glad that I'd shaved my legs the previous day, hoping she'd revel in my soft skin as much as I was hers.

Amber interrupted our thoughts with another command.

"Gently press down and outward with your two hands as you feel you and your partner move your knees closer to the floor. Focus on the pressure and nonverbal feedback from your partner to know how far you can push without causing pain or discomfort. Listen to your partner's body and trust one another to help stretch and relax."

As I pushed gently down on Kayla's thigh and felt her do the same, I felt my adductor muscle begin to relax as our knees moved closer to the floor. I was careful to go slow, paying close attention to the tension in Kayla's leg so I never pushed her beyond her limits. Within a minute or so, both of our legs were pressed flat against the floor. I could still feel some tension in my inner thighs, but much more in my aching pussy from the proximity of her hand to my slit. I hoped that Amber's next instruction would bring us even closer together, where we might actually be able to touch our private parts.

"Now let's turn around facing each other while we twist in the other direction," she instructed. I want you to face each other, returning to the cross-legged Buddha position, with your knees touching one another. Reach as far around your back with your right hand while you extend your other hand forward and clasp your partner's hand behind their back. Gently hold and pull one another as you twist your upper bodies away from one another."

Once again, we watched Amber as she demonstrated the technique with her partner, then we followed suit. I was pleased with how the progression of moves were now being staged in a manner that our level of engagement with our partners increased each time. Kayla and I playfully pushed and pulled each other as we rocked our upper bodies from side to side. It was a fun, stress-free way for us to wind down from the excitement of our last pose, but I was looking forward to rocking our bodies in a whole other way.

"Okay," Amber said. "Now let's see if we can help each other stretch our lower half."

Yes! I screamed inside. *My lower half needs some serious attention.*

Finally, I'd get a chance to touch Kayla where I'd fantasized for so many hours. Our heads turned to look at one another and our eyes widened as we processed the same thought. I could see Kayla's pupils dilating with rising excitement.

"First," Amber instructed, "get into the staff position facing each other with your legs extended straight out in front of you. Touch each other's feet and place your palms face down on the floor beside your hips. Then lean forward with outstretched arms and try to grasp each other's hands. If you can, gently pull one partner toward the other while he or she bends forward with a straight back.

"As always, feel the tension in your partner's body and listen to their feedback so you can help them stretch their muscles without any discomfort. Your goal is to help your partner reach beyond their self-imposed limits, in a safe and supportive role. If you can't reach far enough forward to touch your partner's hands, then simply place your hands on your own legs and try to inch toward him or her with the goal of touching."

This was an easy one for Kayla and me, since we both had excellent flexibility. I was able to guide her all the way forward until her face touched her legs just below her knee, then she repeated the sequence for me. I loved the idea of her head moving closer to my box and it was tempting to separate my legs a little bit to give her a view of my pussy. We were so close together now that our arms bent awkwardly, so we moved our hands further up each other's arms to make it easier to hold each another in the flexed position.

After two or three minutes, Amber asked us to focus on our opposite partner, as she allowed the man to pull her forward, holding her hands. Kayla and I giggled at how we'd gotten ahead of Amber's instruction and simply repeated our steps. After another three or four minutes, Amber asked us to return to the staff position and place our hands in our laps.

"I hope you enjoyed that and found you were able to push yourself a little further than you normally could on your own. Now we're going to stretch another important muscle in our lower legs, which is the adductor muscle between our thighs. I want you to keep your legs extended, but now spread them as far apart as you can. Then move yourself forward until you're touching your partner's feet once again and lean forward to join hands. It should be easier for you to reach your partner this time, as your hips will be closer together. As before, gently pull one partner at a time toward the other while he or she leans forward with a straight back, trying to move your upper body as close to the floor as possible. Breathe deeply, and only go as far as you feel comfortable."

I wasn't sure if the 'feeling comfortable' part Amber referred to concerned the tension we were about to feel in our adductor muscles, or the unease some people might have getting so close to one another's private parts. But I was feeling no such compunction, I wanted to get as close to Kayla's private parts as I could, as soon as possible!

Sensing each other's rising excitement, Kayla and I immediately spread our legs and reached out our arms to one another. I was dying to look at her exposed pussy, but I knew that I'd have a better chance to do so soon. We both hesitated, unsure as to who should 'go down' first, and I gently pulled her toward me to break our little tug of war.

"Feel the pressure in the muscles between your legs," Amber called out. "Only go far enough to where it begins to bind, then pause and breathe slowly until you feel the muscles relax. Listen to your partner's body as you guide them lower and further."

Amber had little trouble bending all the way forward, until once again her upper body was resting flat on the floor between her outstretched legs.

"If you're able to go all the way down," Amber said, "spread your legs further apart and repeat the process, inching closer and closer to your partner. Pay no mind if you notice your partner is getting aroused, as this is a normal and healthy response in this situation. Focus on a spot on the floor in front of you if it makes you feel more comfortable, as you listen to your own body and feel yourself relax and elongate."

Kayla and I pressed our feet together and pushed our legs further apart. Our legs were now at a sixty-degree angle facing one another and there was no escaping the fact that our open pussies were facing one another. I pulled Kayla gently toward me once again, clasping her arms closer to her elbow as she leaned her head down, closer to my quivering love box. I wasn't sure if she was looking at me there as she bent over, but if she was, she must have noticed the widening puddle that was forming between my legs. My labia quivered, and I could feel my hood retract as my excited clitoris pushed out into the open. She couldn't have missed how turned on I was, the closer her head got to my pussy.

Amber's gentle voice continued to encourage us in the background.

"You can focus on taking your partner as far as he or she feels comfortable going in one continuous stretch, or alternate back and forth as each of you extend your position forward."

I glanced in Amber's direction and saw her bent closer toward her partner as he pulled her arms toward him. I could have sworn I saw the head of his erect penis sticking up between his legs as she moved her naked body in his direction. But her flexibility was so pronounced that with her legs spread almost fully apart, her head was closer to his chest than his groin as she bent forward. Perhaps this was by design, as I'm sure it must have been awkward for her to get so intimate with an apparent stranger in this group setting.

I was hoping that Kayla wanted to continue stretching in my direction, until either her head or her pussy touched mine. By now, my clit was throbbing in excitement, and I was gushing lubrication all over the mat. Any kind of direct contact would have pushed me over the edge in an instant, and I was desperately seeking release.

Maybe Kayla was feeling the same way or maybe she was feeling a bit shy, because just as her face got to within a few inches of my steaming pussy, she leaned back and smiled.

"Your turn," she purred.

She started to pull me toward her as we pushed our feet even wider apart. Our legs were now more than ninety degrees separated and our pussies were only a foot or so apart. As Amber had with her partner, we'd spread our legs so wide and were so close together, that when I leaned forward, my head touched her chest instead of her pussy. I was just about to kiss one of her erect nipples and suck her into my mouth when Amber interrupted us again.

"If your feet are wide enough apart that you can no longer lean all the way forward, try having your partner lean back in order to guide you further forward and down. The goal is to stretch and elongate your adductor muscles without actually touching any other part of your bodies. If you can widen your feet still further, your other goal is to bring your Mula Bandha locks as close together as possible without actually touching. We'll save that for your last level of tantric training."

No touching? I thought. *Screw that! If somebody doesn't touch my Mula Bandha soon, I'm going to explode.*

Kayla sensed my desperation and pulled my face toward her chest until my lips touched her skin. She wasn't going to have any part of this no-touching rule either. But instead of allowing me to linger and savor her sweet breasts and nipples, she began to lean back as Amber instructed, pulling me forward and my head lower down her abdomen. But because we'd spread our legs so far apart, we'd gotten too close to bring our heads any closer to our pussies than each other's belly buttons.

Kayla wrapped her arms around my waist and pulled me closer toward her as our legs spread even wider apart. Our pussies were now less than six inches apart with our legs spread in a near one-hundred-and-eighty-degree angle facing one another, and I swore I could feel the heat emanating from her hole as we strained to touch one another. How I wanted to feel her tender clit touch mine and join our love juices together. There was something far more intimate and sexy about this kind of touching than the rough and tumble tribbing I'd experienced in the dark room with my last lesbian lover.

"Remember," Amber intoned from the center of the room, "you should only be touching each other with your hands and feet. Part of the fun is feeling the energy transferring between the two of you as you get closer and closer to reaching your limits. Push your hips forward but respect your partner's space. Get as close to one another as you can without touching and feel the energy passing between you."

I glanced over at Amber and saw that she and the man had reached the point where their chests and hips almost touched, but they had their eyes closed with barely an inch separating them. I felt sorry for her partner, imagining his blue balls and his cock twitching in anticipation with her pussy so close.

Screw that idea, I thought.

Kayla and I both wrapped our arms around one another's waist and we pulled each other firmly toward each other as our sweaty chests rubbed together. I could feel the warm puddle between us on the mat as our thighs connected further up toward our pussies, and we both shifted our hips trying to touch ourselves. When we finally did, the feeling was electrifying. We held each other close and kissed passionately, stifling our moans as we came in each other's mouths. Kayla swirled her tongue in my mouth as she ground her hips against mine, and our chests heaved against one another in simultaneous orgasms.

At that moment, I didn't care who was watching or how many rules we were breaking. Kayla and I had reached a true union of souls and found our own place of enlightenment.

5

———

HARMONY

When the day of my scheduled third session of tantric yoga came around, my entire body was buzzing with excitement. The last session had exceeded my expectations, and I felt I'd formed an amazing bond with Kayla. The connection we'd made was tender, deep, and thrilling. I couldn't wait to touch her again and feel her soft skin against mine. Soraya had said the third level would be where we truly joined our minds, bodies, and spirits and where we'd be able to explore our partner's bodies more intimately. Even though Kayla and I had already broken the rule about no intimate touching at the last session, I felt there was much further we could go.

I arrived at the yoga studio fifteen minutes early so I'd have a chance to chat with Kayla before we began the routines. She hadn't arrived yet, so I walked to the back of the room and placed my mat in a spot near the window. I wanted to have a little more privacy this time, where we'd be more sheltered from the prying eyes of the rest of the group. As more and more people filtered into the room, I watched the clock on the wall move closer to our appointed start time. There was still no sign of Kayla, and I started to worry. We'd promised to meet again for this session, but I'd felt it was too early to ask for her number. Was she having second thoughts? Was she feeling too embarrassed to come back after our intimate exposure at the last session?

The room was beginning to fill and by now there were only a few spots remaining on the floor upon which to lay a mat. An attractive woman in her late-20s paused at an open patch next to me.

"Is this spot taken?" she asked, in a sexy voice.

"Um—no..." I hesitated, looking up at the clock.

"Thank you," she said, smiling at me warmly. She laid her mat about three feet away from me and placed her belongings next to it on the floor. She had long dark hair pulled back in a bun and was wearing loose-fitting sweats and a T-shirt. I could see the outline of her figure in her clothes, and her firm breasts thrust out prominently in her loose shirt. She had an exotic beauty, maybe East-European I thought, with sharp cheekbones and an angular jaw. There was something mysterious and sexy about her that I found uniquely attractive.

"I'm Neve," she said, reaching out her hand.

"Jade," I said, stealing a final glance at the clock as I shook her hand.

At 7:00 p.m., a new instructor entered the room and closed the door behind her. I felt a knot in my stomach knowing that Kayla wasn't coming, and I began to worry if something had happened to her. I was already regretting not getting her number.

The instructor strode to the front of the room and smiled at some of the people she recognized. She had medium length blond hair tied back in a braided ponytail and a petite figure. She was much slimmer than Alexandra or Amber, maybe only five feet three inches tall and barely a hundred pounds. But I could see the sinewy muscles flexing in her tight yoga outfit as she moved. She was pretty in a girl-next-door kind of way, with large brown eyes and fair skin. Could this be the mysterious Soraya that I'd talked to in the online chat session?

"Good evening, everybody," she said, addressing the group. "Welcome to our Level Three Tantric Yoga session—Harmony. My name's Soraya, and I'll be leading this evening's session. I hope you found your last session stimulating. Tonight, we're going to step it up with some new exercises and with a greater level of engagement with your partners. This final level is where we seek maximum enlightenment through the union of our minds, bodies, and spirits. Are we ready to get started?"

Everybody in the room nodded enthusiastically, except me. Even though the 'union of bodies' was what I had signed up for, part of me felt lost without Kayla at my side. It was hard to imagine how I'd be able to engage so intimately with anyone else right now.

"Okay then," Soraya said. "Let's begin by celebrating the freedom of our natural selves by removing our clothes."

By now, everyone had become comfortable with the notion of stretching in the buff, and it didn't long for the group to get naked. I scanned the room through the expanse of mirrors on the front wall and saw many familiar faces. Most of the people from my last class had returned, together with a few new faces who were stepping up from another Level Two class. Once again, the women outnumbered the men by a ratio of two to one, but I noticed that some of the men had paired up next to one another this time. I'd sensed that some of the men attending our previous sessions were gay, and I was intrigued to see how they'd engage one another in this advanced session.

I quickly checked out Soraya's body as my eyes darted across her naked figure. She had a perfect ballerina's figure, with strong slender muscles, small but shapely breasts, and narrow hips with a round, firm ass. She smiled as she appraised the diverse group standing naked before her.

"First," she began, "let's recognize the power within each of us by turning to our partner and celebrating their beauty. Turn to face your nearest colleague and stand with your feet together, with your spine erect. Feel the strength in their body and celebrate the unique beauty each of us embodies."

Up to this point, I'd only seen the backside of Neve as we both faced the front of the room with her slightly in front of me. I'd admired her strong and shapely ass and was looking forward to seeing what she looked like from the front. But as she turned around to face me, my mouth dropped open. A strange movement between her legs drew my gaze down to her midsection, where she had a prominent hanging penis.

My eyes flew open as I caught my breath, and she smiled at me with a knowing gaze. Far from being scared or offended by her transgender appearance, I was fascinated by her blend of masculine and feminine traits. Other than the large phallus hanging between her legs, no one would have guessed that she was transgender. Her arms and legs were slender like a woman's, and her waist tapered in the middle to accent the roundness of her hips. She had a flat and nicely toned stomach that blended seamlessly with her large, firm breasts. I knew that they were likely fake, but I didn't care—they were perfectly shaped, firm, and round. I couldn't see any visible sign of scarring, and her nipples were large and protruded proudly, as if telling me: 'I'm a woman!'

I couldn't help my eyes from darting over her voluptuous figure, but I lingered especially long at her magnificent tool. It was long and thick even in a flaccid state, perfectly circumcised, and a lovely shade of light brown, matching the rest of her beautifully tanned body. She'd shaved her pubic patch to a barely visible light brown stubble, and her tight balls were clean and bare. I could feel my breathing increasing in excitement as my chest rose and fell from the thrill of seeing my first transgender person naked.

Was she a man, a woman, a transsexual, or a lady-boy? I wondered. *What was the correct term to call transgender people these days?*

From the feminine pitch of her voice, I knew she was a man who was probably taking hormone treatment to become a woman, and for all intents and purposes, that's what she looked and sounded like to me. All except that glorious joystick hanging between her legs. My pussy unconsciously began to lubricate thinking of all the fun I could have with her. Suddenly, the image of Kayla was far from my mind.

I looked up at Neve and smiled. The only judging she'd receive from me today was positive affirmation and admiration. I lifted my chest and thrust out my breasts, silently signaling: 'Look at us—two beautiful, strong, proud, women.' She beamed back at me and pulled her feet apart a couple of inches. I glanced down at her member and noticed that it had swelled in size since I last looked at it. Still pointing downwards, it had lengthened to at least six inches in length and five inches in girth.

If this is what her cock looks like when it's tame, I can't wait to see what it looks like fully excited.

The sound of Soraya's voice pulled me out of my trance.

"Now let's loosen up a little bit in preparation for some new poses," she said. "Extend your arms straight over your head and clasp your hands together. Now bend slightly to your right side, keeping your chest parallel with the rest of your body. Bend as far as you can, then pause and hold while you breathe from your diaphragm."

Neve and I swung our bodies in opposite directions as we looked at each other, tilting our heads playfully. After a minute or so, Soraya asked us to bend to the opposite side, and our smiles broadened as Neve and I continued tilting our heads like schoolgirls.

"Now, stand up straight in the Mountain pose, then step back about one leg length with your left foot as you bend your right knee to a ninety-degree angle. This variation on the Warrior pose will strengthen your thighs and glutes, and channel the power within you. Hold for one minute, then switch and repeat with the opposite side."

Neve and I extended our legs and sunk down into the pose, as we looked at each other with exaggerated looks of ferocity on our faces. When we switched to the other side, our eyes widened and our lips puckered, while we continued play-acting. It was nice to have someone to partner with who didn't take the whole naked yoga thing too seriously. Her pecker detumesced slightly, and it swung gently between her legs whenever we changed positions. I could tell she was getting more relaxed and focusing on enjoying the moment.

"Now bend your upper body forward," Soraya instructed, "and place your hands on the floor beside your front foot. You should feel the stretch in your right hamstring and left thigh. Lower yourself as far as you can and hold the position as you look up, breathing slowly."

Neve and I faced each other directly and we continued our little game, holding our warrior expressions as our faces came closer together. I glanced up and down her body to signal I was checking out the firehose between her legs, and with each glance it seemed to get bigger and bigger. It was fun to have so much control over a cock, even if it didn't belong to a man.

"Ok," Soraya continued. "Now let's work on our balance for a little bit before we get into some more serious poses. Turn away from your partners and return to the standing forward fold. Bend over and place your fingertips on the floor then sweep your right leg up to a ninety-degree angle behind you. Now turn your chest to the left and reach up with your left arm until it's pointing toward the ceiling. Hold and pause, trying to center your body over your left leg."

Neve and I watched Soraya demonstrate the technique, then we mimicked her position. We couldn't see each other faced in opposite directions, so I lowered my head and glanced between my legs. She waved her foot that was pointed in my direction as if to say hello and giggled softly. I could see her testicles nestled tightly between her extended legs and her cock pointing straight down. I wondered if she noticed the shining wet spot that was forming between my own legs. Soraya asked us to repeat the procedure on the other side, and once again Neve and I stole glances at each other's backsides between our scissored legs.

"Now we're going to try something a little more risqué," she said. "It's called the Standing Split. Return to the standing forward fold position, continuing in the opposite directions to your partner. Brace your fingertips against the floor and sweep your right leg straight up toward the ceiling. Keep your hips squared and inhale, extending your chest. Now, exhale and lean toward your standing leg, bracing your left forearm against your left calf. Lift your right leg as high and straight as you can, feeling the stretch in your glutes and hamstrings."

As I bent over into the revealing position, I smiled knowing that Soraya could just as easily instructed us to perform the pose facing our partners. But this way, we were completely opening ourselves up to one another, revealing our most intimate parts only inches away from one another.

I was able to lift my foot high enough that my legs were in an almost straight line, with my chest resting against my left thigh. I opened my eyes and looked over at Neve and saw that she was straining to hold the position but had managed to get her legs into a near one-hundred-and-fifty-degree angle. I nodded in approval as she smiled at me, breathing heavily. Her balls had pulled slightly toward her cock from the force of gravity, and I could see her exposed perineum and anus between her upswept leg. I admired how clean and bare everything was, and I hoped she was inspecting me as closely as I was her. I could feel a trickle of lubrication leaking out of my pussy and beginning to run down my leg as I noticed her penis swell and elongate. It was exhilarating to communicate exactly what we were feeling purely through our body language.

After a couple of minutes, Soraya asked us to switch positions and stretch the other leg. I could feel the slick liquid between my thighs as they scissored together. A few people in the group groaned trying to hold the pose, and Soraya asked us to return to a comfortable standing position.

"Okay," she said. "You can turn around and face your partners again. Let's rest for a moment before we try some seated poses. I want you to sit down on your mat and cross your legs in the Buddha position, then place your palms on your knees and close your eyes. Breathe deeply, relaxing your muscles. Empty your thoughts as you feel the energy emanating from within you and from your partner.

"Om," Soraya hummed out loud.

"Om," everyone in the group chanted in return.

"Now let's limber up our back and work on strengthening our core," she said. "Extend your legs straight in front of you, then lift your right knee, placing your right foot against the inside of your left thigh. Now, twist gently to your right and bring your left arm to rest on the outside of your elevated knee. Brace your upper body by placing your right hand behind you on the floor as you try to twist your torso as far as you can in the opposite direction."

I remembered this move from our last class and wondered what Soraya's plan was for this session's development. Maybe it was simply designed to let us come down from the intensity of the last exercise, but I was definitely ready to step it up to the next level of engagement. Neve and I tried not to look at one another as we turned our heads to guide our chests in opposite directions. But when we switched to focus on the other side, we stole a quick glance and smiled at each other.

Maybe there was method to Soraya's madness after all, I thought. The brief pause in the sexual tension that had been building up between us only seemed to heighten my desire.

"Okay," Soraya said, "now let's get down to the serious stuff. Bring your legs back in front of you and extend them straight out until they're touching your partner's feet. Now gently spread your legs as far apart as you can, feeling the stretch in your inner thigh muscles. Extend your arms toward your partner and clasp each other's hands as you brace your feet together. Have one partner gently pull the other forward, bringing your chest as far forward and low as you can. Breathe slowly and deeply, pausing when it starts to bind. When you feel your muscles relax, spread your feet a little further apart and try to bend even lower."

I remembered this pose vividly from our last class. This had been the one that brought Kayla and me close enough where we came together. I wondered if Soraya had a different design for us this time. If this session was all about creating a closer union between partners, I was ready for whatever she had in mind. Neve and I placed our feet together and gradually spread our legs apart as we stared into each other's eyes. Neither of us wanted to be the first to leer openly at the other's exposed genitalia.

When our legs were spread as far as they could go, we hesitated holding hands, wondering who should 'go first'. As with Kayla, I decided to take the lead. I gently pulled Neve towards me, and she lowered her chest and head between my legs. As her head got closer to my throbbing pussy, I wondered what it would be like to make love with a transsexual. I'd never had a transgendered person go down on me, and my clit tingled with the thought of Neve wrapping her lips around my love button.

She wasn't quite as flexible as Kayla, but with her legs swung out over ninety degrees, she was able to get her face very close to my sopping pussy. I held her arms firmly, holding her in the extended position to give her a moment to revel in my womanness. I wasn't sure what her sexual preferences were, but I knew she identified as a woman and I wanted her to see my female parts in all their glory, close-up. I heard her exhale in a muffled moan as she lingered, taking it all in. I was tempted to spread my legs further to see if she could get close enough to touch me, when I heard Soraya's voice again.

"After one partner has stretched as far as he or she can go, switch positions and guide the other to do the same. You may notice your partner's arousal, and this is perfectly normal. If it helps to provide extra motivation for your partner, you may wish to touch each other in the Mula Bandha area to encourage them to go further. Of course, we always want to respect our partner's personal space, so if you want to disengage at any time, just provide the signal."

I released the tension on Neve's arms and she lifted her torso up, looking at me quizzically. I suspect she had the same idea as me and had hoped to go further. I smiled at her and looked down between her legs. Her cock was fully erect and pointing up toward her belly. Now at least eight inches in length, it had to be six inches around. It was perfectly straight and glistening at the tip. I had a feeling she needed to be touched even more than I did.

She nodded to indicate that she understood my plan and gently began to pull my arms toward her. I knew that I'd have no difficulty getting all the way down to her crotch, so I teased her by lowering myself slowly. I could see her erect cock bouncing from the pulse coursing through it, and I licked my lips in anticipation of taking it into my mouth. The angle of our legs was perfectly positioned for my head to reach the top of her erection with my back straight. I paused with my lips inches away from her swelling and glistening head. I was dying to swallow her like a popsicle, but I wanted to build her sexual tension even more. I wanted to hear her gasp when I finally took her into my mouth.

I could see the pre-cum streaming out of her slit as she vainly thrust her hips up toward my face. I paused for one last moment, then placed my lips around the head of her dick and sucked her into my mouth. She let out a guttural moan as I felt her lingham swell in my mouth. I pictured her sitting on her yoga mat, sitting with her legs spread wide, with everyone watching me suck this beautiful woman's cock into my mouth. Maybe they were doing the same thing at this moment, because I could hear muffled moans coming from the people around me. Whether they were getting turned on watching us or getting some of their own action, it didn't matter. At this moment, I was at one with my partner.

As I swirled my tongue around the head of Neve's cock and pushed myself down deeper over her shaft, I heard the pace of her breathing increase. She started to whimper when I flicked the sensitive part of her coronal ridge under the head of her frenulum. I sensed that she was getting close to cumming, so I moved my hands from my sides and cradled her balls, rolling and squeezing them gently in my hands.

"Oh God," she gasped, as l felt her hard cock flex in my mouth.

It won't be long now, I thought.

Just then, I heard Soraya's voice again, as she instructed us to move into a new position.

You've got to be kidding me.

"I know many of you are feeling an intimate connection with your partners," she said. "If you wish to continue exploring this position, you may. But we have one last pose that I think you may find even more empowering. It's called the Buddha Straddle, and I believe you may find it brings you even closer together and elevates your spirits even higher. When you're ready, sit up and face your partner in the seated Buddha position."

I paused for a moment with Neve's throbbing cock in my mouth, and she froze, unsure what to do next. Then she gently placed her hands under my shoulders and encouraged me to lift myself up. I withdrew her cock from my mouth, kissed the tip, then sat up. The look we shared when our eyes met said everything we needed to express. Her eyes were glazed over and she gave me a thankful smile. Whether she was trying to respect Soraya's commands or she was trying to save herself for the main event, I wasn't sure. I simply smiled back at her as I gazed deeply into her eyes.

"Okay," Soraya said, after everyone had moved into the new position. "Place your hands together in front of your chest and bow toward your partner to acknowledge each other's divinity."

Neve and I pressed our hands together in a steepled prayer position and bowed.

"Namaste," Soraya said.

"Namaste," Neve and I said, saluting each other.

"In this last exercise," Soraya said, "we're going to move as close together as we possibly can to combine our life energy into one. I'd like one partner to move forward and lift yourself up so your hips rest between the straddled legs of your other partner. Then wrap your legs around your partner's hips and interlock your feet to pull yourself toward him or her. You may choose to simply rest in this position as you listen to each other meditate, or you may engage your Mula Banha directly in order to exchange your energy more intimately. Either way, focus on each other's breathing and move slowly to celebrate each other's life flow."

I smiled at Neve and scooted toward her, then lifted myself up into her lap. We both knew who should be on top in this case. I could feel her cock pressing against my stomach, and I paused as I looked into her eyes.

"Enjoy," I whispered softly.

Then I tilted my hips forward and grasped the shaft of her cock between my slick labia and rocked slowly back and forth to massage her gently. She closed her eyes to savor the sensation, and I moved forward to kiss her. Her lips were soft and pliant, and I pushed my tongue inside her, allowing her to taste her own honey. We kissed for a time with me rubbing her shaft up and down my slippery slit, then we both tilted our hips at the same time and her cock slipped inside me. We both moaned as we held each other close, then Neve titled her hips further as I sunk down onto her throbbing member. I was surprised I could take all of her inside me, and we began to rock our hips faster together.

"Remember to go slow," Soraya admonished. "One of the joys of tantric yoga is the savoring of each other's Chi as we interweave our bodies and join together in intimate connection. Enjoy the feeling and savor each moment, as you prolong the build-up of your pleasure and intimacy. Feel the power coursing through your bodies and the joy that you're able to share with one another."

Neve and I slowed our rocking down and I placed my head beside hers as we held each other close. I looked behind her for a moment and watched some of the other couples in the room. Some of them were engaged in girl-girl coupling and some were engaged in man-to-man intercourse. But most, like Neve and me, were engaged in heterosexual coupling. As I ground my hips against Neve's cock, I watched the other couples moving in a similar fashion. Many were looking into each other's eyes or were locked in a passionate kiss.

Grunts and moans were coming from around the room now, and I could hear the passion rising between each couple. Not far away, I could see two men rocking their hips together, as their joined cocks poked up from their laps, their tips shining in the bright light streaming in from the window. It was an incredible turn-on watching everybody connecting with their partners as they focused on being in the moment.

I could feel my juices starting to flow more freely now as they dribbled out of my hole and down Neve's balls onto our shared mat. I could feel her tight balls rubbing against my perineum and knew she was getting close. But I was determined not to be the first ones to come this time, and I slowed down our rhythm to give her a chance to ease off. I think she had the same idea, and she stopped rocking her hips to let me take over creating the friction. I could feel the warmth of her cock deep inside me as the heat radiated between us. I began kissing her again and we closed our eyes as we rolled our tongues inside each other's mouths.

"Feel the energy radiating between you," Soraya said from the front of the room. For a moment, I felt sorry that she hadn't been able to partner up with anyone else, since there was an even number of participants in this class and everyone was coupled up. I wondered if she might be playing with herself watching this incredibly erotic show. I could hear the breathing and moaning of my colleagues around me, and Neve and I began to increase our pace. We wouldn't be the first to come, but I didn't want to be the last, either.

As we heard some couples groan out loud in the obvious throes of orgasm, Neve suddenly began moving her hips again, thrusting her cock deeper inside me. I returned the favor and pressed my cunt as hard as I could against the base of her cock and balls. We were joined as deep and close as two people could be, and I could feel her breathing increasing in speed and intensity as she neared the precipice. With one final thrust, she pushed inside me as I clamped down on her penis and felt the throbbing of her cock as she emptied her potion inside me. That was enough to put me over the edge, and I pulled her hips toward me as I locked my legs around her. I arched my back and came in one long stream of continuing spasms for what seemed like a minute. My body shook as I savored every last second of the euphoria we shared.

When we finally came down from our powerful orgasms, we held each other close and touched our foreheads as we closed our eyes. There was utter silence in the room as everyone including Soraya concentrated on the fulfillment we all felt. I said a silent prayer as I thanked the universe for sharing its energy with me and Neve.

"Om," I purred into her ear.

"Om," she replied, as I felt her cock twitch one last time inside my pussy.

VOLUME FOUR

THE COSTUME PARTY

1

———————

I woke up to the sound of my best friend Hannah calling me from the other end of my house. She'd let herself in early on a Saturday morning and for some reason was yelling at me as she ran up the stairs.

"Jade!" she hollered. "Where are you? I've got some exciting news!"

I rolled over and squinted at my clock on the nightstand. It was a little past eight. Saturdays were the only day of the week I allowed myself to sleep in, and I was more than a little ticked at her rude intrusion.

"Aren't you up yet?" she called. "Get up—you're not going to believe what I just heard."

I rolled over and wrapped my pillow around my ears as she dashed into my bedroom. She paused for a minute smiling at my feeble attempt to block her out of my morning daze, then she pounced on the bed below my curled-up knees.

"Wake up, sleepyhead!" she squealed, pushing my shoulders to rouse me from my slumber.

"This better be good," I said, raising my pillow a few inches and peering at her through thin eyes. "You know how much I worship my weekend sleep-ins."

"You'll be glad I woke you when you hear what I have to tell you," she said. "Besides, you're gonna want to get up and begin planning your day right away. We're going to need a few extra hours to go shopping."

I pulled my duvet cover over my shoulders and huffed.

"What could possibly be so important to drag me out of my soft and cozy bed this early in the morning?"

I peered outside, looking at the gray clouds hanging low in the late October skies. I was in no hurry to venture out into the chilly autumn air.

"Only the biggest private shindig of the year. Steve Bannon is hosting his annual Halloween party at his mansion on the lake, and we're invited!"

"Isn't that the party with all the A-list celebrities? How did you score an invitation?"

Hannah peered at me with a wicked look in her eyes.

"Let's just say I know somebody who knows somebody. Someone with whom I may have pulled a few strings to earn some special favors."

"I bet that's not the *only* thing you were pulling to earn those favors," I said, raising an eyebrow.

"Possibly," she smirked. "But I apparently impressed him enough with my naked gymnastics to land an invitation to this special event. Except this year, it's got an extra twist. This time it's going to be a *nude* costume party."

I lifted my head and propped the side of my face on a crooked elbow, suddenly intrigued.

"Isn't that an oxymoron? How can you be in costume and naked at the same time?"

Hannah smiled and handed me a gold-embossed card inscribed with fancy calligraphy writing. I felt the raised surface of the script on the tips of fingers, rubbing it gently trying to divine its meaning through my still bleary eyes. Somebody had gone to a great deal of effort to create an invitation card on par with the most extravagant wedding.

I pulled myself up and leaned against my headboard, slowly reading the message.

You are cordially invited to attend my annual Halloween costume ball at my estate overlooking Lake Michigan.

This year I've added a special twist to make it even more interesting. You're encouraged to wear as little or as much trappings as you feel comfortable—including nothing at all beyond a simple mask. With everyone baring a little more than usual, who knows what kind of shenanigans might break out, and we're always mindful of protecting the anonymity of our special guests.

Of course, I encourage everyone to be playful and creative with their choice of costumes, as this is always the highlight of the event. As in previous years, there will be a special prize for the best costume of the evening and we hope you'll be suitably daring and inventive.

Feel free to bring a partner and let down your britches! As always, what happens at the Bannon residence stays at the Bannon residence. I look forward to seeing you this Saturday, starting at midnight. We'll all have a ghoulish good time!

I peered up at Hannah and grinned.

"No RSVP?"

"There's no need with a Steve Bannon invitation," she said. Everyone who's invited always goes. It's the go-to event of the year in the Chicago area. Models, actresses, rock stars, billionaires—everybody who's anybody in this town will be there. There's even a rumor that the Governor and his wife will attend this year's event."

I looked down at the card, rubbing my fingers over the embossed script.

"The invitation says you're allowed to bring a partner. Was that a condition of your little tryst with your friend—that you accompany him as his plus-one?"

Hannah peered at me devilishly as a tiny curl formed on the sides of her mouth.

"When I told him I had a friend who was even prettier than me and had a body to die for, he didn't hesitate to hand me an extra invitation. *You're* my plus-one, girl." She pulled another card out of her purse and handed it to me. "You know I'd never pass up an opportunity like this without bringing my bestie along to share in the fun."

I looked at Hannah with a quizzical look and shook my head in confusion.

"How are we ever going to find a decent Halloween costume on the Saturday before the end of the month? All the costume stores will be sold out of the best stuff."

Hannah kicked off her shoes and lifted the covers, then scooched in excitedly next to me against the headboard.

"I've been searching online for some ideas. We don't have to wear anything too elaborate, and there's no reason why we have to stick to a Halloween theme. Remember, this is a *nude* costume party. We already look pretty hot for a couple of girls nearing middle age. The less we wear, the better. Let's flaunt it while we've still got it!"

She pulled an iPad out of her purse and tapped the screen. A website opened showing a collection of sexy models wearing risqué costumes. She scrolled through the images, commenting on the various themes.

"Just look at some of these possibilities. We can play any role we like, wearing as much or as little as we please. Most of these costumes can be put together with a simple trip to Walmart and maybe a bit of needle and thread. Plus, we can easily remove one of two pieces from each outfit to reveal a bit more skin. The most important element is the headpiece. We just need something to conceal our identity and highlight our girly figures with a bit of flair."

Hannah paused at a picture of a sexy blonde wearing a Playboy bunny costume. She wore a tight corset and a rubber mask that covered the top half of her face with tall ears pointing up in the air.

"What about this one? You have to admit, it's pretty hot. You'd could even dispense with the bodice altogether and just keep the bunny tail on your naked ass. Imagine the looks you'd get prancing around his mansion in that costume!"

The images of sexy half-nude models wearing unusual masks

reminded me of my encounter at the Fantasy Feast naked dinner party. Suddenly, I became mindful of the wetness that had begun building between my legs.

"Not bad," I said, shifting my weight uncomfortably off the wet spot on my sheets. "Show me some more."

Hannah flipped through a few more images and stopped at a picture of a sexy maid wearing a lacy dress, holding a feather duster in her hand. Her firm tits pressed against the flimsy fabric, creating an irresistible focal point from the sensuous shadows on her bosom.

"How about this?" she said. "You'd look stunning in this outfit. You'd be covering up just enough to drive every man and woman at that party absolutely crazy. And imagine all the fun you could have teasing the naked guests with your little duster!"

"*Intriguing...*" I said as I squeezed my thighs together, trying to quiet my burning clit.

The more images Hannah showed me, the more turned on I got. Whether it was from me imagining myself in the costumes or imagining myself playing with the guests dressed up in the provocative outfits, was unclear. Either way, the more my mind began to ponder the possibilities, the more excited I became about going to this event.

"The only problem is, it will be difficult to cover my face without looking unnatural in that outfit," I frowned. "Show me more costumes with masks."

Hannah refined her search by typing in the words *sexy mask costumes* and the screen refreshed showing a new set of models in racy outfits. Many of the themes revolved around superheroes, with the male models sporting Batman and Superman motifs and the female models wearing Wonder Woman and Batgirl-type costumes.

"Not very original," I frowned. "I bet there'll be a ton of superhero costumes among all those egotistical celebrities. I'm looking for something a little different."

Hannah paused for a moment, then tapped on her photo library pulling up an image of me wearing a business suit painted on my naked body.

"Remember that time you went to the nude bodypainting workshop? You're a graphic artist. You can be virtually anything you want and show off all you wish with a little bit of well-disguised paint. Whether it's Catwoman, Black Widow, or Wonder Woman–all these characters wear is a mask and tight outfits to show off their beautiful physiques. You could even dress up like Mystique in the X-Men movie and wear absolutely nothing other than a full coat of body paint."

"Been there, done that," I said. "If I'm going to really enjoy myself, I want to wear something I've never worn before that will absolutely blow everyone away."

"You sure are a tough customer," Hannah said, shaking her head. "Let's try something a little different..."

She reopened her browser and typed in the words *naked masquerade costumes*. A gallery of Google images popped up with a collection of half-naked men and women.

"*Now* we're talking," I said, squirming on the bed as I scanned the toned bodies of the sexy models.

"Look at that one," Hannah said, pointing at the screen. "It's a picture of Rihanna at last year's Met Gala dressed as Nefertiti. With her sheer lace dress and silver headdress, it doesn't leave much to the imagination. A bit more makeup around the eyes, and you'd be able to mask your identity quite easily."

"That's pretty hot," I said, beginning to feel the sheets getting wetter and wetter between my legs. "She definitely looks fuckable. But it's been done before. I don't want to wear something half of these people will have already seen."

"Damn, girl, you're *impossible!* Remember, less is more. The idea is to show as much of our bodies as possible to attract the attention of all these beautiful people. You could get away with a simple mask, a painted emblem on your chest, and a shiny belt. Who really cares what you're wearing as long as you get the attention of the guests?"

"Humor me for a little longer," I said, squeezing Hannah's leg. "I'm starting to get a few ideas. I just need a bit more inspiration."

Hannah began flipping through the images more quickly until one picture suddenly caught my attention.

"Wait!" I said. "Go back a few frames. I saw something

interesting..."

She scrolled back until an image of six men dressed in contrasting costumes popped up.

"That's the one," I said, scanning the image slowly.

"*The Village People*?" Hannah said. "That might be okay for a gay guy, but how could you possibly look sexy wearing any one of those cheesy costumes?"

My eyes darted back and forth between the sexy cowboy wearing chaps and the indian warrior wearing a feathered headdress and a skimpy loincloth. Suddenly I nodded as a mischievous smile formed on my face.

"What?" Hannah said. "What could you possibly be thinking?"

She glanced down at my breasts peeking above the covers, noticing my hardening nipples.

"Because I know gay dudes—even ones with hard bodies like these guys—don't do it for you. Where is your mind going with this idea?"

"I've decided what I'm going to wear," I said, crossing my arms over my chest. "But I'm going to keep it a secret until we get to the party. It'll be all the more fun and surprising if I reveal it at the last second. But I promise you, it'll be one-of-a-kind and extremely provocative."

Hannah's eyes darted across my face, trying to imagine what I had in mind.

"Now you've got *me* all excited thinking what you're going to do. Judging by your obvious state of arousal, your head is already at the party. Can I crawl under the covers with you and have some fun fantasizing which one of those costumes you're going to wear?"

"By all means," I said, disappearing under the covers with her. "Just imagine me as one of those hot dudes with his clothes off."

"Mmm," Hannah purred, slithering between my slippery thighs. "I'd rather imagine you as a hot *chick* with her clothes off."

"In a couple of days," I said, spreading my legs further apart and pulling her face into my steaming crotch. "You might be able to have it both ways."

2

———————

J ust after midnight on the day of the party, I pulled my car up beside a call box in front of a large wrought-iron gate protecting the entrance to Steve Bannon's estate. After providing our names and the identification numbers on the front of our invitation cards, the gates opened and we followed the curved driveway up to the front of a giant French-styled chateau. As a parking attendant approached our car, I turned to Hannah seated next to me and smiled.

"It's show time," I said.

"Not a moment too soon," she huffed. "I've been dying to see what you're wearing under that coat ever since you picked me up."

I'd intentionally worn a long western duster to cover my body all the way from my shoulders to my ankles. Part of it was meant to surprise Hannah when I finally reached the event, but it had much more to do with my desire to shock everyone else once I got in the front door. I reached behind my seat and pulled a thin black mask out of a bag on the floor and wrapped it around the top of my face.

Hannah's forehead wrinkled as she looked at me, still confused.

"Let me guess: Kato, Zorro, Nightshade?"

"You're moving in the right direction with the first two," I smiled, reaching back into the bag and pulling out a pair of western boots.

"Cowboy boots?" Hannah squinted. "I don't know my cowboy characters quite as well—"

"Maybe this will help," I said, donning a white Stetson.

Hannah looked at me blankly for a moment, then her eyes lit up, recognizing the familiar image of the famous cowboy with the white hat and black mask.

"The Lone Ranger?"

"Yes, but with a little twist. You'll have to wait for the full reveal until we get inside."

"You're such a tease," she said as I handed the attendant my keys and we stepped out of the car.

We paused for a moment, taking in the full scale of the Bannon estate close-up. The four-story mansion extended almost a hundred feet in either direction, with tall arched windows and ornate brickwork. The bright spotlights illuminating the front of the house lit up the entire courtyard, reflecting off Hannah's shiny Batgirl outfit.

"Holy shit!" she exclaimed. "This place is gigantic. We're going to have to drop *breadcrumbs* to not get lost in there."

"More like *caviar* or *foie gras*," I chuckled. "Something tells me everything about this affair is going to be top shelf."

"What are we waiting for?" Hannah giggled, rushing ahead of me toward the front door.

My gaze drifted down while I soaked up her tight ass in her black latex outfit. She had a beautiful hourglass figure, and the tight Batgirl costume highlighted every curve of her sexy body. I smiled as I imagined the two of us mingling among the high rollers. But I had a feeling they'd be focused on someone *else's* ass tonight.

With the large double entrance doors pulled back, we peered into the bright marble-floored foyer as we approached the front steps. A large crowd of costumed guests had already begun to gather in the main ballroom, and we could hear soft jazz music wafting out into the courtyard.

"Good evening ladies," a man wearing a crisply tailored tailcoat and black tie said as we stepped into the entrance hall.

He looked at my long shawl and smiled.

"May I check your coat, Madam?"

"Yes, thank you," I said, turning my back to assist him in its removal.

When he pulled the cape off my back and viewed my naked backside, I heard him gasp. To complement my Lone Ranger disguise, I'd chosen to wear a tight-fitting black leather vest and long black chaps with nothing underneath. My tight ass poked out the back of the open leggings, and I could feel him running his eyes up and down my body as he hesitated hanging my coat in the closet.

But when I turned around, both Hannah and the doorman took a step back in shock. On the front of my open pants, I wore a large dildo fashioned in the shape of a man's cock and balls, framed by two silver pistols on either side of my hips. The long phallus slapped against the sides of my naked thighs as it swung from side to side.

"Holy *fuck*, Jade!" Hannah squealed. "That's *outrageous*! Where did you ever come up with that idea?"

"Remember the Village People picture you showed me a few days ago? I decided to borrow elements of both the cowboy and the indian characters to create my own design." I shook my hips to juggle my equipment and smiled. "I thought it would be kind of fun playing *both* sides of coin, so to speak."

"Uh—*yeah*," she said, flicking her eyes between my tight bosom spilling over the top of my vest and my faux genitals. "I'd have to say you pulled it off. With that getup, I expect you'll be the center of attention all night long."

"Um," the doorman said, shyly interrupting. "May I have your tickets, please?"

"Of course," I said, rustling my rubber balls as I fished in the pocket of my chaps for my ticket. When the butler turned to collect Hannah's ticket, I could see the front of his pants tenting in obvious arousal.

"Enjoy your evening," he said, motioning for us to enter the ballroom.

"Oh, I have a feeling we will," Hannah winked, as she nodded toward the lengthening pole pushing down his pant leg.

A waiter approached us with tall glasses of champagne on a silver tray and did a double-take when he noticed the swinging package between my legs.

"Whoa boy," Hannah said to the server, taking two glasses off his unsteady tray. "We wouldn't want you to spill your load before we've sampled the goods."

As we moved into the main entrance hall, the patrons milling in small groups began to turn around to view the newly arriving guests. Suddenly, the gentle buzz of group conversation receded until the only sound we could hear was the hum of the background music. Everyone was so stunned taking in my outfit, they were literally dumbstruck with their mouths agape.

Many of the guests had chosen to wear predictable Halloween costumes with little bits of flesh showing here and there, but nobody was letting it all hang out quite as brazenly as I had. Amid the predictable sprinkling of ghosts and goblins, there was a profusion of superhero figures and Disney characters bedecked in various stages of undress. I shook my head at the lack of imagination of the high-powered group and began to wonder if the event was going to live up to Hannah's hyperbole.

"Damn, girl," she said. "It looks like you're going to be this evening's scene-stealer. You've already stopped the show. I don't know what everybody's thinking right now, but that thing looks so realistic, they must be wondering if you're a legit tranny wearing that impressive package."

I smiled a crooked grin, suddenly feeling self-conscious with all of the eyes in the room surveying my exposed body. Fortunately, a handsome couple dressed as Anthony and Cleopatra began to approach us, providing some distraction.

"Welcome to our little costume party," the man said, extending his hand to Hannah and me. "I'm Steve Bannon and this is my wife

Genevieve. You'll have to excuse me, but I don't recognize either of you under your—*interesting* disguises."

I was taken aback by how handsome the eccentric billionaire looked close up. With his square jaw, dimpled cheeks and thick head of salt-and-pepper hair swept back in a dense poof, he looked like a slightly older version of the famous actor Patrick Dempsey. He wore a loose toga draped over his well-muscled chest, and I could see his pecs flexing as he shook my hand.

But I found his wife even more beguiling. Wearing a tight-fitting gold-lamé dress slitted at one side of her hips and a pretty beaded headdress, she looked like a dead-ringer for a young Elizabeth Taylor. As I ran my eyes shamelessly over her luscious figure, I felt a sudden dampness building under the weight of my latex balls pressing against my flaring clit.

"Jade," I introduced myself, not yet wanting to reveal my full identity.

"Hannah," my partner responded, politely shaking their hands.

"It appears that you two have already captured the attention of my guests," Bannon said, turning to appraise the congregation still gazing awkwardly in our direction. He extended his arm in the direction of the main hall and nodded. "Please, come in and mingle. There are so many fascinating people to meet. I'm sure we'll catch up with the two of you a little later this evening."

"I'll look forward to that," I said, smiling at Genevieve, lingering for a moment longer at her dazzling figure. She returned the gesture, widening her eyes as my member twitched while I held my palm over the handle of one of my six-shooters.

"Holy shit," Hannah said, as Bannon and his wife melted back into the crowd. "Did you see the way he was looking at you? He was practically *raping* you with his eyes. Something tells me this is going to be a very interesting night. It seems the men are even more enamored with your disguise than the women. Either there's a lot of bi-curious guys in here, or they're attracted to that whole futa thing."

"I dunno," I said. "I'm showing off a lot of *girl* parts too. Who's to say what they're more attracted to? But did you notice his wife? I'd far rather get into *her* pants."

"It's too bad that thing isn't animated," Hannah chuckled, glancing at my pendulous dick. "If you could actually get it up, you could probably have your way with just about everybody in this place."

"Who knows?" I said, winking at Hannah. "In my current state of arousal, I wouldn't be surprised if this thing had a life of its own."

Little did she know how much truth in this statement I was about to reveal before the evening was over.

3

____

After Bannon and his wife resumed mingling with the rest of the crowd, Hannah and I wandered into the main ballroom. At first, most of the assembled groups gave us a wide berth, unsure what to make of the two girls dressed in such revealing costumes. Hannah's latex Batgirl outfit clung to her naked body like a second skin, the shiny fabric accentuating every crease and curve like it was painted on her. And the cutouts on both sides of my leather chaps left little to the imagination, even with the modicum of cover provided by my fake genitals covering my bare mound.

I was glad to have the freedom to mill about the room for a while, surveying the faces and costumes of the high-powered gathering. I recognized a fair number of public figures from the senior ranks of the local political, business, and media fields. The mayor was there with his wife, dressed as Little Red Riding Hood and the Big Bad Wolf, which seemed fitting given the ongoing level of corruption at City Hall. Bannon's business partner and fellow billionaire Kent Schiffer circled the room with a familiar supermodel, outfitted in matching red tights as Mr. Incredible and Elastagirl. And our local news anchorman was paired with his pretty sidekick, dressed as Woody and Bo Peep from the movie Toy Story.

Many of the guests were dressed as famous characters from superhero movies or nursery rhyme stories, with most of the men playing the more dominant role. *Typical display of macho-entitled privilege*, I thought. *Why does it seem every man who achieves a certain degree of power have to lord it over everyone else, thinking they're better than the rest of us?* My cheeky cowboy costume seemed a perfect counterpoint to the heavy dose of testosterone permeating the room, mocking their oversize male egos as I swung my big dick around like I owned it.

As Hannah and I began mingling with the small cliques scattered around the room, I found it amusing that while most of the women praised my cocky outfit, their male partners seemed threatened by it, silently stealing glances at my huge dong while their wives and girlfriends chatted with me comfortably. I wasn't sure if it was because they felt intimidated by my outsize genitals, or because they were secretly fantasizing about fucking me.

As more and more people began gravitating toward us, intrigued by my outrageous costume, Hannah slowly drifted off to the other side of the room. I couldn't blame her, with everyone asking me silly questions like what it felt like to be a woman carrying a man's dick. For a while I amused them, swinging my hips from side to side and playfully grabbing my balls, flaunting my male persona.

But I soon tired of the incessant stares and never-ending quips about my tranny disguise, and began looking for an excuse to break away. Just as I was about to excuse myself to go to the ladies' room, the governor and his wife approached our group and introduced themselves. They were dressed in matching his and hers chef outfits, the only difference being that his wife wore a less poofy hat and a backless apron that showed off her sexy ass and legs.

"That's quite a provocative costume," the governor said, extending his hand to me. "I'm Jack Scanlon and this is my wife, Alicia."

"Pleased to meet you, Mr. Governor," I said, quickly seeing through his thin disguise. "But no less daring than your wife's, which I dare say is even *more* revealing."

"In some respects, possibly," he said. "Except you're revealing both sides of the coin."

"Heads *and* tails, you mean?" I smiled.

"In a manner of speaking," he said, temporarily at a loss for words by my sassy attitude. "Are you here alone tonight?"

I scanned the room and noticed Hannah chatting it up with a hunky guest dressed in a Tarzan outfit.

"It seems my partner is out looking for greener pastures. I guess she felt this one had been fully tilled."

"Oh?" the governor said, glancing at my pendulous prick. "Who's been doing most of the figurative plowing—you, or all these other farm animals?"

"At this point, I'd say everybody's just getting the lay of the land," I said, dragging out the metaphor. "Surveying the landscape, deciding the best place to position their hoes."

"I see what you mean," the governor said, his eyes widening from my double entendre. "You seem to be particularly–*ambidextrous* in that respect."

"I'm just having fun pretending what it might be like to cultivate both sides of the field," I said, running my eyes up and down his wife's sexy body before locking eyes with her. "You never know when a particularly fertile plot might need tending."

"Well put, my lady."

"Please—call me Jade," I said, turning my attention to his wife, who'd been staring at my outfit the entire time. "What about you, Alicia? Have you been enjoying the evening so far?"

"Yes," she said, happy to deflect attention away from her overbearing husband for a moment. "So many interesting people and costumes."

"I find yours very alluring also," I said, staring at her plump breasts pressing against the front of her skimpy apron. "But it seems that all your fun parts are hidden from view, at least while we're talking face-to-face. It's only when you turn around that you reveal your adventurous side."

"I guess you'll just have to catch me when my back is turned then," she said, winking at me sexily.

"I'll definitely be keeping a lookout. Hopefully we can catch up later."

As much as I wanted to continue our playful flirtation, I knew I'd never have a chance for some alone time with her as long as I continued to engage them as a couple. Besides, I was getting tired of her husband's thinly veiled sexist comments.

"Will you excuse me for a moment while I use the restroom?"

"Of course," she said. "But be careful in there. It's not as simple for us ladies to pee standing up as it is for the men."

"Not to worry," I smiled. "Fortunately, this thing is easily removed. Though it might be kind of fun to try it just once."

"Will you be using the men's or the ladies' room?" the governor smirked.

"I'm pretty sure the toilets are unisex in this place," I said, gently admonishing him for another chauvinist remark. "Which will be a refreshing change from the usually cramped ladies' rooms we have to endure in other public places. Enjoy your evening. Perhaps we'll see each other a little later."

"We'll look forward to that," the governor smiled.

As I pulled away from the crowd, I shook my head at the impudent tone of the governor, ignoring his beautiful wife while he shamelessly flirted with me. Little did he know that I was far more impressed with Alicia than by the trappings of his high political office. I felt like I needed to wash myself off after dealing with his sexist attitude and while looking for a place to freshen up, I recognized the familiar red and white uniform of the mayor's wife as she waited outside the closed door of an adjacent anteroom. As I approached her from the side, I admired her shapely legs and full bosom pressing against her tight bodice. Her Little Red Riding Hood costume seemed the perfect outfit to highlight her youthful face and figure.

"You'd think we wouldn't have to wait to use a toilet in this place," I said, sauntering up next to her. "There must be at least twenty washrooms in this mansion."

"No doubt," she laughed. "But even in a place like this, with this many guests, unfortunately we ladies still have to wait to use the lavatory." She glanced down at my faux genitalia and smiled. "It's too bad they don't have his and hers toilets like in most public settings. With that getup, you'd probably get away with slipping into the men's room."

"Maybe," I said. "But I'd still have to pee sitting down. I'm just looking to freshen up anyway. I was hoping for a respite from all the overcharged testosterone out there."

"Tell me about it," she nodded. "I've been dealing with city politics from the other side for almost twenty years now. It's still very much an old-boys network in this business. Women are just treated as chattel, to be trotted out as eye candy whenever there's a public relations opportunity like this."

"That's partly why I wore this outfit," I admitted. "I thought it would be kind of fun to swing my own dick around all these heavy hitters at this posh event."

The washroom door suddenly swung open and a woman wearing a Victorian costume brushed past us, sneering at our haughty outfits.

"Judging by the heft of that thing," she said, "I'd say yours is the biggest one here by a large margin. Do you want to join me while I freshen up inside? It looks like the last thing you need right now is to stand outside alone while everybody wags their tongues at you."

"Thanks," I said. scurrying in behind her as we locked the door, giggling like two schoolgirls. "I'm Jade, by the way," I said stretching out my hand.

"Haley," she said, grasping my hand firmly as she smiled into my eyes.

As we leaned in to the doublewide mirror over the marble vanity to check our lipstick and mascara, I noticed Haley's gaze drifting lower to check out my package.

"You know, if it weren't for the straps holding that apparatus onto your hips, I'd swear that thing was real," she said. "It's so life-like. Even your *testicles* look authentic."

"The whole thing is made out of a special latex engineered to mimic real skin. With all the advances in artificial dolls these days, it's amazing what they can do with sex toys."

"Do you mind if I—*touch* it?" she asked.

"I thought you'd never ask."

As I stepped back from the vanity, Haley turned to face me, reaching her hand down to touch my artificial cock.

"My God," she said, squeezing it firmly. "It even *feels* like a real dick. If only it could get hard, I shudder to think how big it would be angry."

As she reached further down to cup my balls, her face came closer to mine, and we kissed. I pressed my tongue into her mouth and she reached lower still, running her fingers over my moist labia. I purred in pleasure, pressing my crotch harder into her hips. She hiked up her skirt, and I was pleasantly surprised to see that she was completely naked underneath. Recognizing my opportunity to have a little fun, I positioned my hand over my right pistol, gently pumping the trigger. Slowly, my synthetic cock began to fill with air and inflate between her legs.

"What the—" Haley gasped, pulling back to see what was happening. "You've got to be kidding me. You can *animate* that thing?"

"In a manner of speaking," I said. "You want to give it a try?"

"*Hell* yes!" she said. "I'm so horny right now, I could fuck just about anything. But first, let me take a closer look at what I'm working with."

As I smiled at her wickedly, I pumped my trigger harder until my organ rose to a full ten inches of erect flesh. Haley couldn't help herself as she fell to the floor and took my member into her mouth while she proceeded to give me a pretend blowjob. As I watched her stretch her lips around my thick pole, I placed my hands behind her head and imagined fucking her face like a man. Although I was being far gentler than most, it was fun fantasizing being in the man's role for a change, having my way with my muse.

"That's it," I purred. "Suck my big cock, baby. Squeeze my balls while I fuck your pretty face."

Without hesitating, Haley reached underneath me and began

rubbing my balls against my raging clit. The sensation was not unlike what I imagined a real man would be feeling as she stimulated my sex organ.

"Fuck, yes," I panted. "That feels good, Haley. I want to fuck you so bad."

Suddenly, she stood up and smiled at me.

"That makes *two* of us. I'm so turned-on, I could pop off any second."

She reached behind her, placing her hands on top of the vanity and lifted herself up onto the counter, hiking her skirt all the way up. I took one look at her glistening pussy and leaned in to kiss her passionately. She reached down and pointed my hard pecker toward her opening and when I pressed it into her, she gasped.

"Oh God, Jade," she groaned. "Your cock feels so good. Fill me up with your big dick. I want to feel your balls slapping against my pussy."

Her dirty talk got me even more worked up, and as I pressed my hips forward, she moaned loudly. As we began to grind our hips together, our tongues danced in each other's mouths. Haley flapped her thighs against me as I plowed in and out of her, grinding my clit against the underside of my rubbery balls. While we grunted and moaned with abandon, anybody who might have been waiting to use the restroom must have surely known what was going on inside. But neither one of us cared, lost in the moment by the rising feeling of ecstasy engulfing our joined bodies.

Suddenly, Haley wrapped her legs around my ass and pulled me even deeper inside her pussy.

"*Damn*, girl," she panted. "You're going to make me come with that big thumper of yours. Fill me up while I come all over your pretty pussy."

"Yes," I groaned. "I'm close too. I'm going to cum with you. God damn, I like fucking you."

"Here it comes," Haley moaned. "Take me over the edge."

I grabbed Haley's hips by both sides and pulled her strongly toward me, grinding my cock and balls as hard as I could against her while ramming my cock in and out of her sloshing pussy. Suddenly, a wave of passion rolled over me as my clit began pulsating against the underside of my faux balls.

"Oh God, Haley," I groaned. "Cum with me baby. Come all over my big dick."

"Yes!" Haley howled. "I can feel you pounding my G-spot. It feels soooo good!"

Suddenly, I felt Haley spraying all over my balls and mound as her pussy clenched down over my phallus while we ground our hips against one another. We moaned inside each other's mouths as we locked lips in a tight and passionate kiss. After what seemed like a full minute of shaking and convulsing in each other's arms, our breathing finally returned to normal, while we kissed with me still inside her.

"*Ahem*," a woman's voice called impatiently from outside the door, from someone waiting to use the facilities.

"I guess we'll have to vacate the premises," Haley smiled. "Though I could make love to you all night long."

"Same here," I said. "Let's clean up and get out of here. Maybe we can find a more private place to continue our fun."

While Haley pulled down her skirt and reapplied her smudged lipstick, I unfastened my appendage and washed it under the tap before reattaching it to my mound. When we finally got ourselves put back together, we opened the door and walked past a long line of stunned onlookers as their eyes widened in shock ogling my still-dripping, semi-hard cock.

4

It didn't take long after Haley and I returned to the main ballroom for her husband to spot us. While we giggled amongst ourselves about the pretentious costumes of all the men in the room masking their tiny peckers, the mayor approached us with an angry scowl on his face.

"Where've you been?" he barked at Haley, his ruddy, pockmarked face making his wolf costume look all the more ridiculous. "I've been looking all over for you. There are a lot of prominent people I wanted to introduce you to."

"Jade and I were just freshening up. No need to get your knickers in a twist, dear."

"*Freshening up*?" he said, darting his eyes back and forth between Haley's face and my tumescent cock. "How long does that take? You must have been gone for at least a half hour!"

"Well, you know how we women are when we hang out in the ladies' room," she replied with a straight face. "There's no telling how long it might take to get ourselves put together in front of the mirror. You *do* want me to look pretty and proper for all your important friends, don't you?"

"I—suppose so," he stammered, distracted by my glistening

joystick. He grabbed Haley's hand, trying to drag her away from me. "Come, I want you to meet one of my biggest fundraisers, Kent Schiffer."

As he steered Haley toward a gathering in the center of the room, she looked back at me with an apologetic expression, mouthing the words *later*. Soon after, Hannah came up behind me and cupped one of my bare cheeks with her hand.

"What was *that* all about?" she said. "It looked like the Big Bad Wolf was about to bite off his wife's head."

"He might as well have," I huffed. "The way he was acting as if he owned her. All these upper-class snobs seem interested in is congratulating themselves around their buddies while showing off their arm candy."

"He did seem a little distracted by you," Hannah said, noticing Haley peering in my direction with a flushed face. "And he wasn't the *only* one. What kind of trouble did you get into with his wife? You've got a strange glow about you."

"Nothing much," I lied. "We were just freshening up in the ladies' room, looking for an escape from all the overbearing egos in this place."

Hannah looked at me suspiciously, pinching her eyebrows as she peered at my puffy appendage.

"Well, judging by the flush on your chest and the sweat dripping down your ass, I'd say you were up to a little more than just fixing your makeup. If I didn't know better, I'd swear even your *dick* looks more excited than usual."

"We may have been touching up a bit more than just our *faces*," I admitted. "We started admiring each other's costumes and one thing led to another..."

Hannah reached down and squeezed my tumescent dildo, then her eyes widened as her lips curled up into a knowing smile.

"Is it just my imagination, or does it seem a little *bigger* than when we first came in? You better be careful—you could poke somebody's eye out with that thing."

"That's not the only thing it's good for poking," I grinned.

"No way!" she said, stepping back in mock indignation. "You were *fucking* the mayor's wife in the washroom? Did he have any inkling?"

"I don't think so. But judging by how much noise we were making in there, I imagine it won't take long for word to spread around the room."

"Not to worry–just stick with me, girl," Hannah said, moving closer to protect me from everyone's disapproving glares. "If any of these jokers cause you any trouble, I'll give them a batkick to the groin."

"I doubt that'll be necessary," I sighed, catching Hannah's Tarzan friend stealing glances at me from the open bar on the other side of the room. "Most of the men in here seem reluctant to engage me in any kind of conversation, let alone actually approach me in this getup. I don't know if they're more threatened by my provocative outfit or they're just afraid to admit they're attracted to a pretty girl with a big cock."

I noticed Tarzan moving to the other side of the bar to get a clearer look at me. I found it strange that he seemed so focused on me after Hannah had spent so much time with him earlier. Unlike me, I knew she had a preference for men, and I suspected she was hoping to land a wealthy boyfriend at this event.

"What about you?" I said, shifting my position to deflect Tarzan's gaze. "What kind of trouble have you been getting up to around all these society types?"

"Not as much as I'd like," Hannah frowned. "I've found a few interesting candidates, but so far everybody's been politely keeping their dicks in their pants."

"Well, you know how it is. With all their extra ornamentation, it might be kind of hard to just whip it out. Most of these guys seem to have gone to great lengths to gussy themselves up with all this embellishment."

"I know what you mean," Hannah said, pulling her tight latex skin down uncomfortably under her crotch. "I guess I didn't give this costume as much forethought as I should have. I'm sweating like a pig under here. I have to dismantle the whole thing just to go pee."

"Not exactly conducive to pulling off a quickie in this place," I chuckled.

"Not as easily as you," she grumbled. "You don't have to remove a single stitch of clothing to get your freak on. All you have to do is find a willing accomplice and insert your magic wand."

With Hannah's back turned away from the bar, I saw Tarzan adjusting his equipment under the counter. His loincloth had begun pouching in front of his penis, and he seemed to be getting more and more aroused watching me.

"What about that hunky Tarzan character I saw you flirting with earlier?" I said, hoping to redirect his attention. "He seems worthy of a little deconstruction."

"It crossed my mind, believe me," Hannah said. "But he seemed more interested in talking about everyone else in the room. Either he's just here for the people watching, or he's gay. I mean, I'm still a *catch*, right? Who can resist a sexy chick in this tight outfit? I was practically throwing myself at him."

Tarzan turned away from me holding his hands in front of his crotch, trying to keep his rising member from making too obvious an appearance. Then he suddenly stood up and exited through a door next to the bar.

"He's probably just trying to keep up appearances," I said. "It's a pretty snooty affair, you have to admit. People would likely get their nose out of joint if they caught a couple getting too carried away in public."

"That's what *powder rooms* are for, right?" Hannah grinned.

"Speaking of, I gotta go pee for real this time. Catch up with you in a bit?"

"Sure," Hannah said. "Just try not to dip your dick anywhere it doesn't belong this time. There's no telling what kind of hullabaloo it might generate if one of these heavy hitters caught you getting it on again with another one of their wives."

"Don't worry," I smiled. "I'll be staying far away from the ladies this time."

As soon as I left Hannah, a flock of men suddenly converged on her, no longer threatened by the presence of her sexy androgynous partner. But I was happy for the distraction, because there was something about this Tarzan hunk I needed to check out. He was the first man I'd met at the ball who'd demonstrated any genuine interest in me, and I wanted to see which persona he was more attracted to.

I meandered through the crowd making small talk with some of the guests then I ordered a cocktail at the bar and slipped quietly out the same door I'd seen Tarzan use. It led to a large wine cellar, darkened and chilled to a frigid fifty degrees. I looked around the room, catching sight of Tarzan huddled between two kegs with his hand moving suspiciously between his legs.

I strolled over in his direction and smiled when I noticed his predicament. His cock was at full mast, flapping up over his flimsy loincloth, high up against his belly. I nodded when I saw how well hung he was, his organ standing a good eight inches in length and at least two inches thick.

"Aren't you a bit underdressed for this place?" I asked.

"I suppose so," he said in a shaky voice. "But I didn't know where else to go." He looked down at his crotch with a sheepish expression, vainly trying to cover up his erection. "It seems I'm having a bit of a wardrobe malfunction."

"Is *that* what you call it?" I said. "Can I offer some help? Provide a little body heat at least? You're shivering in that skimpy outfit."

"Maybe," he hesitated, peering down at my even bigger cock hanging down over my naked belly. "At least you can provide some cover if anyone else comes in here."

As if on cue, the door on the other side of the wine cellar opened, and a uniformed waiter entered the room, walking in our direction. He appeared to be looking for a particular bottle, but when he caught sight of the two of us, he stopped and did a double-take. Without pausing, I stepped closer to Tarzan and flung my arms around him, pretending to make out. It was just the cover he needed, and this was the perfect excuse to get a little closer. The waiter smiled as he nodded toward us, then collected his items and exited the room.

"Thanks," Tarzan said, pulling away awkwardly. "This is beyond embarrassing. I can't seem to make this thing go down and I have nothing to cover up with."

"I can't imagine why you'd *want* to," I said, running my fingers over his hard chest muscles. "With a body like this, you should be showing off as much of it as you can."

He glanced down at my full breasts pressing up against him in my tight leather vest.

"I hadn't counted on getting quite so—*aroused* at this event," he stuttered. "I thought I'd be able to keep it together around all these stiff necks. This has never happened to me before in a public place..."

"Not to worry," I said. "This little accident will stay between us. But if you don't mind my asking, may I ask what's gotten you so worked up? I saw you looking in my direction, and all of a sudden you wanted to hide."

"I'm sorry," he said, his face flushing like a teenager. "I just couldn't help staring at you. I find you incredibly sexy, and with so much of you hanging out for everyone to see, I guess I just had a visceral reaction."

"I understand," I said, darting my eyes over his handsome face, finding myself getting surprisingly turned by his shy demeanor. "But which *part* of me were you most attracted to? I'm hanging out on both sides."

"Both," he said, without hesitation. "You have a sexy body and you're absolutely stunning. But there's something especially alluring about a woman flaunting a man's genitals overtop their naked body. It's very—*ballsy* of you."

"You like *cocky* women, do you?" I said, leaning in towards him as I brushed my thick cock against his tight balls.

"In a manner of speaking," he huffed.

"Did you want to play with it?"

"May I?" he said. "I've never really touched another penis before..."

"You mean besides your *own*?" I kidded. "Is that what you were doing in here? Stroking it trying to make it go down before you went back into the ballroom?"

"I was so turned on, I didn't think there was any other way to get myself back together."

"Maybe I can help you with that," I smiled, reaching down and grasping his throbbing cock with my left hand. "Is this warming you up a little bit?"

"Yes," he panted, clutching my ass while he rocked his hips toward me, trying to create some much-needed friction against his throbbing hard-on. "But you've got goosebumps too. How can I help warm you up?"

I wasn't sure what he had in mind, but I wasn't interested in him fucking me in the usual manner. I'd long been fascinated seeing gay men play with themselves. I found one of the most erotic things was when they rubbed their erect cocks together. Something about the playful jousting of their erogenous parts always got me turned on.

"Well, we're both equipped with similar equipment," I said, raising an eyebrow. "I've always wondered what it would feel like to rub two cocks together..."

"Oh my God," Tarzan said. "I've fantasized about that too. But you're not exactly *functional* in the way most men are—"

"You might be surprised what this ladyboy is capable of," I grinned. "This little package comes equipped with a few extra features."

As I began stroking his hard-on, I squeezed the trigger of the pistol on my right hip, slowly inflating my rising pecker. Tarzan looked down and widened his eyes, seeing my love muscle inflating to its full ten inches. When it reached its maximum length, I placed it against the underside of his prick and began rocking my hips in tandem with his. Even though he was better endowed than most men, my giant phallus looked like an anaconda slithering up next to his garden snake. As the rubbery veins of my dildo rolled over the sensitive flesh on the tip of his rod, he shuddered and emitted a drop of dew out of his hole.

"Uhnnn," he groaned. "This is incredibly hot. I've always wondered what this would feel like, but to do it with such a sexy woman is a dream come true."

"You've always wanted to get it on with a *tranny*?" I smirked. "Well now you've got your wish."

I reached down and cupped my hands around both of our cocks and began humping him more vigorously. Tarzan groaned as he placed his hands against my chest, squeezing my breasts over my cowboy vest.

"Open it up," I nodded. "See what it's like to fuck a real ladyboy. I want to feel your hard pecs rubbing against my tits."

He didn't need any more encouragement as he fumbled with my buttons until he freed my boobs from their tight enclosure. When he saw my firm breasts bouncing on my chest, he circled them with his hands and pinched my nipples gently while I continued frotting our cocks together in my hands.

"Fucking hell," he said. "You are so hot. You are truly the woman of my dreams."

"And *man* also?" I smiled.

"Yes," he admitted. "I've long fantasized what it would be like to hold another man's penis in my hands."

"Why don't you take the driver's seat then?" I said, acknowledging his bisexual nature. "Let me admire the scenery for a while."

When I removed my hands, he placed his palms around our joined cocks and squeezed them together firmly. More precum oozed out of the head of his pole, and he moaned as he began to pick up the pace of his rocking motion. Neither one of us seemed interested in kissing, fixated on the appearance of our two big cocks frotting in and out of his hands. As he began to moan more loudly, I slapped my sweaty breasts against his hard chest. I could tell he was getting close to the point of no return, and I was eager to watch him cum with our cocks joined together.

"Yes, baby," I purred. "Let it come. Cum all over my big tits. Let me hear Tarzan's call of the wild."

Suddenly, he arched his back and thrust his dick as hard as he could against my organ, pressing his balls tightly against mine. My clit throbbed as he shot one giant geyser after another between my boobs, cumming all over the underside of his chin and face.

"Fuckkkk!" he growled with each spurt. "I'm cumming all over your cock. *Uhn, uhn, uhn!*"

With each throb and spasm, he grunted like a wild animal until he was fully spent. When he finally recovered his strength, he looked up at me with gratitude.

"Thank you," he said. "I needed that. You were even more magnificent than I imagined."

"Glad I could be of service," I said. "Now you should get yourself back in there. Somewhere out there is your *real* Jane, waiting for you to scoop her up and take her away to your jungle."

"What about you?" he said, looking at me confused.

"I'm still looking for my Jane, too," I smiled.

The whole time neither one of us had so much as touched lips. All either one of us wanted was a quickie in the wine cellar, where we could live out one of our mutual boy-on-boy fantasies. As Tarzan tucked his pecker back under his loincloth and staggered out of the cellar, I smiled.

That's one way to get it on with a man, I thought. I wondered what other fantasies awaited me before the night would be over.

5

____

After Tarzan left the wine cellar, I found a sink nearby and cleaned myself up, removing all the cum that he'd splattered over my dildo and chest. Feeling flushed and sweaty, I decided to catch some fresh air before going back into the main room. A side door from the cellar led onto an expansive terrace overlooking the lake. Standing alone in a corner of the balcony stood the governor's wife Alicia with her back toward me. Her arms rested on the stone railing as she puffed a cigarette, leaning over with her naked ass jutting out behind her backless apron. My pussy fluttered as I admired her shapely figure, feeling the moisture accumulating on my lips tingling in the cool autumn air.

Alicia had one of the most magnificent backsides I'd ever beheld. Her long, slender legs were taut and shapely like a professional dancer's and her ass was as tight and firm as a teenager. The rising moonlight reflecting off Lake Michigan shimmered between the space in her thighs, illuminating the dark pit under her mound. It was almost as if she were daring me to approach her and fuck her from behind.

I surveyed the rest of balcony and seeing that we were alone, I began tiptoeing toward her. It was a calm and cloudless night and the light of the full moon shone brightly over the Bannon estate, revealing the splendor of its manicured gardens. Amidst autumn-speckled trees and perfectly manicured flower beds, lay a geometric hedge maze accented with stone sculptures and a flowing water fountain.

I paused for a moment to breathe in the floral scent of the breeze wafting in from the shore. I couldn't imagine a more romantic setting for a private encounter with my pretty temptress. As I edged closer toward her, I stepped on a small pebble and it went skittering over the stone tiles in Alicia's direction. She cocked her head and turned slightly in my direction, then bent lower on the handrail, taking another puff of her cigarette. Whoever she imagined approaching her from behind only increased the boldness of her seductive pose.

Maybe being the wife of the most powerful figure in the state gave her the confidence to blow off any would-be interlopers. Or maybe she was just bored and looking for an anonymous fling to mix up her dull political life. Whatever the reason, her self-assured nature turned me on even more and as the glistening slit of her pussy came into focus, I felt the wetness from my own sex beginning to run down the insides of my thighs. When I came within a few feet of her, she stood up with her arms extended on the balustrade and blew a stream of smoke high in the air.

"Beautiful night, isn't it?" she said to no one in particular.

"Spectacular," I said. "The view is truly magnificent in this light."

"Mmm," she replied, oblivious to the identity of her midnight paramour. "Were you admiring the landscaping?"

"Among other things," I said, staring at her bald snatch. "Everything is so perfectly balanced and neatly trimmed. It really makes you want to pause and appreciate Mother Nature."

Alicia took a step back with one of her legs, arching her ass higher.

"It would be a shame just to *look* at it," she said, "Nature is meant to be immersed in, don't you think?"

"Absolutely," I said, taking a step closer, brushing my bare breasts against her chilly back. "You never know what you might find until you make contact."

"Like the way a woman's nipples pucker when it's cold?"

"Or when they brush against a soft surface," I replied.

"Or her lover's skin," she said

She pressed her ass further toward me and touched my protruding organ, then gasped and turned her head in my direction, checking it before we made eye contact.

"And sometimes—" she mused, recognizing the familiar shape of my leather chaps. "Nature has a way of *surprising* us with her wonderful diversity."

"Do like surprises?" I teased.

"In the right circumstances."

I reached under the front of her apron and squeezed her breasts, pressing my cock harder between her legs. She reached underneath and began stroking my dildo against her wet cleft.

"I particularly like the way nature has a way of adapting to its surroundings—" I said, beginning to inflate my rubber penis with my pistol trigger. "Like the way it expands and contracts to fill the void in any particular situation."

"Yes," Alicia panted, running her hand up and down my giant shaft. "I'd like you to fill *my* void."

By now, my inflatable penis had reached its maximum length and Alicia was busy rubbing the bulbous head against her inflamed clit.

"Fuck me, Jade," she said, dispensing with any further pretense. "I've been fantasizing about you banging me with your beautiful dick all night long."

"As have I," I panted, angling the tip into her dripping opening. I've dreamt of pounding your beautiful ass from the moment we met."

"*Fuck* yes," she grunted, as I pressed myself inside her. "Pound me with your big cowboy dick. Let me feel your balls slapping up against me while you ride me."

As I began to hump her, I marveled at how enthralled all the guests seemed to be with my transgender persona—both male and female. Everyone seemed to want a piece of my girl-cock, no matter how they could get it. While I watched my drumstick pounding in and out of her hole, I had to admit it was kind of fun assuming the male role for a change. There was something strangely empowering about being connected to a man's cock, watching all these strangers bow to my made-up masculinity. As I grasped the sides of her hips and pulled her toward me, she moaned and gyrated her hips, holding on to the rail for support.

"God damn, girl," she hissed. "You feel so good inside me. I've never had a man fill me up quite this way before. I only wish you could cum inside me. I want to hear you get off with me."

There was something about the sight of my big phallus plowing into her tight little ass that was getting me especially worked up. Even though she wasn't providing direct stimulation to my lady parts, I could have come just watching the incredibly sexy scene that was unfolding before my eyes. But I'd been saving up one more special secret. I pressed a button on the inside of my handle and suddenly my balls began vibrating from a battery-operated motor embedded inside. As I pressed my scrotum against her underside, I was instantly taken to a whole new level of excitement.

"Holy shit!" she squealed. "That's *definitely* something no man has ever done to me. Grind your nuts against me, Jade. Trib me with your big fat balls."

"Fuck, yes," I growled, feeling the rising tide of ecstasy building within me.

I couldn't help smiling, acknowledging the multipurpose capability of my male equipment. Not too long ago I was frotting a man with my big firehose, and now I was tribbing a sexy woman with my vibrating balls. For a brief moment, I felt envious of a man's equipment, but as my pussy began throbbing and dripping over my strap-on apparatus, I became acutely aware of my true gender. I leaned forward and rubbed my tits against Alicia's back, pinching and rolling her nipples between my fingers.

"Can you feel my wetness, Alicia?" I panted. "Can you feel how much you're turning me on?"

She reached under my vibrating balls and inserted two fingers inside me, stroking the front of my G-spot.

"Yes," she grunted. "You feel exquisite. You're going to make me come soon. I want to feel you come with me."

"With every part of my body actively engaged in fucking her, I didn't need any further encouragement. Within seconds, a surge of energy coursed through me, as my pussy began clamping down over Alicia's fingers. At the same time, she hunched over and began shaking wildly as she gripped the railing with all her strength.

"Fuck, Jade!" she hissed. "I'm cumming! Pound my ass with your big dick. God, I'm cumming so hard!"

As the two of us grunted and shook in simultaneous orgasm with my buttocks clenching as I pressed my cock deep into her, I suddenly became conscious of the extra light that was being cast onto the terrace from the open windows of the ballroom. When we finally came down from our powerful climax, she turned around and gently kissed me.

"It seems we have an audience," she smiled, directing her eyes toward the adjacent wall.

I peered in the direction of the ballroom and noticed a giant crowd of onlookers staring out the windows with their eyes and mouths agape.

"Good," I said. "It's about time some of these snobs got a taste of the real world outside their sheltered cocoons. "Maybe this will open their minds about the natural order of things."

With that, I lifted Alicia up onto the stone abutment and spread her legs far apart, pressing my still buzzing cock back inside her.

"If they want a show, let's really give them a show."

6

———————

After Alicia and I came a second time in full view of the crowd, we took a moment to compose ourselves then walked back into the main ballroom as if nothing had happened. Neither one of us seemed to care that virtually everyone was staring at us as they continued gossiping in their little cliques. I didn't even bother to refasten my leather vest or deflate my dildo as my breasts bounced freely on my bare chest in tandem with my turgid hard-on.

The two of us approached the bar and ordered matching margaritas then giggled amongst ourselves about the way everyone was trying not to stare as they talked amongst themselves. In spite of the fact that they pretended to carry on normal conversations, it was obvious that they were still highly aroused by our little tête-a-tête.

"I think Mr. Incredible is regretting his wardrobe choice right about now," Alicia chuckled, motioning toward the billionaire and his supermodel girlfriend.

I stole a glance in their direction and noticed Schiffer had a pronounced erection tenting the front of his tights.

"He's looking more like *Mr. Fantastic* with that cucumber wedged between his legs," I joked.

"And check out our favorite newscaster," she said. "It looks like Woody's popping a little Pinocchio of his own."

I peered at the anchorman and noticed him rearranging the front of his denims as a prominent bulge ran down one side of his pant legs.

"Ha," I chuckled. "I bet he's wishing he wore chaps like me."

I had to admit that I was enjoying the attention of all the powerful people in the room, particularly amongst the men who seemed especially attracted by my naked ladyboy costume.

"I don't know about *Jack* though," she said, furrowing her brow as her husband marched toward us with an angry expression on his face. "I have a feeling that his little willie will be even more shriveled than usual after watching you pound me with your big tool."

The governor stormed up to the bar and grabbed Alicia's hand, trying to ignore the pink pole jutting up from my lap.

"What is it, dear?" Alicia said, feigning surprise at her husband's indignation. "I was just enjoying a quiet drink with my new friend."

"That was hardly *quiet*!" he huffed, dragging her off her barstool. "Come on, it's time for us to go."

"But the party was just getting started," Alicia protested. "I was just starting to get warmed up."

The governor glanced down at my flaring joystick then glared at me.

"It looks like the two of you were getting more than just *warmed up*."

"Oh, come on, Jack," Alicia said, trying to resist his advance. "We were just having a little fun. You said that you wanted me to get more comfortable around your political friends."

"Not *that* way!" he fumed. "You've made a fool out of me and embarrassed me in front of all my colleagues!"

Alicia tried to protest, but the governor pulled her away from the bar and stormed toward the entrance. After collecting their coats from the butler, they soon disappeared out the front door. Alarmed by the commotion, Hannah joined me at the bar and sat on Alicia's stool, taking a sip of her cocktail.

"Jesus, Jade," she said, slapping my dripping dildo. "You sure know how to rock the boat in these genteel affairs."

"That's not the *only* boat I was rocking around here," I said. "Were you watching the show like everybody else?"

"How could I miss it?" Hannah chuckled. "It only took one person to catch you fucking the governor's wife before the entire room joined in the spectacle. Not like they could have *ignored* it, with all the grunting and groaning the two of you were doing."

"I wasn't paying much attention. I was kind of lost in the moment."

"You sure looked like it," Hannah said. "I have to say, It was an incredible turn-on watching you fuck her from behind. I could actually see your buttocks shaking when you came." She glanced down at my swollen cock and shook her head. "How does that work, exactly? I thought you were kind of detached from that thing."

"Not as much as you might imagine," I smiled. "Touch my balls to see for yourself."

Hannah placed her hand over my rubber scrotum and I switched on the vibrator, then her eyes suddenly flung open.

"Holy shit!" she said. "That thing really *is* fully animated. What else can it do? Spurt out fake cum?"

"As much as I wish it could, no. But these two extra tricks seem to be providing all the entertainment I need."

"I'd say so, judging by how loud the two of you were howling out there on the balcony. I fact, I've got a little girly hard-on of my own thinking what that would feel like inside me. I don't suppose we could find our own private alcove for a little fun, could we? I'm so horny right now, this costume is practically glued onto my body."

I glanced around the room and noticed that everybody was staring at us with disapproving expressions.

"Why not?" I said. "After that last escapade, it looks like all bets are off. There's not much to hide any more at this point."

I took Hannah's hand and began heading in the direction of the wine cellar, but Steve Bannon and his wife stepped in front of us, smiling like Cheshire Cats.

"It appears you've been enjoying my party even more than I could have imagined," he smirked, peering at my dripping dildo. "You seem to have gotten a rise out of more than a few of our guests this evening. I'd have to say you win the prize for the most inventive costume."

"I have to admit, it's been far less of a stuffy affair than I imagined." I glanced at Genevieve, noticing the slit in the side of her dress looking even more pronounced than before, revealing her hip bone above her barely concealed pussy. "I've found the conversation very stimulating."

"So it would seem," he said, staring at my tumescent totem. "Would you like to join my wife and me for a little nightcap in our private lounge? We've been admiring you all night long and would love to continue the conversation."

"Hmm," I said, raising an eyebrow toward Hannah. "Do you mind if I bring my friend along? We were just about to explore some private time of our own."

Bannon leered at Hannah's costume then smiled at her.

"I don't see why not," he said. "What do you think dear? Would you like to bring another partner into our little meeting?"

"The more the merrier," she smiled, jumping at the chance to have some more alone time with me. "Besides, now it'll be more evenly balanced. I'm not sure I could manage the two of you all by myself."

"Come then," Bannon said, leading us to a private elevator at the base of his stairs.

As we crossed the ballroom floor, the entire room followed our movement while my protruding penis waggled playfully between my legs. When we got in the elevator and the doors closed behind us, Bannon pressed button number four and smiled at Hannah and me.

"You've already explored many of the rooms in my house," he said. "But I think you'll find the view particularly appealing from the top floor."

I glanced toward Hannah and saw that her pupils were already dilated in excitement. I didn't know if she was more impressed by the fact that Bannon's mansion had four floors and a personal elevator or that she was about to participate in a private orgy with the richest man in the Midwest.

When the lift stopped and the doors opened, we both gasped at the view. The elevator opened to an enormous bedroom with floor-to-ceiling windows providing a panoramic view of Lake Michigan. As impressed as I'd been with the view from his main floor balcony, from this elevation the lake seemed to stretch out in every direction forever. But the view on the *inside* was even more spectacular. Bannon's bedroom was almost as large as most people's houses, with giant expressionist paintings hanging on the walls, a huge wood-burning fireplace next to the bed, and a separate bar beside the sliding glass windows.

"Would you like something to drink?" he said, lifting a crystal decanter off the table. "Perhaps a glass of brandy? I've got a thirty-year-old bottle of Hennessey that I've been meaning to open for a special event."

As much as I admired his impressive collection of personal effects, I was far more attracted to the elaborate trimmings of his beautiful wife.

"That would be lovely," I said, smiling at Genevieve.

Bannon handed each of us a large goblet filled with cognac, then he pressed a remote control device and the large window panes began to separate, bringing in a gust of cool air.

"Would you like to move to the balcony? The view is even more magical at this time of the night."

"Sure," I said, checking with Hannah to make sure she was still feeling comfortable. She simply peered back at me with wide eyes and nodded silently. We stepped out onto the deck and Bannon motioned to a wicker settee encircling a bubbling Jacuzzi.

"It might be a bit warmer next to the hot tub," he said, extending his hand toward the tub. "Please—make yourselves comfortable."

Hannan and I took a spot next to one another, while Bannon and his wife sat kitty-corner to us, a few feet to our left. The view of the lake was magnificent with the light of the full moon reflecting off the ripples like an evening sunset on a secluded beach. A cool breeze wafted in from the shore, and I pulled my vest over my exposed abdomen.

"Feel free to dip your toes in the water," he said. "Or climb right in if you prefer. It's chillier outside than usual tonight."

"I wouldn't mind getting out of these boots," I said, kicking off my footwear and placing my feet in the churning water.

Then I turned to Hannah and smiled.

"This feels heavenly, Han. Why don't you join me?"

She motioned to her all-in-one ensemble and frowned.

"It's not quite as simple for me as it is for you."

"Don't be concerned about *us*," Bannon grinned. "We're all adults here. Besides, I think we've seen just about everything already tonight. No one's watching this time besides Genevieve and me."

Hannah peered at me for a moment and I nodded. I'd never known her to be shy in these kinds of circumstances and it didn't take long for her to shed her clothes and slide under the bubbling water.

"Mmm," she purred, glancing up at me. "It's lovely. You should come in. These jets are good for massaging more than just your feet."

I looked toward Bannon and his wife and they smiled with a knowing grin.

"You said you wanted to find a private spot to continue your engagement," he said. "Don't let us stop you. We'll just finish our brandies while you two make yourselves comfortable."

He glanced down at my bobbing tool then peered back up at me.

"Is your equipment waterproof?"

"It should be," I said, winking toward Hannah. "Would you like me to keep it on?"

"I think we would," Bannon grinned. "I'd love to see how you use that thing close-up. How about you, dear? Are you interested in watching Jade play with her magic wand again?"

"Absolutely," Genevieve said, staring me directly in the eye. "I'd love to see her make another pretty girl come with her big man-cock."

I pulled off my chaps and vest and squeezed the trigger on my pistol to re-inflate my shaft to its full length then pressed the button on the handle to turn on the vibrator. Bannon and Genevieve squinted at the humming device, and I smiled at them as I slipped under the surface next to Hannah.

She scooted up next to me and lowered her hand under the water, stroking my phallus as she caressed the inside of my thighs. I turned toward her and we embraced in a passionate kiss. I could feel the jets of the Jacuzzi shooting between our breasts as we rubbed our tits together while she lifted her leg, straddling my hips. Within seconds, she lowered herself onto my pole and wrapped her arms around my back. As she began to rock her hips together with mine, I glanced up and made eye contact with Bannon and his wife. I noticed the front of his toga was tenting between his legs and Genevieve's hand was moving up and down as he smiled lasciviously toward us.

"Damn, Jade," Hannah groaned as I embedded my rod deep inside her. "That thing feels amazing. Fuck me with your big cock. Rub your balls on my cunt. I can feel it vibrating."

"Mmm," I sighed, as her tits mashed up against mine in the swirling water. "Squeeze my dick, Hannah. Let's put on a nice show for our hosts."

By now, Bannon had dispensed with any form of modesty, flinging his toga to the side where I could see his throbbing erection standing up between his spread legs. Judging by the size of his wife's hand, he appeared to have a decent-sized hard-on, but nowhere near as large as my own. Genevieve had apparently gotten just worked up watching Hannah and me fucking under the swirling water, and before long she kicked off her heels and hiked up her dress, sitting down over her husband's cock while she faced us. As I darted my eyes between her husband's prick thrusting in and out of her pussy and her dark eyes, our mouths began to open in mutual pleasure.

It was an incredible turn-on watching Genevieve's sexy body squirming over her husband's cock as she watched the two of us writhing in the churning water. Whether she was more excited getting fucked by her husband while two pretty girls watched them get it on or by the sight of Hannan and me enjoying ourselves underneath the surface, it didn't matter. Before long, all four of us were moaning loudly as we watched each other fuck our partners with abandon.

Hannah was the first to go off, as she started shaking wildly on my hips.

"Oh God, Jade," she groaned. "I'm cumming! Ram it inside me. Let me feel your balls slap up against me. Uhnnnnnn!"

Seeing Hannah having a powerful orgasm on top of me soon put Bannon over the edge as he grunted with his shaft pulsing inside his wife's pussy. Although he was staring at me, I was more interested in watching the expression on Genevieve's face as she returned my gaze with glassy eyes. I could tell that she was close, but needed a little extra stimulation to reach her goal.

As she locked eyes on me, she placed her hand over the front of her mound and began jerking her protruding nub. As her eyes opened progressively wider, I leaned forward and lifted my ass over one of the jets behind me. While the water gushed against my quivering opening, the vibrating balls pressed against my clit, and I felt a surge of pleasure engulfing my body.

"I'm close," I panted, locking eyes with Bannon's wife. "Come for me, Genevieve. Let me watch you come all over my big dick."

Even though she was planted on her husband's cock, we were both thinking the same thing. In that moment of mutual ecstasy, we were both imagining that it was *my* cock embedded in her pussy instead of her husband's.

"Yes, Jade!" she howled. "I'm cumming! I feel you inside me. I want you so bad. Oh *Gawd*..."

While the four of us panted and groaned in simultaneous climax, I glanced at Bannon, noticing him watching me with a wild look in his eye. Locked on me with laser focus, he had a strange, almost animalistic expression. I wasn't sure what he was channeling at that moment, but I could tell it wasn't his wife he was thinking about.

After we all settled down, Genevieve lifted herself off her husband's cock and slid in the water next to Hannah and me. She cuddled up beside me and her hand disappeared under the water, and soon after I felt her caressing my vibrating dildo. As Hannah leaned over to kiss her, Bannon stood up with his penis dripping a string of cum, motioning with his head inside his bed chamber.

"Why don't we all go back inside?" he said. "There'll be more room for us to play and we can watch each other better on the bed. Something tells me there's still a lot of pent-up energy between you girls."

Genevieve stepped up out of the tub first and led me by the hand into the bedroom as Hannah scampered in behind us, shivering. Bannon returned from his washroom and threw each of us a towel. Then he walked over to the bed and sat on the edge, beckoning for the rest of us to join him.

"Come," he said. "Let's share the wealth. There's plenty to go around."

"What did you have in mind?" I said, raising my eyebrows. After the Tarzan episode, I wasn't sure what part of me he was more interested in.

"There's enough parts between us for us to create an interesting *foursome*, don't you think?" he smirked.

As we all lay down on the bed and began exploring each other's bodies, Bannon seemed immediately drawn to my cock. As he sucked on my nipples, he reached down and began stroking my phallus while he masturbated himself with his other hand. While Hannah and Jenny intertwined their legs and began rubbing their pussies together, Bannon lowered himself down my abdomen until his face was directly in front of my giant pole. Suddenly, he stretched his lips around the head and began sucking it while he jerked his hand over his own dripping dick. Within seconds, he began moaning loudly, as he jetted squirts of cum all over his stomach.

Seeing her husband getting off so quickly again, Genevieve sat up and peered at the two of us with a sly smile.

"You seem quite enamored with Jade's cock, dear. I have an idea, if you're game for a little four-way fun. How would you like a *real* cock inside you this time, Hannah?"

Hannah looked at Genevieve then back at her husband, and smiled. There was little doubt that she'd fantasized about being fucked by the hot billionaire for a long time.

"*Definitely*," she said.

"Lie down face up on the bed," Genevieve instructed. "That way we can *both* have access to you. And *Jade*," she purred, with a gleam in her eye. "Why don't you choose whatever outlet looks most enticing to you among the three of us?"

As Genevieve spread her thighs over Hannah's face and lowered her pussy onto her lips, Bannon pulled Hannah's legs apart and straddled her opening with his dripping dick. As I watched them begin to fuck my best friend like she was a piece of meat, something inside me snapped. There was something about the way Bannon thought he could use her any way he wanted that pissed me off.

Just another self-righteous rich asshole, I thought. *This guy needs to be put in his place.*

As I kneeled behind him watching the two of them grinding their bodies against Hannah, Genevieve looked up at me and smiled. She glanced down toward her husband's ass and nodded. It was almost like she was *begging* me to fuck him from behind.

As the sides of my lips slowly curled up in acknowledgement, I brushed my erect dildo over Bannon's cheeks. Instead of flinching, he leaned further forward until I could see his balls waggling above Hannah's pussy. His asshole puckered as he thrust in and out of her, and for the first time in my life, I sensed the attraction of anal sex. There was something incredibly sexy and empowering about fucking a man up the ass. Now I knew why gay men separated into tops and bottoms. Just as with lesbian couples, one had to be the dominant one and one was meant to be the submissive one.

And *this* time, it was *my* turn to be the dominant one. Only in a way I'd never envisioned.

I lifted the tip of my pole, still glistening with Hannah's juices, and pointed it toward Bannon's opening. As I pressed it against his pucker, he grunted and pushed back gently.

So he likes being fucked by a woman? I thought. *It's time to show him who's really in charge here.*

I grabbed the sides of his hips and slowly pressed my cock deeper inside him. It felt strange and titillating at the same time to be fucking a man with my faux hard-on. As my balls pressed back against my clit, I imagined what it would feel like for a man to fuck another man this way. Suddenly, all the times I'd felt used by men who fucked from behind came flooding back. I thrust my dick as far into Bannon's ass as I could and began pounding my hips against his butt cheeks.

As his hole stretched as far as it could go by my coke-can-width hard-on, I found myself enjoying the feeling of thrusting in and out of him. Strangely, Genevieve seemed to be enjoying the show almost as much as me, as she writhed and moaned on Hannah's face while watching the two of us.

"Yes, Jade," she grunted. "Fuck Jack's ass. Make him your bitch. I want to watch him get off while you have your way with him."

Whether it was the sight of her pretty body twisting over Hannah's face or the sense of power I felt fucking her husband, I soon felt the familiar wall of pleasure beginning to overtake me. As I pressed my balls tight against his ass, creating more friction against my clit, I began to moan approaching my peak.

"Damn this is hot," I grunted. "I'm going to come soon. Watch me cum inside your husband's ass, Genevieve."

"Yes," she groaned, suddenly shifting her gaze to her husband's eyes.

I wasn't sure if she was communing with him at that moment or she just enjoyed seeing him at his most vulnerable moment. Either way, the sight of her convulsing over Hannah's mouth as she reached her own orgasm soon opened my floodgates. I pulled Bannon's ass hard toward me as I thrust my cock one last time deep into him, squirting all over my vibrating balls and Hannah's pussy. Within seconds, all four of us were howling in mutual ecstasy as we pounded and quivered atop one another in a mass of sweaty flesh. When we finally collapsed onto the bed in exhaustion, Genevieve leaned over and kissed me, whispering in my ear.

"Thanks for putting my husband in his rightful place," she mewed. "You have no idea how much both of us needed that."

VOLUME FIVE

LADYBOY

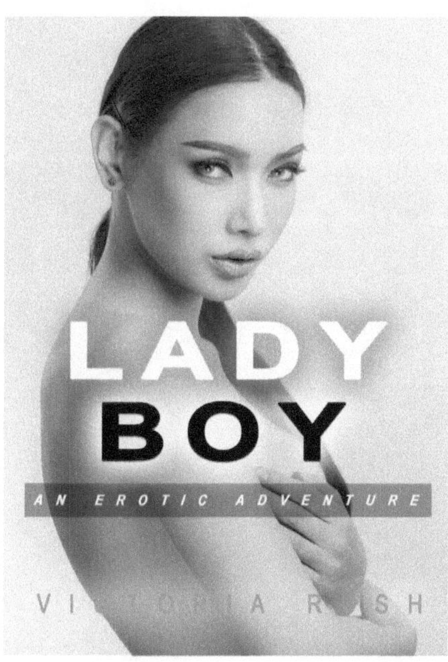

I'd been looking forward to this night out for a long time. It had been ages since I'd been out to a show, and the live cabaret act that my best friend Hannah had invited me to promised to be a lot of fun. Starring female impersonators, there'd be plenty of singing, dancing, comedy, and campy good fun.

In the spirit of the theme for the night, Hannah and I had agreed to dress up in cross-gender outfits, and I was eager to see what she'd chosen to wear. I'd found an old padded-shoulder pantsuit in my closet and paired it with a see-through chiffon blouse, skinny red tie and matching high heels. Deciding at the last moment to go topless underneath, the lapels of my blazer and the narrow strip of silk down the front disguised just enough of my bosom to look half-convincingly like a man. To accentuate the appearance, I'd trimmed my hair and slicked it back over my head with some heavy gel. Of course, the six-inch-high Louboutin pumps and my curvy figure in the tight suit left little doubt as to my real identity. But something told me not many people would be looking at my *shoes* this evening.

When my doorbell rang, I finished applying mascara and blush then ran downstairs excitedly to greet Hannah. But as I swung open the door, I gasped and had to hold onto the handle to steady myself. She was wearing a Scottish kilt, replete with high white knee socks, leather sporran, and a glengarry hat. But instead of the usual argyle jacket or waistcoat up top, she wore a thin plaid sash running diagonally over the front of her bare chest. Covering only half of her torso, her right breast poked brazenly out next to the flimsy tartan strip.

"Holy fuck, Hannah!" I said. "I didn't know you were going to go full *Mel Gibson* on me tonight!"

"You *told* me to dress up like a man," she deadpanned.

"Um, well yeah–dressed up in a man's outfit, but not with your *tits* hanging out!"

"Well, technically I've only got *one* tit hanging out," she said, stretching the ribbon to pull it over her other breast. "But at least the sash is pleated, so I can look a little more demure if the mood pleases me.

"Besides," she said, glancing at my see-through blouse. "You're not exactly leaving much to the imagination with that outfit. If it weren't for that skinny tie barely covering your cleavage, you'd be putting most of it out there on display too."

"Not quite as blatantly as you," I huffed, pulling my lapels tighter over my shoulders.

"Come on," she winked. "Tonight's all about having fun, remember? What good is it going to a queer revue if we can't let our hair down?"

"Speaking of," I smiled, tracing her strawberry-colored ringlets down over her bare shoulders. "I like your hairstyle. It goes nicely with the tartan theme."

"Yours too," she said. "Kind of minimalist, but it matches the power suit, and it highlights your cheekbones."

"Thanks," I said, looking at my phone to check the time. "Are you ready to do this? We better leave soon if we're going to get there in time for the start of the show."

"I've been ready all day," she said. "Let's go get our Vogue on."

When we got to the theater, there was already a long line stretched along the side of the building, but we found a spot to park on the side of the street not far away. As we approached the venue, the crowd was pumped up, chatting and joking boisterously in flashy drag costumes. With their heavy makeup, colorful wigs and over-the-top costumes, it was hard to tell the men from the women. Everybody seemed to have gotten into character, mimicking the campy personas of the female impersonators inside.

"Looks like a raucous crowd," I said, pulling up at the end of the line.

"These shows typically involve a lot of audience participation," Hannah nodded. "Kind of like the Rocky Horror Picture Show. That's part of the fun."

I looked up at a neon sign flashing on the brick wall above us.

"'*Lips?*'" I said. "Isn't that a bit of a strange name for a cabaret show?"

"Not for a *queer* cabaret show," Hannah said, smiling at a pretty girl wearing a feather boa next to us in line. "If you think about it, it's actually the perfect name for a female impersonator act. It's mostly about the singing, but it's also a metaphor for a woman's anatomy. These girls take their act pretty seriously."

"Except they're not really *girls*," I chuckled.

"You'll be amazed at how authentic these performers look and sound. You'd never know they were actually men under all their makeup and bodily enhancements."

"Enhancements?"

"Some of these performers take hours to get into drag. Between the makeup, wigs, and all the extra padding, it's quite a production. But the final results are quite astounding. Some of them are actually quite gorgeous."

"You make them sound almost fuckable."

"Well most of them are *men*, after all, under all their entrapments. It's kind of fun imagining taking a pretty girl to bed only to find she's equipped with a real functioning cock."

"Like in the song by Lou Reed, *Take a Walk on the Wild Side*?"

"Yeah, kind of like that."

"You said most of them are men. What about the others?"

"It's hard to say, because everybody's so well camouflaged. They're all *gay* of course, but I suspect there's a fair number of transgender girls who are transitioning one way or the other. That's just another aspect that makes it all the more interesting. You never really know what's going on behind their stage personas. But it's all very inclusive and accepting."

I glanced down the line, surveying the mix of primping and preening theatergoers. Everybody seemed to have taken the theme to heart, dressing in provocative outfits. Whether adorned as a man or a woman, they all looked sexy and hot. As I squinted my eyes trying to decipher each person's gender, my eyes stopped at a platinum blonde dressed in a tight corset with cone-shaped cups and black garter stockings. With her hair pulled back into a tall pony tail and pointy eyebrows, she looked like a dead-ringer for Madonna during her *Blind Ambition* days. She caught me staring at her and shook her chest from side to side, playfully twirling the tassels hanging from the tips of her bra as she smiled at me. I pulled my shoulders back, stretching my suit lapels to reveal the erect nipples showing under my sheer blouse.

"I see what you mean," I said. "I'm already getting excited about meeting some of these girls."

When we got inside the theater, the hostess escorted us to a table near the front of the stage and we ordered some cocktails as a loud buzz began to fill the room.

"How'd you score us such primo seats?" I said to Hannah. "I was afraid showing up so late, we'd be stuck in the bleachers."

"Nothing a little extra *lubrication* can't fix," Hannah smiled, rubbing her fingers together, indicating she'd tipped the hostess handsomely. "The closer we can get to the action, the more immersive the experience will be."

"Mmm," I nodded, as the room lights dimmed and a spotlight lit up the stage.

Suddenly a tall redhead wearing a feathery costume with black fishnet stockings and high hells pulled the drapes aside and strutted out onto the stage.

"Good evening, ladies and *wannabees*!" she shouted into the mic. "Are you ready to have some fun?!"

"*Woo hoo!*" the audience wailed, stomping their feet excitedly on the floor.

"My name's Ginger Snaps, and I'll be your MC for the evening," she said. She placed the side of her hand over her eyebrows and peered out into the crowd. "Do we have any *queens* in attendance tonight?"

Another loud cheer arose from the crowd as many patrons waived their hands proudly over their heads. I peered up and down the MC's figure, inspecting her long slender legs, curvy hips, and full bosom. With her arched eyebrows, pouty lips and bright red wig, she looked just like a sexy, full-blooded woman.

"That's a *man*?" I said, whispering into Hannah's ear.

"Uh-huh," she nodded, smiling up at the MC.

Ginger caught Hannah's gaze and moved closer towards our table.

"I see we have a few other Scarlet O-*Hair*-ahs in the room," she said, flipping her poufy mane dramatically behind her shoulder.

"What's your name, sweetheart?" she said, kneeling down and extending the mic in our direction.

"Hannah," my friend blushed.

"I like your costume," Ginger said. "Goes nicely with your fiery hair. Why don't you stand up and show the audience what you're wearing tonight? Don't be shy, sweetie. We're all queens tonight."

Hannah stood up and turned around, pulling her sash to the side to flash her bare breast then jerked her hips, flipping up the leather pouch between her legs. The crowd hollered its approval and Hannah sat down, as a crimson flush spread over her chest.

"That's pretty hot, honey," Ginger said. "But do the curtains match the carpet under that kilt of yours? Have you got a tinge of the *ginge* in your minge?"

Hannah glanced at me for a moment, contemplating lifting her skirt for everybody to see what lay underneath, but I shook my head in horror, already embarrassed enough by all the attention we were getting from the bright spotlight focused on our table.

"Do you guys want to hear some good redhead jokes?" Ginger said, turning to the crowd.

Everybody hollered in encouragement and Ginger stood back up, raising the mic to her mouth.

"What do you call it when a redhead squirts when she comes?"

"*A Fanta blast.*"

The audience roared in laughter.

"How many redheads does it take to screw in a lightbulb?" Ginger continued.

"*None. They prefer to hide in the dark.*"

Hannah grinned good-naturedly, but I could tell she was beginning to feel the sting from the pointed jokes.

"What's the difference between a ginger and a brick?" Ginger said.

"*At least the brick gets laid.*"

Hannah placed her hands on her hips and pouted, pretending to be hurt.

"But that's not true, is it Hannah?" Ginger said. "We gingers know better. We get plenty of action. You've heard of *yellow fever* for people who like to have sex with Asians? Except in our case, the obsession with carrot tops is called *gingivitis.*"

As the crowd chuckled and howled, Ginger finally turned away from our table and motioned toward the red velvet curtain at the back of the stage.

"Enough redhead jokes," she said. "Who's ready for some *diva delights*!?"

"Woo hoo!" the audience hollered.

"Well then, let's hear a big round of applause for the hottest girls this side of the Mississippi!"

She waved her hand toward the curtain, and it suddenly parted as five flamboyant girls strutted forward in unison singing *It's Raining Men.*

Hi, hi, we're your weather girls and we've got news for you, they warbled.

As they swiveled their bodies in harmony to the women's empowerment anthem, I ran my eyes over their sexy figures. Every one of them had long slim legs, curvy hips with narrow waists, and full, realistic bosoms. As they belted out the song in full soprano voices, I watched their lips trying to detect if they were lip-syncing to the music. But I didn't notice any gaps or disconnects between what their mouths were saying and what the music was projecting.

I turned to look at Hannah, dumbfounded. Besides having pitch-perfect, exquisite feminine voices, every one of them was drop-dead gorgeous.

"You've *got* to be kidding me," I shouted over the music. "You can't be serious that these are *men* dressed up as women?!"

"I told you they took their act serious," Hannah nodded. "They go to extraordinary lengths to play their part convincingly."

"But," I protested. "Their legs, their asses, their *breasts.* They look like real women!"

"It's part diet, part genetics, and the rest is just good makeup."

"But those hips! And their tits! How can they make them look so real?"

"It's amazing what a little bit of strategically placed padding and waist-cinching will do. Do you like it?"

"I guess so," I said. "I mean, there's no denying that they're all hot. It's just weird knowing they're actually men underneath all that makeup."

We've got news for you, you better listen up, the girls continued singing.

"Don't think about any of that," Hannah said. "Just sit back and lose yourself in the fantasy. Enjoy the ride!"

I nodded at Hannah, then turned back to watch the performers.

Get ready all you lonely girls, they sang.

And leave your umbrellas at home...

As they twisted their bodies and shook their hips to the beat, I watched the muscles in their arms and legs, looking for the telltale signs of any masculine features. But their limbs were smooth and slim, and their calves as long and skinny as any woman's. Even their tits and asses giggled like a real woman's. As each girl took a turn singing a solo part, I studied her facial expression and skin tone, looking for any evidence of a five o'clock shadow.

'Cause tonight, for the first time in history, a sexy brunette wailed, *it's gonna start raining men.*

As they all joined together in formation to sing the song's chorus, moving to within a few feet of our table, I felt goosebumps from the excitement of witnessing such an electrifying performance.

It's raining men, hallelujah, it's raining men, they trilled.

I'm gonna go out to run and let myself get wet, absolutely soaking wet.

As I began to get caught up in the act, a strange feeling came over me. Even though I identified as a lesbian, I was beginning to get wet myself watching these female impersonators shaking their sexy bodies and singing such an empowering song. By the time the song was over and the MC came back out to work the crowd with some more light-hearted jokes, I was already shifting uncomfortably in my seat, feeling the wetness in my tight-fitting pants spreading down my thighs.

"Pretty sexy, huh?" Hannah said, noticing my disequilibrium. "Bet you never thought you'd get this excited watching a bunch of guys performing on stage."

"I still can barely believe it," I said. "They just don't have any of the normal manly features. No sinewy muscles, broad shoulders, or square jawlines..."

"I suspect a lot of them are drawn to this line of work because they're already blessed with naturally effeminate features. If you look closely, you can see their Adam's Apples when they turn a certain way. But who cares, anyway? All the power to them if they can entertain a whole room full of admirers to this degree."

"They're *entertaining*, alright," I said, adjusting my tight pants bunching up around my moist crotch.

"Don't tell me you're actually getting *turned on* watching these guys?" Hannah said, raising an eyebrow. "I thought you just liked women?"

"I do, for the most part. I guess my mind is just playing tricks with my body. When they're doing their schtick, I can't help imagining them as sexy women."

"I suppose they've accomplished their goal then," Hannah nodded. "For all intents and purposes, when they're on stage, they *are* women."

The MC suddenly raised the volume of her voice, interrupting us.

"What do you guys think?" she said. "*Are you ready for some more T-girl action!?*"

As the crowd roared, she stepped toward the side of the stage, swinging her arm back toward the red curtain.

"*Let's spice it up then!*"

The curtain parted again, and the five performers sashayed slowly onto the stage, while the music from the Spice Girls' hit song *2 Become 1* filled the room. As the opening verse started, one of the girls separated from the rest, slinking toward the front of the podium. Everyone had changed their costumes to look like one of the original Spice Girls, and this time it was 'Sporty Spice's' turn to introduce the song.

Candlelight and soul forever, she purred.

A dream of you and me together,

Say you believe it, say you believe it...

I marveled at how beautiful and authentic her voice was, and before long I found myself swooning at the intoxicating lyric.

Next, it was the Scary Spice character's turn, looking for all the world like a young Mel B in her caramel-colored afro wig.

Free your mind of doubt and danger, she crooned.

Be for real, don't be a stranger,

We can achieve it, we can achieve it...

I'd always thought Scary Spice was the sexiest Spice Girl, and as she warbled the suggestive lyrics, I crossed my legs together, squeezing my throbbing clit, remembering how I'd fawned over her as an adoring adolescent. By the time her set had finished, I was feeling so hot I had to take my blazer off and hang it over the back of my chair to let my body breathe. With the spotlight focused on the girls on the stage, I felt confident in the shadows that no one would notice my rapidly hardening nipples under my flimsy see-through blouse.

But it was the *next* performer that really got my juices going. As the spotlight swung to the other side of the stage, the performer resembling Baby Spice began singing the next verse. With her parted pony tails and tight lamé dress, I practically melted when she began walking toward our table and locked eyes on me.

Come a little bit closer baby, get it on, get it on, she teased.

'Cause tonight is the night when two become one...

As I stared at her with wide fawning eyes, she gazed at my chest, noticing my nipples protruding like doorbell buttons under the glow of the spotlight cascading toward our table. By the time she'd finished singing her part, I'd already begun to fantasize about joining together with her every way I could. But as much as I tried, I couldn't see any sign of an Adam's Apple in her throat while she flexed her muscles belting out the song. Even her *hands* looked feminine and petite as she caressed the microphone erotically, tormenting me with her dark brown eyes. When the five girls came back together and began to sing the chorus, I'd already transported myself back twenty years when I used to fantasize as a teenager about making love to each of the Spice Girls one at a time.

I need some love like I never needed love before, they sang.

Wanna make love to ya baby,

Wanna make love to ya baby,

Set your spirit free, it's the only way to be.

Even though each of the T-girls had her own individual vibe going on, there was only one I was fixated on now. As I watched Baby

Spice mouth the words sexily to me, I felt the puddle between my legs expand further and further down my pant leg, and it took everything in my power not to mouth the words back to her.

I want to make love to you too, baby, I dreamed.

2

———

For many days after the cabaret show, I dreamed about the sexy T-girls prancing around the stage, crooning their songs as they took turns shimmying up to my table and peering into my eyes. I imagined going to bed with each one, but in every case I ended up disappointed when they disrobed and revealed their fake padding and flapping dicks. It wasn't so much that I was turned off by them being men under their suggestive costumes–after all, I'd enjoyed my fair share of hard cocks in my life. It was that the fantasy bubble I'd created in my mind's eye had been so rudely popped.

But my thoughts kept returning to the pretty blonde one who seemed so much more feminine than the rest. Even though Hannah had warned me that she was probably just another gay guy dressed up in a convincing outfit, I wanted to *believe* that she was something more. Maybe it was the sweet Spice Girls character she played in one of her sets that had got me going, but there was something about her that I found different, and highly alluring.

I was already planning to go back to the venue to take in their next show and wait by the exit door after the performance to see if I could catch sight of her out of costume. I wasn't sure how or whether I could approach her, I just needed to know one way or the other what her deal was. I knew that I was probably deluding myself into thinking we'd made any kind of meaningful connection during her performance, knowing that she, like most of the rest of the performers, was just play-acting for the benefit of their fans' prurient fantasies. But my steadily throbbing pussy whenever I thought of her told me I couldn't let it go.

Trying to take my mind off my never-ending obsession, I decided to go grocery shopping at my local supermarket to find a temporary distraction. When I walked into the store and saw all the bright produce displayed on the stands and smelled the aroma of freshly baked bread, I smiled knowing this was just the remedy I needed. Collecting the ingredients for a home-cooked meal would soon refocus my attention on my rumbling stomach instead of my other aching body part.

As I began assembling the ingredients for a cucumber salad, I couldn't help imagining each item as a symbol for the female impersonators I'd seen a few days before. I picked up a large red onion and squeezed it to make sure it was properly firm, wondering if their silicone implants felt equally hard. Then I ambled over to the refrigerated display case and lifted a tuft of fresh dill to my nose. It smelled grassy with a hint of licorice, and I closed my eyes wondering if that's the way my Baby Spice T-girl might smell if I got her naked.

Naked, nothing but a smile upon her face, I hummed the melody to their hit song Naked.

I grabbed some garlic powder, sour cream and white vinegar to make the dressing, then angled back to the produce section to pick up some radishes and cucumbers. As I approached the cucumber stand, I smiled inspecting the long green tubers which always reminded me of a certain well-hung porn star. I occasionally liked to use English cucumbers as a substitute for rubbery vibrators, reveling in the natural texture and flexibility of the phallic-shaped objects. I picked up one of the larger ones and bent it sensuously in my hands, sensing another customer hovering behind me, waiting for me to finish fondling the merchandise.

"Are you more interested in *length* or *girth*?" she said with a sultry voice.

I swung around to see a pretty blonde woman about my height, smiling at me as I held the long vegetable upright in my hand.

"Oh, ah, *yeah*," I stammered. "It *does* have a certain suggestive shape, doesn't it?"

"I prefer zucchini squash, myself," she said, running her fingers delicately over my cucumber's shaft. "It's a little shorter and stubbier, but it has that lovely bulbous tip that makes it feel a little more authentic."

I blushed, suddenly feeling embarrassed by her cheeky manner.

"Oh, I'm just planning to use this to make a *cucumber salad*," I lied.

"Whatever you say, sweetie," she smiled. "It works well for *that* too."

I darted my eyes back and forth across her face, recognizing something familiar.

"Do I know you from somewhere?" I said. "It feels like I've seen you before."

"I don't think we've met," she said, holding out her hand. "My name's Shae. But I get around quite a bit, so there's a good chance we've crossed paths one place or another."

"Jade," I said, I squinting my eyes trying to place the recollection.

Then my eyes suddenly flew open. Her pointy nails gave it away. *It was Baby Spice from the cabaret show!* And she looked even prettier and sexier in street clothes. Wearing a tight wool sweater and skinny jeans, I ran my eyes shamelessly over her curvy figure.

"Oh my God!" I gushed. "You're one of those girls from the *Lips Cabaret Show*, aren't you? I barely recognized you out of costume. I absolutely *loved* your act! If you don't mind my saying, I thought you were one of the sexiest performers."

"Thank you," she said, lowering her voice. "I try to keep a low profile when I leave the stage. There's a lot of fanatics out there who are obsessed with T-girls. You never know when you might run into someone who's got a more insidious intention in mind..."

"Sorry," I apologized. "I didn't mean to invade your privacy. You must get accosted everywhere you go..."

"It's okay, honey. You're one of the few people who've recognized me offstage. And besides," she said, scanning my pointy nipples pressing against my cotton T-shirt. "You don't strike me as one of the dangerous types." She glanced around her, noticing other supermarket customers eyeing us suspiciously. "Why don't we continue this conversation in a quieter place? There's a Starbucks just a few blocks down the street."

S hae and I drove our separate cars to the coffee shop, then we went inside and ordered a pair of lattes, finding a quiet table in the corner to chat.

"I hope you don't mind my asking," I said, pulling up a chair. "You don't seem like the other performers. I mean, you look like a–"

"*Woman*?" she chuckled. "Most of us girls put on a pretty convincing act. It's all part of the game. It takes quite a few hours behind the scenes to get into character."

"It doesn't look like you need much *help*," I said, still intrigued by her evasive answer. "You're already gorgeous and plenty curvy..."

"I guess I've been blessed with some natural genetics," she said. "Some of my gay friends have to work a little harder to create the look. May I ask what brought you to our show? Were you just looking for a little fun, or are you another one of those drag queen groupies?"

"I guess I was looking for a little change of pace. I've been flitting from one flighty relationship to another, and I needed a little distraction..."

"Are you attracted to *T-girls*?" Shae asked. "How do you identify, sexually?

"I've tried it both ways," I said. "But I seem to have settled into a comfortable groove with other women. Though I *have* had the occasional fling with a transitional girl."

"*Oh*?" Shae said, raising an eyebrow. "Which way? I mean, was she transitioning from a boy to a girl or a girl to a boy?"

"Boy to girl, I think. She looked for all intents like a woman, but still had all the functioning boy parts."

"Did you *like* having it both ways?" she smiled.

"It was definitely interesting," I nodded, happy to see her becoming more interested in my sex life. "Ever since then, I've been kind of intrigued with the whole *ladyboy* thing, if I can use that term. I even dressed up at a masquerade ball once wearing a strap-on dildo, and I've fantasized more than once about being one for real."

"It sounds like you're a little obsessed with ladyboys," Shae said, running her eyes over my chest. "I think I remember you now. You were the hot chick sitting near the front of the stage with the slicked-back hair and the chiffon blouse. I'd recognize those tips anywhere."

"Yeah, sorry," I said. "It was getting a little hot in there and you were kind of getting me worked up–"

"Maybe that's why you came to the show," she grinned. "To live out your fantasies of getting it on with a real T-girl?"

"I dunno," I said. "There's something strangely arousing about being with a transsexual person. I get to imagine them as a woman while still experiencing the act of penetration..."

"Mmm," Shae nodded, adjusting her position in her chair, obviously getting as excited as I was by our conversation. "You're not alone. There's a whole subculture of futa-loving fanatics out there. Both men and women."

"Does that make me a freak or something?" I said. "It doesn't quite seem normal..."

"No less than the people plying their wares on the other side of the coin. Everything's pretty gender-fluid these days. Nobody can seem to make up their minds what they want to be, or who they want to be with."

"You almost make it sound like a *bad* thing," I said, still searching for clues as to her real sex. "How did you get into this line of work anyhow?"

"I kind of fell into it. I have a lot of gay and bisexual friends and when I went to my first T-girl revue, they thought I'd be a natural at it. It's kind of fun to vamp it up and put on a different persona for a bunch of adoring fans. I find it very invigorating to receive that kind of affirmation from the crowd."

"How do you identify *yourself*, if you don't mind my asking?" I said, growing more confident with her increasing transparency. "I mean, do you consider yourself gay, bi, or trans?"

"I prefer not to pigeonhole myself into any particular corner," she said, placing her elbows on the table and leaning forward to gaze into my eyes. "I consider myself *pansexual*–I enjoy having sex with anyone who turns my crank."

"I feel exactly the same way," I smiled, sensing an opportunity to move our conversation to the next level. "Are you feeling hungry? Maybe we can get out of this place and find a bite to eat."

"I'm absolutely famished," she said. "I could really go for a cucumber salad about now."

"Oh?" I said, raising an eyebrow playfully. "Would you like to come back to my place? It would be a shame to waste all those tasty vegetables on just myself."

"I thought you'd never ask," Shae said. "But something tells me you won't need that cucumber after all. I think we might find some *other* ways to satisfy our appetite..."

The moment we got to my place and I set the grocery bags down in my kitchen, Shae and I fell into each other's arms as we groped each other and pressed our bodies together against the island. I could feel her tits mashing against mine and all I wanted to do was get her naked as quickly as possible to ravish her body. Besides, I was dying to see what she'd been hiding so carefully from me ever since we met. I still wasn't sure if she was a natural woman, a pretty boy pretending to be a woman, or someone transitioning from one gender to another.

"Let's go upstairs where we can get more comfortable," I said. "I'm dying to touch you *everywhere*."

"Same here," Shae panted. "I want to have you every way I can."

I held her face, plunging my tongue into her mouth, then grabbed her hand, pulling her down the hall and up the stairs into my master bedroom. We both dropped down onto the bed and I ended up lying next to her with her back leaning against my front side. Feeling all the more excited still not knowing what I'd find, I began taking off her clothes.

I reached around and pulled off her sweater then unclasped her bra, squeezing her breasts tightly in my hands. They felt full and natural, and I ran my fingers around the base of her mounds, trying to feel for the telltale ridge of a silicone implant. But they felt as soft and natural as any woman's. Then I lifted my fingers and rolled them gently over her areolas as she sighed and arched her back in pleasure.

No sign of scars either, I thought. *Whoever did her boobs must have been a very skilled surgeon.*

As I traced my fingers down her quivering abdomen, her skin felt as smooth and soft as a baby's. I didn't detect any sign of hard abdominal muscles or any stubble from recently trimmed hair. I could even feel the thin indentation of her linea alba running down the middle of her stomach, something I'd always found attractive in fit women. As I traced the line toward her crotch with my middle finger, she grabbed my hand and stopped me just above the top of her jean's waistline.

Instead, she slowly unclasped the button and pulled her jeans down over her hips, then shimmied out of her panties and threw them near the base of the bed. Shae was now completely naked facing away from me, and I could feel her hot body radiating next to me. I was dying to reach around and touch her loins to see what surprises lay in wait for me, but I decided to go slow and torment her just as much as she was me.

She pulled her right knee forward, separating her legs a few inches, and I caressed the inside of her thigh from the base of her knee all the way up to her curvy, tight buttocks. I felt a slippery film of fluid as I got close to her crease, and I rubbed my fingers and together, trying to divine its source. It didn't feel thick and mucousy like a man's precum, and I pressed my hips harder against her ass, rejoicing in the knowledge that I was holding a real woman in my arms.

She turned her head around and we kissed softly while I caressed the curvature of her ass, inching my hand toward her steaming cleft. When I felt her slippery slit, I pressed two fingers deep inside her hole, and she moaned into my mouth as our tongues swirled together in delight. As I began to fuck her with my fingers, she rocked her hips along with me, and I felt her juices begin to trickle down over my knuckles. Eager to please her even more, I removed my fingers and traced them forward along her valley, seeking to caress the sensitive nub at the top of the fold.

But when I reached the base of her mound, instead of finding a little clit, I felt a huge, throbbing phallus pointing upward toward her stomach. Hardly believing what I was feeling, I placed my fingers around the shaft and squeezed it tightly to see if it was real. Unlike any strap-on dildo or faux penis I'd ever felt before, this one felt warm and spongy in my hand. And unlike the plastic or silicone fake dicks, this one *pulsed* in my hand as I felt the rush of blood coursing through its shaft.

I suddenly felt a charge of electricity running through my body, realizing I was lying next to a true hermaphrodite for the first time in my life. My pussy gushed in excitement as I traced my fingers further up her shaft, feeling the flare of the coronal ridge encircling the crown at the tip of her cock. Her head was coated in a viscous layer of precum, and she groaned as I swirled my fingers over the sensitive tissue.

"Oh my God, Shae," I whispered. "I had no idea–"

"You said you had a *thing* for ladyboys," she smiled, turning around to face me directly. "Well now you've got your wish. The real question is, have you got the skills to take full advantage of my special equipment?"

"*Fuck* yes," I growled, ripping off my clothes, pressing my tingling body up against hers.

3

———

"What do you feel like first?" Shae smiled after I'd removed all my clothes. "There's a lot to choose from."

"Mmm," I purred. "Indeed there is. Do you mind if I play with your big thumper first? I've never experienced a real cock attached to a girl before. Just plastic dildos and other artificial toys–"

"Like long *cucumbers*?"

"Ha, yeah–sometimes. But it's not quite the same," I purred, stroking the underside of her shaft with my fingers. "This one you can actually *feel*..."

"Yes, I can," she sighed. "Have at it. That's all anybody seems to want, anyways."

I lifted my hand from Shae's crotch and looked into her eyes, realizing I was treating her like a piece of meat.

"I'm sorry," I said, pulling away. "I imagine this can be awkward for you sometimes. With your fans already expecting to find boy parts under your clothes, they must be even *more* obsessed with your body when they discover you're more than you seem."

"You mean a full-fledged *tranny*?" Shae said. "*Dick girl*? Anatomical *freak*?"

"No," I said, caressing her face softly with my fingers. "I'd never call you any of those things. To me, you're just a girl with a bit of a...*twist*. A very sexy, *surprising* twist."

"Mmm," Shae said, leaning in to kiss me back. "I like the sound of that. I didn't mean to sound so defensive. It's just that I kind of–*like* you. I was hoping we'd have something a little more meaningful than a quick fling."

"I feel the same way," I said. "We can slow down if you want and take some time to get to know one another before we escalate things any further. I've got some food downstairs if you're hungry–"

"No," she said, pressing her hips against me, coating my belly with her dripping cock. "I only want *you* right now. I want to feel your lips all over my body..."

"With pleasure," I purred, kissing my way down her neck. As my face nestled between her cleavage, she arched her back and moaned.

"Suck my tits, Jade," she mewed. "Take my girls into your mouth and tease them like you do your other lovers. Make me feel like a real woman."

"You *are* a real woman to me Shae," I said, peering up at her. "I love your body–*every* part of your body."

I traced my hands down over her shoulders and encircled her full breasts, squeezing them gently. Then I lifted my head and sucked on each of her nipples, making a playful popping sound.

"Yes," Shae moaned. "That feels so good. You're not like most of my other lovers. They just want to *fuck* me or have me fuck them. I like the way you make love to my whole body."

"Mmm," I hummed as I swirled my tongue over her fat teats. I could feel them lengthening in my mouth and I sucked on them like lollypops as she writhed in delight on the bed.

"I need you Jade," she groaned. "My *cock* needs you. Make love to the rest of my body the way you're worshipping my tits."

I didn't need any further encouragement, and as I slid my body down the front of her slippery abdomen, I pointed her member between my breasts and pressed them together, feeling her heat throbbing between my flesh. The precum dribbling down the underside of her shaft provided ample lubrication, and I proceeded to caress her cock with my melons as she rocked her hips in pleasure.

"Oh God, Jade," she moaned, lifting her head to watch her purple tip poking in and out of my cleft. "I love fucking your tits. You look incredibly hot."

"So do you," I smiled, watching her big pole sliding between my cleavage.

Part of me wanted to continue fucking her with my tits, intrigued to see if or how much she could cum when she reached orgasm. But by now I was burning up with desire also, and I had to feel her in my mouth. I wanted to make love to her most sensitive part and feel her jetting inside me when she came. I lowered my body a few more inches, kneeling between her legs, and looked up at her with a devilish grin. Her pole was bouncing in excitement between her legs, and I grasped it with two hands, beginning to jerk her off slowly.

As she threw her head back in ecstasy, I watched her body writhing on the bed. There was something incredibly erotic about watching a beautiful woman squirming in pleasure while I felt her burning sex in my hands. It was strange to see her breasts jiggling on her chest as I stroked her cock with both hands, her nipples peering up at me like two beacons in the dark shadows of my bedroom.

"Jade," she panted. "You're going to make me come soon. I've never had someone give me such a delicate hand job before. Look into my eyes when I come. I want to see your pretty face."

"Yes, Shae," I hissed, feeling my own juices beginning to run down the inside of my thighs. "Come for me, baby. I want to watch you cum in my hands."

Shae began rocking her hips more urgently then she slammed her hands down onto the bed, clenching the covers between her fingers as she curled her body up toward me, staring into my eyes. Suddenly her cock erupted, spewing ropes of cum all over my tits and face, as I gushed simultaneously all over the sheets. The intense eroticism of watching her beautiful body come alive as I held her tightly in my hands had turned me on so much that I'd come along with her even without any direct stimulation.

As I watched Shae's chest heaving in excitement as she recovered from her powerful climax, we clasped hands, and she pulled me down gently on top of her.

"That was incredible," she panted. "I've never had someone touch me like that before."

I lay down beside her, pushing some loose strands of hair back over her face.

"You've never had someone give you a hand job before?" I asked.

"Not like *that*," she said. "Usually they just want to see me cream, like I'm some kind of robot. But this time it felt like you were making love to me with your eyes. Knowing you were watching me that way made me cum a thousand times harder."

"I could tell," I said, wiping some of her cum off the side of my face with the back of my hand. "I enjoyed watching you respond to my touch just as much as you did."

Shae slid her knee forward, feeling the big wet spot I'd made on the sheets.

"So it would appear," she said, wiping my face to remove the last traces of cum from my skin. "I've never seen a woman squirt so much before."

"You're not the *only* one with special powers," I smiled.

Shae grabbed my head and thrust her tongue deep into my mouth, pressing her dripping cock up against my stomach.

"I want to return the favor now," she said. "It's *my* turn to watch you while I give you some pleasure."

"I won't say no to that," I purred, rubbing my slippery tits against hers. "What did you have in mind exactly? Like you said, the combinations and permutations are practically limitless."

"As much as I'd like to focus entirely on you, I desperately need to make love to you. I want to be *inside you* this time when we come together."

"Mmm," I smiled, grabbing her ass and pulling her tighter toward me. I felt her burning cock resting against my abdomen, and I swiveled my hips to see if she was still hard. "Are you ready to go at it again this quickly?"

"I've been ready from the moment I met you," she said. "As long as you're lying naked next to me, I don't think there's any risk of my cock flagging."

I reached between our two bodies and squeezed her throbbing member in my hand.

"Should we be taking any precautions?" I said, pinching my eyebrows.

"You mean regarding pregnancy?" she said. "We don't have to worry about any of that. As you can see, I don't have any balls, so I can't produce sperm."

"But you produced plenty of fluid–"

"That comes from something else. Just like a man, I've got a prostate and seminal vesicles. Ninety percent of a man's ejaculate is produced by those glands–it's just that in my case it's *all* of the cream."

I pulled back momentarily, intrigued to learn more about her unique features.

"What about the rest of the package, if you don't mind my asking?" I said. "You seem to have all the other lady parts. Do you have a uterus and ovaries, like a regular woman?"

"The chromosomes got a little mixed up in my case," Shae said, shaking her head. "I got a little bit of this and a little bit of that when they were handing out the DNA. Every intersex person is born differently. Some have mostly boy parts, some have mostly female parts, and some have a few parts of each."

"Well, I think God endowed you with the *best* combination of parts," I said, tracing a line down the side of her jaw with my finger. "I can't imagine a more perfect specimen than you. You look more beautiful than any woman I've met, and you *still* get to have it both ways."

Shae chuckled softly, then her expression turned more solemn.

"For the longest time, I felt like a freak. When you're a kid, you want to be like all the other kids. But I've learned to make peace with my situation and I hardly think twice about it anymore. I'm just Shae–unique and special in my own way."

"I couldn't have said it better myself," I said, beginning to feel closer to her as she grew increasingly candid. "But I know there's a lot of gender-confused people out there, even without your ambiguous anatomy. Did you ever consider–"

"Surgery?" Shae said. "Not for a moment. I kind of *enjoy* having two sets of organs to play with. You have no idea how much experimenting I did growing up."

"I can imagine," I smiled, thinking about all the different ways I'd found to self-pleasure myself. "But what about your parents? Didn't they want you to fit within society's expected stereotypes? Wasn't there a lot of pressure to choose one clear sex or another?"

"Thankfully, I had pretty progressive parents," Shae nodded. "They loved me for who I am and never pressured me one way or the other. I can't imagine being any different than the way I turned out."

"Neither can I," I said. "I love you just the way you are."

"*Love*?" Shae said teasingly. "Isn't it a bit early to be using those kinds of words? I mean, I just *met* you..."

"I know," I said. "But it feels like I've known you my whole life. There's something deeply spiritual about you. You're unlike any other woman I've met before–"

"That's because you've never met another woman with a real cock before."

"That's not what I mean," I said. "I just feel a special connection with you. I knew you were different the moment I laid eyes on you. I've fantasized about being with you ever since the cabaret show–"

"Being with me, or *being* with me?" Shae said, furrowing her brows. "I don't want you to love me the way all those other ladyboy fanatics do."

I shook my head as I wrapped my arms around her back and pulled her closer.

"I know it's weird to say so soon after we've met, but I want to be with you forever. As friends, partners, lovers. I'm stuck on you like no one I've met in a long time."

"I feel it too," Shae said, gazing into my eyes. "Let me make love to you properly now. I'm thinking of *another* way for you to be stuck on me."

"Mmm, I like the sound of that," I said, rolling on top of her. "Stick me with that big cock of yours. I want to feel you creaming inside me this time."

Shae tried to turn me over so she could be in the superior position, but I pinned her arms on the bed and smiled mischievously at her.

"Let me be on top. I want to watch you when we join our bodies. *All* of you."

"Same here," Shae smiled. "This time I want to watch you to gush all over my cock when you come."

"Damn straight, girl," I said, rubbing her throbbing pole against my wet labia. "This time I'm going to surround your cock with a *different* part of my anatomy."

"*Yesss*," Shae purred. "Fuck me, Jade. Fuck me with your wet pussy."

I lifted my hips over her quivering dick, then I pointed it toward my hole and slowly lowered myself over her shaft. As she penetrated deep inside me, we both groaned in pleasure. It felt strange having a woman's cock inside me, not just because of the absence of testicles slapping against my ass. The combination of her pretty face, sexy tits, and throbbing hard-on was something I'd never experienced before. As I began to pump my body up and down over her throbbing organ, I gasped when I felt her reach the end of my tunnel.

"*Fuck*, Shae," I groaned. "I've never felt so filled up like this before. Fuck me with that big tool of yours."

Shae grabbed my hips on either side and pulled me harder toward her as she began thrusting deeper inside me. I tilted forward and grabbed her tits, squeezing them tightly. It was nice to have something substantial to hold on to while I bounced on her joystick, and we both smiled at how perfectly we'd melded together.

"I love looking at your pretty face while I fuck you," I purred, gazing into her eyes as my juices dribbled down over her slit and between her ass.

"I want to look into your eyes when you come this time," Shae said. "I haven't felt this close to anyone in a long time. Make love to me, baby."

I lifted my arms and held my hands out to her, and she grasped my hands again, interlocking her fingers tightly with mine. As we rocked our hips together, gazing lovingly into one another's eyes, our grip grew progressively tighter the closer we edged toward orgasm.

"Fuck, Jade," Shae hissed. "You feel so good. Squeeze my cock with your tight pussy. I want to watch your tits shaking over top of me when you come with me."

"Yes, baby," I panted. "I'm almost there. Pound me with your big dick. Let me feel you spurting inside me."

"Oh God, Jade," Shae grunted. "It's coming. Look at me while I come inside you. Oh *fuckkk*..."

Shae squeezed my fingers so tightly they began to turn blue and her whole body began shaking as she fell over the precipice. With her tits shaking in orgasmic tremors, I arched my back, pointing the tip of her cock against the G-spot on the front side of my pussy. As I watched her mouth gape open in the throes of a powerful climax, I clenched down hard on her pulsating prick and sprayed all over her quivering pussy. Feeling me come on her slit, she angled her hips toward me, jetting her cum hard against my cervix. Feeling her touching my furthest reaches heightened my pleasure all the more, and I shuddered in joy as we gripped each other's hands and peered at one another with watery eyes.

As I collapsed on top of her feeling her warm body pressed against mine, I closed my eyes and rested my head on her chest. For the first time in ages, I felt like I'd found my soulmate.

4

———————

For many long moments, Shae and I lay next to one another, softly caressing each other's skin. I could feel her heart pounding next to my head on her chest, and I wasn't sure if it was because she was still coming down from her high, or if it signaled her joy at being next to me. Either way, I smiled, knowing we'd made a powerful connection and that this was just the start of something wonderful. After a few minutes, I felt her heartbeat returning to normal, and I peered up at her.

"How are you feeling?" I said.

She peered into my eyes and smiled.

"Happy. Content. Euphoric."

"It's probably just the endorphins still floating around your system," I said.

"No," she said, shaking her head. "It's much more than that. With all my other partners, it was mostly about the sex. Like they were using me as a novel plaything. But with you, I can feel something special. I haven't felt this close to anyone in a long time."

"Did you know there's a special hormone that's released when we have an orgasm with someone? It's called oxytocin, sometimes referred to as the love hormone. It creates feelings of belongingness between partners and promotes a sense of togetherness. Psychologists believe it's an evolutionary adaptation in humans to encourage couples to stay together long enough to raise their children. I've often thought it plays an important role in same-sex relationships too."

"Oxycontin?"

"No," I chuckled. "That's a whole other type of drug. That one produces an intense artificial high, much like heroin. This one's all natural and lasts a much longer time."

"Are you saying these feelings we're developing for one another aren't *real*? That it's just due to the hormones produced when we have sex?"

I could feel Shae's heart racing again under my ear, and I reached up to squeeze her hand reassuringly.

"No, I just think it's interesting how it's all interconnected. How sex and love are mutually interdependent. But true lasting love is something that develops over time. You have to work at it. It's a give-and-take process, where each partner supports one another as they learn each other's wants and desires and learn how to make each other happy in more substantial ways."

"Well if love depends on sex, and sex depends on love," Shae mused, "and the strength of our bond depends on getting to know each other's desires better, then we better get *busy*. Tell me what you like—in *bed*, I mean. What turns you on?"

"Until I met you, I thought I knew. But you're kind of a game-changer. Suddenly, I have so many more...*options*."

"Because I have a cock?"

"Kind of. With other girls, it was all about tribbing and licking and that sort of thing. You know, mostly focusing on the external organs. But with you, I can feel you *inside* me. I've got a whole new exciting toy to play with. Now I can throw away all my vibrators and dildos—"

"Not so fast," Shae smiled. "I enjoy playing with those things as much as you do. Sometimes it's just as much fun to watch your partner pleasure herself. Besides, I can think of a number of ways we can incorporate those into our sex life to keep it fresh and exciting. Starting with that big vegetable of yours..."

Shae's mention of the cucumber got me thinking about all the new ways I could use it with her. After all, she also had a fully functioning *vagina*, and there was nothing I loved more than using a double-sided dildo with my partner while we ground our pussies together. Only this time, I could watch and play with her pecker too while we fucked each other.

"Mmm," I said. "I like the sound of that. Shall I run downstairs and bring it up for us to play with? I want to fuck you so bad right now."

"In a little while, maybe," Shae said. "First, I want to taste you and make love to you with my mouth. I'm dying to suck your pussy."

My cunny suddenly twitched at the thought of her going down on me.

"I've been dying to take you into my mouth too," I said. "Maybe we can do it at the *same time*. Do you feel like a little sixty-nine action?"

Suddenly Shae's heart began thumping rapidly against the side of my face again.

"Yes," she nodded. "We'll be able to rub our bodies together and hold each other close that way. *Fuck*, yes. I want to bury my face between your legs."

I lifted myself off her body and turned around, lying beside her on the bed with our faces positioned in front of each other's crotch. Her flagpole was already ramrod straight and bobbing inches away from my mouth. I grabbed it gently with my fingers and rolled my tongue around her crown in slow circles.

"Oh God," Shae groaned. "Lick my cock, Jade. Make love to me with your mouth. I'm gonna suck your pussy and taste your honey. I want to feel you gush all over my face when you come this time."

I spread my legs and felt Shae's face press against my dripping hole as she began lapping her way up toward my clit.

"Yes, baby," I panted. "Lick my pussy. Taste my love for you while I suck you off. I love your beautiful rod."

I grasped her prick with two hands and engulfed her head in my mouth, sucking her pole feverishly while I slathered her shaft with my tongue. At the same time, Shae wrapped her arms around my ass and pulled me tightly toward her, encircling my bud in her mouth. We both moaned, thrashing our hips against each other's faces.

As we pressed our bodies together with our tits sliding against each other's abdomens, I rejoiced in the knowledge that I was making love to someone I'd never imagined being with in my wildest fantasies. It felt strange to be sucking a cock that didn't belong to a man for a change and to feel someone kissing me in my most intimate areas that wasn't a regular woman. It was like she had some kind of superpower, like she was my very own *Wonder Woman*.

As our moaning began to rise in urgency and volume, and our pleasure arced inexorably toward orgasm, I slipped my hand inside Shae's pussy and curled my fingers toward her G-spot. She hummed excitedly, thrusting her cock deeper into my mouth, and I tried to relax my throat to take as much of her as possible. Normally, I'd gag on a man's dick this size, but somehow with Shae I didn't have the same sense of fear being taken advantage of by someone far stronger than me. I knew that Shae would be gentle with me, not fucking my face just to get her rocks off. We were truly making love to one another, and I savored every moment feeling her warm, throbbing organ in my mouth.

I could feel myself nearing the point of no return as she teased my burning clit with her tongue, sucking and teasing my nub as she squeezed my buttocks with her hands.

"Mmm-mmm," I grunted, signaling that I was about to come.

"Mmm-*hmm*," Shae nodded, clenching her buttocks as I relaxed my throat while she sank her cock all the way into my mouth.

Suddenly, the walls of her pussy began contracting against my fingers as I felt her pole pulsing while she poured her jism down my throat. Feeling her coming both ways soon put me over the edge, and I groaned as I clamped down hard and sprayed my juices onto her face, coming in a series of powerful contractions that never seemed to stop. All the while, we gnashed our tits against each other's tummies, feeling every square inch of our bodies tingling in euphoria.

I held Shae in my arms until her contractions subsided then I drew my head back, closing my lips around her crown. I wanted to taste her for the first time–even her *milk* tasted sweet and creamy.

"Mmm," I purred, feeling her pussy twitching as I milked the last drops out of her trembling hard-on.

Shae kept her face planted between my legs while she caressed my ass and nibbled on my jewel. As we held each other lovingly in our arms, there was no longer any doubt in either of our minds that we'd created something special and neither one of us wanted to pull away anytime soon. Within a few minutes, we both drifted off to sleep, dreaming of nymphs and mermaids gliding through an ethereal realm.

5

____

When we woke up a few hours later, we snuggled next to each other, kissing softly and talking about our plans for the future. We were both giddy as schoolgirls talking about all the places we wanted to go and all the different adventures we wanted to have. But before long, we realized how much of an appetite we'd worked up, and we went downstairs where I cooked up some fresh seafood and prepared the cucumber salad. When we finished, Shae looked at me and smiled.

"That was a lovely dinner, Jade," she said, raising a playful eyebrow. "But now we don't have one of your favorite sex toys to play with any longer. Whatever are we going to do with ourselves?"

"Oh, I've got plenty of _other_ toys to play with," I said, looking at her with a mischievous grin. "Why don't we go back upstairs and see what we can find to work with? I'm intrigued to see how we can incorporate some of them with your special features."

"I'm guessing you don't have too many cock rings or Fleshlights in your bedroom," she grinned. "They're probably all designed for clitoral or vaginal stimulation."

"I think we might be able to find a way to make a few of them work for both of us," I said, grabbing her hand. "Come on, I've got a few ideas I want to try out."

When we got back upstairs, I pulled open my nightstand and showed Shae my collection of sex toys and dildos. Most of them looked like the normal female stimulators you'd find at any sex shop, but there was one that she seemed particularly interested in.

"What's this thing?" she said, picking up a long silicone wand with a bulb on the end and a mysterious hole in its base.

"That's one of my favorite sex toys," I smiled. "It's called an Osé vibrator, and it works in a very unique way."

"How so?" Shae said, placing the tip of her finger into the little hole.

"Let me *show* you instead," I said, pulling it away from her. "I've got a special idea for how we can adapt it for you to use." I shimmied up against the bed's headboard and spread my legs, tapping the mattress between my thighs. "Sit in front of me and rest your back against my chest. I think you might kind of like this."

Shae peered into my eyes and smiled.

"I'd like *anything* we do together," she said. "As long as I'm lying next to you."

"This time, it will be a little different. It'll give me a chance to stimulate and explore *every* part of you at the same time."

"Mmm, I like the sound of that," Shae said, shifting her ass up next to my crotch.

I could see her cock angled at half-mast, unsure of what to expect. I grasped the Osé vibrator and slowly bent the flexible wand in the reverse direction. Unlike its normal use in the missionary position with the wand curled upward to stimulate a woman's G-spot while the other part caressed her clit a few inches higher, in *Shae's* case we'd have to make some adjustments. For one thing, she didn't have a clit to stimulate, but she was also faced in the opposite direction, so the wand would have to be turned the other way around.

I reached down and caressed the sides of her lips to prepare her for the insertion. She'd have to be good and wet to enjoy the tool's unique movement, but I also wanted to get her fully hard so I could play her *other* part while she was being stimulated internally.

"Mmm," she purred. "I like it when you stroke me like that. It makes me feel very...womanly."

"Oh you're a *woman*, alright," I said, slipping my fingers inside her box to see how wet she was becoming. "A *super* woman—my own very special action hero."

"Mmm," she panted, rocking her hips against my fingers deep inside her. "You know I'd protect you against anyone who'd try to take you away from me."

"You don't have to worry about any of that, sweetheart. I'm stuck on you like glue now, remember?"

"Right, hormones, and all that," she smiled, turning her head toward me. "But right now, I'm stuck on you in a very different way."

"You *like* that?" I said. "Do you like the feeling of my fingers fucking your pretty pussy?"

"Yes, Jade," she sighed, resting her head against my chest. "Fuck me with your fingers while I play with my cock."

As she moved her hand up toward her throbbing pole now flapping straight up against her tummy, I batted it away gently.

"Let *me* have the pleasure," I said. "I'm going to have my hands freed up soon enough."

"Oh?" Shae teased, looking at the strange sex toy lying on the bed a few inches from her watering pussy.

"I think you're about ready to try this thing," I said, picking it up and pointing the bulbous tip toward her opening.

I turned it around with the hole facing her anus, then inserted the tip slowly into her slit. Shae tilted her hips forward to accept the instrument and hunched down a few inches to allow it to penetrate all the way inside her.

"Mmm," she purred. "That's a pretty big cock you're wielding there, my love. But I'm not sure it can do all the things your fingers can do for me."

"I wouldn't be too sure about that," I grinned, reaching down to tap the button on the base of the unit with my finger. The device began humming, and Shae's body jerked in surprise as she twisted her head to look at me with wide eyes.

"What the *hell*?" she said. "What is that thing? It doesn't feel like any vibrator I've used before."

"It's not really a vibrator," I said. "As you're about to see. It's more of a human *simulator*. Can you feel it caressing the inside of your pussy?"

"Yes," Shae said. "It feels like a finger stroking me. A very long and *soft* finger."

"I knew I'd be able to make you forget about my own fingers soon enough," I smiled. "I've got other plans for them."

Part of the attraction of using the special vibrator with Shae was that it would free up my hands to play with her cock while her pussy was being stimulated in other ways. I wanted to feel her burning flesh in my hands again while I watched her hips trembling from the feeling she was receiving inside. In her position faced away from me, it gave me an opportunity to caress every part of her body while the sex toy did its work on her lower parts.

I poured some baby oil into my palms and encircled her python with both hands as I began pumping her shaft up and down while the Osé finger caressed the inside wall of her pussy. Shae threw her head back against my chest in pleasure and I plunged my tongue into her mouth, kissing her passionately while she was being serviced below. I could feel her hips cavitating wildly against my crotch as she received stimulation simultaneously in both of her erogenous zones. As she rocked her body against my hands and the finger probing deep inside her pussy, I watched her pretty tits bouncing on her chest.

"*Fuck*, Jade," she hissed. "That feels incredible. I've never–"

"Been fucked and caressed at the same time?"

"Not like this," she panted.

"Mmm," I said, taking one hand off her cock and squeezing her breast while I twisted my other hand around the tip of her pole. "I like being able to feel and touch all of your parts this way."

"Fuck yes," she squealed, pumping her big dick into my hand. I could see precum pouring out the top of her slit, and the mix of her creamy emission with the watery baby oil made for an even silkier lube. "I can't imagine anything more heavenly than having you caressing every sensitive part of my body."

I grinned at her devilishly as I reached between her legs to tap the button on the base of the Osé vibrator one more time.

"I'm not quite sure we've finished caressing *every* sensitive part of your body," I said.

Suddenly, a snake-like appendage hidden under the hole of the vibrator emerged and began licking her twitching anus with its realistic tongue-like action.

"*Uhhn!*" Shae groaned, flexing her abs as she pressed her hips harder against the device. "What the hell is *that*?"

"I told you this was a special vibrator that was capable of stimulating you in many places. Just sit back and enjoy while you let *both* of us pleasure every part of your sexy body."

Shae leaned back against my chest and rested her head against my shoulder as I watched her face grow redder and redder from the rising tide of pleasure within her. I glanced down at her throbbing member and saw some pulses of precum dribbling over the top of her crown and down the underside of her shaft. I placed my other hand back on her throbbing meat and began pumping it tightly between my two fists. As I watched her purple head poking in and out of my hands, a bright flush began to spread over the top of her chest.

Suddenly, her face tightened up and her stomach muscles flexed as her body jerked against mine. While I pumped her raging dick and the Osé wand caressed her G-spot, with its tongue teasing her quivering rosebud, she wailed at the top of her lungs and wrapped her hands around mine as her prick jetted thick streams of white cum high into the air. I watched with amazement as she ejected one long string after another, arcing high into the air before landing with a loud plop onto her shaking chest.

When she finally stopped cumming, I took my hands off her cock and rubbed the creamy dew all over her plump tits and hard nipples.

I'd never seen anything so erotic in all my life, and to have held her in my arms while I beheld the spectacular fireworks show was just icing on the cake. I turned my head to kiss her gently, and she squeezed her hands three times against mine still wrapped around her throbbing member as if to say 'I love you.'

I squeezed her pole three times back to return the sentiment as I watched the last bit of cum dribble over the tip of her magnificent flute.

That's one instrument I'm never going to get tired of playing, I said to myself as I held her softly in my arms.

Threesomes

THE LESBIAN COLLECTION

VICTORIA RUSH

2 + 1 = a hundred ways to have fun...

Sometimes the biggest turn-on is knowing you might get caught...

First
Time
A LESBIAN ANTHOLOGY
VICTORIA RUSH
It's never as good as the first time...

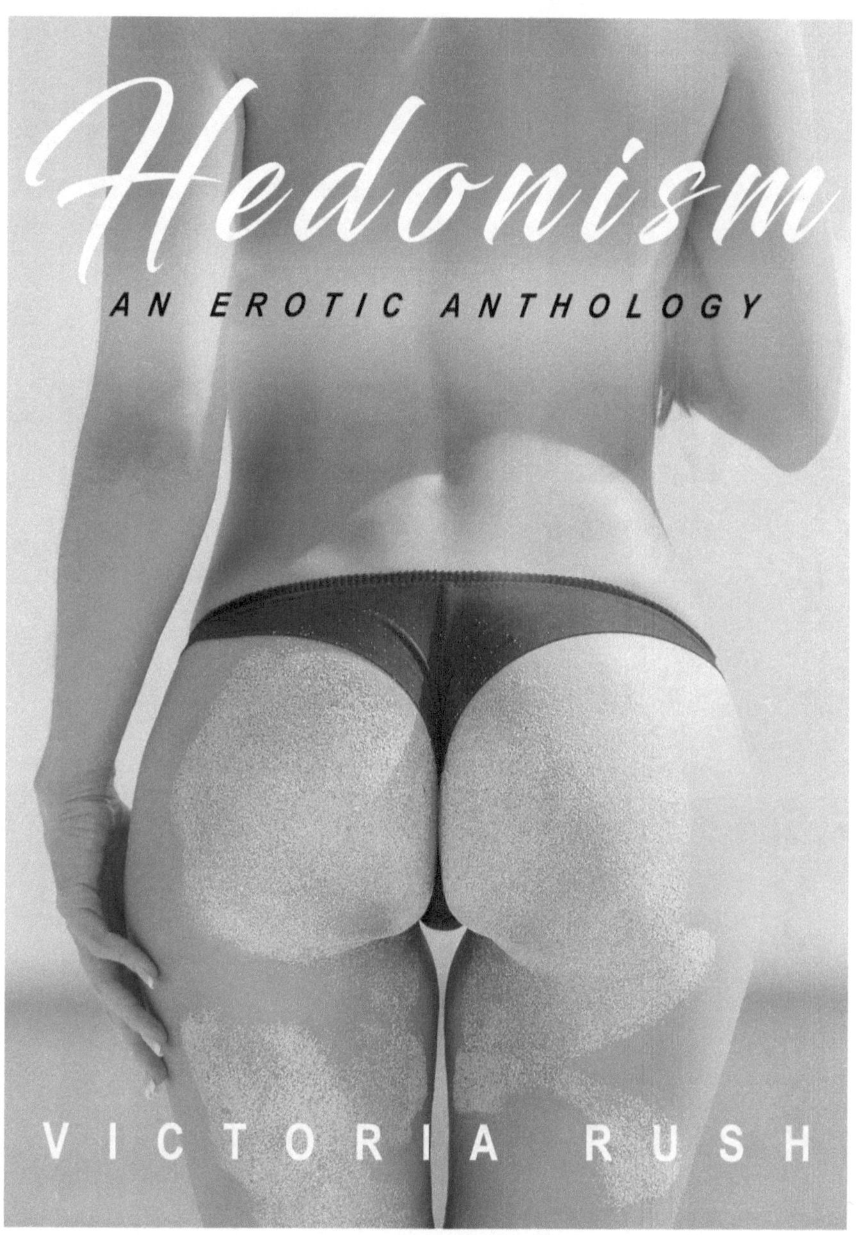

Hedonism

AN EROTIC ANTHOLOGY

VICTORIA RUSH

Sometimes all you need to spark up your love life is a little change of scenery...

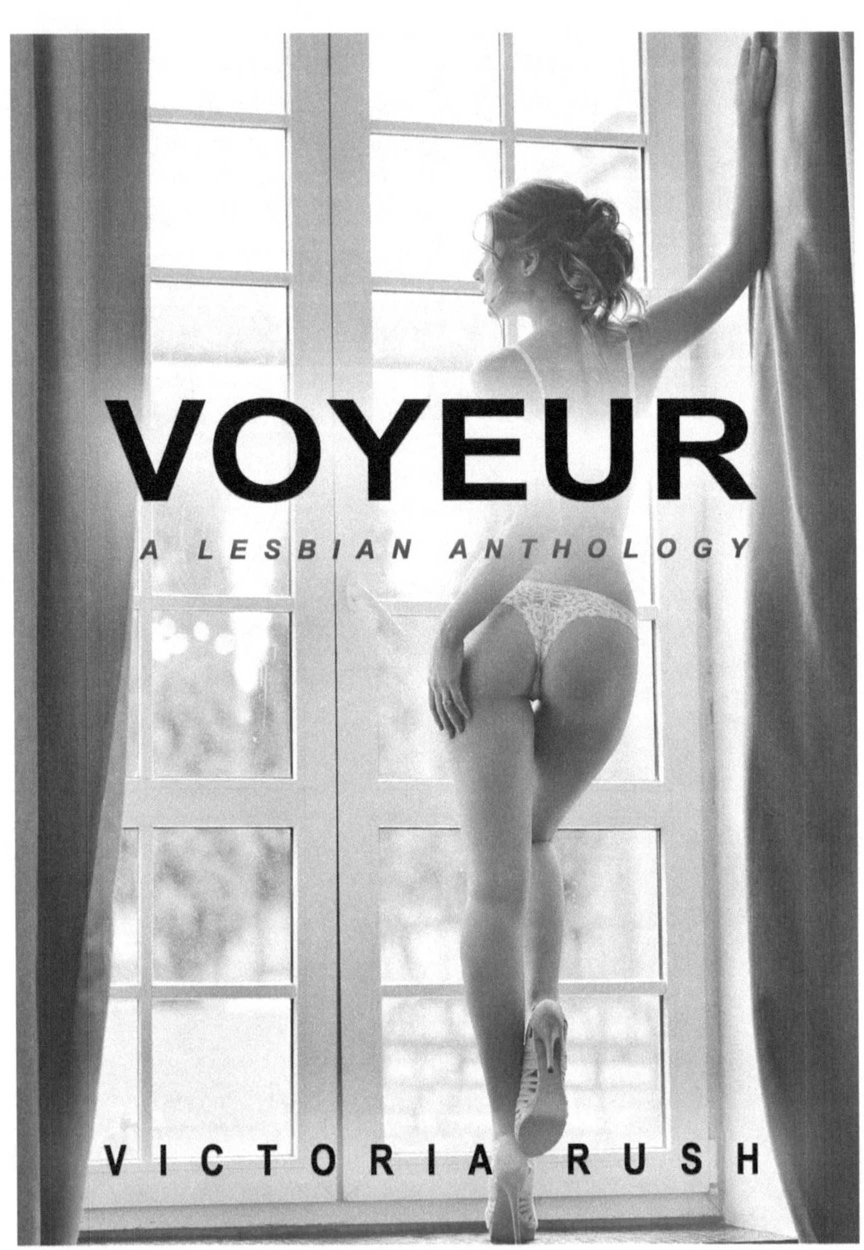

Sometimes it's more fun to watch...